I0633584

THE POWERS THAT BE

BROKEN CONTRACTS

∞

HAZEL DOMAIN

ANGLERFISH PRESS

Riptide Publishing
PO Box 1537
Burnsville, NC 28714
www.riptidepublishing.com

Broken Contracts

Cover art: Simone
Editor: Rachel Haimowitz

ISBN: 978-1-963773-22-4

First edition
November, 2024

Also available in ebook:
ISBN: 978-1-963773-20-0

THE POWERS THAT BE

BROKEN CONTRACTS

∞

HAZEL DOMAIN

ANGLERFISH PRESS

For Rachel. Here's your damn world-building.

TABLE OF CONTENTS

∞

CHAPTER ONE

February 2012

A Adam Slate tapped his desk. "I need something of yours."
The man—Slate had already forgotten his name, Charles maybe—blinked stupidly.

"Something of . . . mine?"

"Of the company's, yes. Something I can use as a placeholder for the organization as a whole."

And maybe those words were too long, Slate thought in the silence that followed. The man—Henry? Benedict? One of those old money names—didn't have much going for him, and barely ten minutes into this meeting, it wasn't hard to see why.

"A business card will usually suffice," Slate said, and that seemed to break Quincy's stupor.

"Of course," he said, nodding. He set his suitcase on the e-ink map that covered the top of Slate's desk, and rummaged inside for the card. He might have set it on his lap, if there had been a second chair in the room. There wasn't. Taking a seat encouraged people to stay.

Lance, the card read, when he handed it over. *Lance Richardson.* Of *Richardson Subsidiaries, LTD*, presumably.

That would explain it. Nice suit, good haircut, not too bright, and barely any connections. A couple of weak ties, probably to classmates or coworkers, and then one thick tether, vital as an umbilical. Possibly literally. Rich mommies could be just as nepotistic as rich daddies, and Lance had one of them wrapped around his mediocre little finger.

Slate set the card on the desk, over the black-and-white representation of New York City that defaulted as the center.

Lance cleared his throat. "Do you want to see the business plan?"

"No," Slate answered. "Move your suitcase."

"Oh, right." Lance hesitated. "So are you gonna do your . . .?"

"I'm already doing it," Slate answered. On the desk, the card began to sprout tendrils. Flat and wet, they crawled away from the card and across the desk like slime mold in an agar plate. Slate let his fingertips rest lightly on the surface, changing the scale and focus of the map as the tendrils spread outward. They grew and stretched, combined, found nourishment and branched again, withered, and finally settled.

"The West Coast expansion's a poor choice," Slate said, studying the patterns. Lance leaned in, trying to discern what Slate was examining. To him, it would look like a paper card on a map. Nothing more. "You'll be better off redirecting that energy toward your operations in the Gulf."

Lance blinked. "The Gulf project isn't even in the briefing, how did you—"

"The same way I know the bulk of your finances are actually located in Barbados," Slate interrupted. He resisted the urge to rub his eyes. Of his three offices, the one in Manhattan was easily the most tiring. Business majors and business masters, meeting after meeting after meeting as he tried to explain the obvious to people who couldn't wipe themselves without having the toilet paper approved by a focus group first.

"You researched us beforehand," Lance said, narrowing his eyes, and Slate gave in and rubbed his temples. He was too fucking old to still be having this conversation.

"You came to *me*," he said, still watching the energy slithering contentedly across his desk. "*You* came to *me* because I've proven myself invaluable to projects significantly larger and more complicated than yours. You came to me because what I have to say is *worth* something, worth enough that they spared *you* for the day to come collect it."

Lance stared at him, angry but not clever enough to express it politely. As Slate watched, one of his stronger connections thinned, dried, disintegrated.

The West Coast project had been his, then. Some quid pro quo deal that Slate had just killed, taking Lance's influence from unremarkable to poor.

Something on the map shifted minutely, not enough to affect the outcome, barely enough to catch his eye. One tiny little cluster in Miami, a connection opening because another had closed. It wouldn't affect anything.

"So what have you got to *say*, then?" Lance sneered, and Slate only blinked at that one remaining tether: the doting, overbearing parent without whom he could simply strangle this arrogant brat. People without connections could be vanished. The ones around Slate, more than most.

"I'll send you my analysis by Friday," he said, his voice too even. Lance took half a step back. "Go."

Lance didn't even consider arguing, just picked up his briefcase and left, shutting the door behind him. There was the mumbled sound of social pleasantries as he said goodbye to Slate's receptionist, an indentured woman named Megan, who was two years into her lifetime contract.

Slate sat alone at his desk, scrutinizing the map. He'd have to translate this all into words. It was, at this point, almost the only part of his job that he hadn't yet managed to automate or delegate.

He had to do the translation himself because he was the only one who could *see*. What looked to him like a straightforward graph of resources and opportunities was, when drawn for anyone else, a stringy blotch. Even explaining it didn't help, no matter how many times he'd tried.

Sighing, Slate slid his chair back, drawing a keyboard tray out from beneath the heavy mahogany desktop. On it lay a slim silver computer, a new model since the last time he'd been here. Megan must have replaced it. He opened it and checked his calendar. He had four hours until his flight to Rochester. More than enough.

He opened up a word processor and began writing, taking what he saw on the map and turning it into instructions. Listed the chokepoints and described how to bypass them. Exposed the unexploited resources and explained how to seize them. In three hours, he wrote a business plan that would dictate the company's next five years of decisions. Following his plan would net them somewhere in the vicinity of 9.8 billion dollars of additional revenue. Between the bonuses, stock options, and base pay, roughly twelve percent of it would be his.

With his remaining hour, he fucked the receptionist.

The auction in Rochester was so desperately esoteric it was almost boring.

There was the magic, of course. The magic was what had originally drawn Slate to the scene. He liked magic.

He was slightly less thrilled with the company this put him among.

These aspiring sorcerers called his ability magic. A "Gift." But it wasn't *real* magic.

He'd started being able to see the connections in his late teens, and it had seemed so obvious he'd simply taken it for granted. He hadn't realized other people *couldn't* see what he did until he started betting on fights. A lot of fights.

He couldn't see who would win, and if the fights had been fair, he would have been just another gambler. But they weren't. And Slate could see both how and why.

He made his first million that way, and then gave it up while he was ahead. It didn't feel like cheating—sure, no one else could do what he could do, but the information was all *there*, all anyone had to do was *look*—but he'd suspected that the people losing might have begun harboring grudges, and so he'd quit.

But he'd met a lot of people in the meantime. Interesting people. Lose-ten-grand-in-a-bet type people. And they thought he was *fascinating*. They had things they wanted him to look at.

That felt like cheating. Like a parlor trick, becoming a god among dogs for the ability to sort by color. But once everything was sorted, the dogs wanted to talk about magic. Real magic. Different magic. And that was a conversation Slate wanted to have.

That was how he got his first auction invitation. A woman who thought he could see auras wanted him to tell her which items were real. He couldn't help her with that, but he had made new friends. Interesting friends.

Buy-people-like-they-were-contracts friends.

He'd thought it was a joke at first, done for show . . . but the indentured woman being sold had no connections. None. Slate had never seen anything like it. Not a flicker of a single other person who would help her, vouch for her, do her a favor . . . look for her.

By the time she'd sold, Slate had been rock-hard. He'd invented excuses, made his way awkwardly to the gentlemen's, and beat off violently against the back of the wooden stall door. He'd tipped the attendant a fifty and gone back to the bidding.

That had been twenty years ago.

Nowadays, Slate was a fixture at those sorts of auctions. To date, he'd discovered six members of undercover law enforcement, nine escape attempts, and countless indents with too many loved ones to safely go missing. He'd taken a furtive, underground ring and created an *industry*. It was still illegal, of course . . . but there hadn't been so much as an indictment in two decades. Not for the people Slate worked with.

That was what had brought him to Rochester. His usual fee for inspecting the merchandise, and the hope that he'd find something to spend it on.

He wasn't overly optimistic.

The slave still had clothes on, which Slate found amusing to no end.

The slave—*indent* was the proper term, but Slate was well beyond transparent euphemisms at this point in his life—strode confidently to the center of the dais, preening for the collection of gathered bidders. The auctioneer clearly wasn't sure what to do with him and looked to the audience for clues. A couple of people muttered disapprovingly; someone else whistled. The slave took a little bow, evoking scattered laughter from the crowd.

"That's not fair," someone called. His voice was good-natured, despite the complaint. "Show us what we're buying!"

The auctioneer murmured to the slave, who looked back into the shadows. His owner, presumably, must have given him the nod, because a moment later he reached down, taking hold of his shirt and beginning to strip it slowly, almost languidly, off.

Slate smirked. The slave was beautiful, but then, of course he was. They all were.

The body revealed inch by inch was lithe but not overly muscular, tanned by lights rather than days in the sun. The barcode marking his lifetime contract stood out on his arm. He was one of Arabelle's trainees—a hint of her tattooed Signature peeked from beneath the low-slung waistband of his black cotton pants.

Slate narrowed his eyes. As he'd seen in his earlier checks, this man had no connection to anything or anyone. The smallest, flimsiest tether indicated an owner who would argue that, if nothing else, he was worth money. But there was something there, just for a moment as he turned . . . Not a connection, but . . . *something*.

The slave's torso caught the light enticingly as the shirt was pulled over his head. Messy, dark hair tumbled out of his shirt collar and over his shoulders. His arms flexed as he folded the shirt into rough quarters, then tossed it aside. Slate smirked. The slave was putting on a deliberate show, but he was almost, *almost* good enough to make it look natural.

That attention to detail appealed to Slate more than the slave's body ever could. The slave hooked his thumbs into the waistband of his pants and slid them down, slowly, as the auctioneer began the bidding. And Slate saw what had caught his eye.

Right below the slave's belly button, there was . . . a *space*.

Not a physical mark—the man's skin was smooth in the way that only regular descarring could achieve—but a vague, dark place Slate couldn't see.

Or . . . that he could *see* that he couldn't see.

He'd missed it while doing his inspections because the slave hadn't stripped, and this wasn't a connection. It didn't extend away from his skin. It was . . . the *absence* of a connection. An *anti*-connection.

A hundred auctions identical to this one, and a lifetime of watching the people around him, and Slate had never seen anything like this.

A thrill went up his spine.

Settling back into his seat and putting on a casual air, Slate began to bid.

CHAPTER
TWO

∞

It was another three days before Slate actually got around to summoning the slave. He was approached about a new project—something marginally more complicated than usual—and spent eighteen straight hours translating before passing out at his desk, having forgotten to eat.

It took a day to recover from that, and then he remembered his purchase almost with surprise, and instructed that the man be readied and sent to his office after dinner.

And then of course Slate found the slave was there, waiting. The members of Slate's household staff were where he told them to be, when he told them to be there. Being new wasn't an excuse, and the others would have made sure the slave knew it.

He stood before Slate's massive mahogany desk, eyes down, forearms crossed behind his back, tattoo facing out. The wait had been long enough that he *probably* would have been justified in switching to a kneel, and yet, he stood.

Good form, Slate thought, approaching the man and circling him without a word. Without any further instructions, the slave had once again been dressed in a black cotton uniform, similar to the one he'd worn at the auction. He didn't move as Slate examined him, and kept his eyes fixed stubbornly on the floor.

No, Slate thought, looking closer. Not stubbornly. Resolutely.

It was a subtle difference, to be sure.

Slate reached out, lifting the slave's chin with a finger. There was no resistance to the action. No flinch. His breathing stayed even, his eyes on the floor.

Slate felt a shiver run down his spine. The slave was doing his best to follow his training, and like the others Slate had deigned to actually buy, he was doing a superb job so far. But this man wasn't just being stoic. His body language was utterly absent the fear, the anger, even the subtle humiliation that Slate saw so frequently in the others. Slate wasn't sure which would be more interesting—actual nonchalance, or the ability to so superbly mimic it.

"Whose idea was it?" Slate asked. Then, when the slave hesitated, "The clothes. Whose idea was it to send you onto the dais clothed? Yours or your master's?"

"My mistress's," the slave answered.

"What was her reasoning?"

"She didn't say."

"What do *you* think?" Slate pressed, stepping in closer. He was fully in the man's space now; social conventions and basic animal instinct would be telling the slave to step backward. He didn't.

"I think . . . she was trying to draw attention. Interest."

Slate let the statement hang between them, showing neither pleasure nor displeasure. The slave's form held perfectly, and he didn't rush to babble out a clarification.

A connoisseur of lesser taste might have missed the way his breath came ever so slightly faster.

"Are you *interesting*, then?" Slate asked, leaning forward and looking up, directly into the taller man's lowered eyeline.

The slave met his eyes then. "She thought so, sir," he said, a flirting undertone to the phrase, and Slate laughed.

He stepped back, leaning casually against the desk. "Good. I detest boring people. So tell me what I've bought. What will you do to interest me?"

The question wasn't as casual as it seemed.

For a fraction of a second, the slave hesitated, before looking up at Slate through thick lashes. "Whatever you'd like, sir," he answered. His voice was low, sultry, almost a purr. Slate felt his body reacting, that voice trailing down his belly like a warm breath.

He slapped the slave across the mouth.

For an instant, he saw the shock and disbelief on the man's features. Confusion, hurt, and then nothing.

"I told you not to bore me," Slate said casually, inspecting the fingernails of his stinging hand. He expected indignance here, possibly even anger. It wasn't there. "*Obviously*, you'll do whatever I like."

"I can—"

"And if I wanted my dick sucked, I'd have said so," Slate interrupted, putting a note of regret into his voice as he correctly predicted the slave's next suggestion. The man's face didn't change, but he didn't speak again, either.

He was trying to keep his body language neutral, casual, but Slate could see him calculating. He'd be running through every skill he had, every option he could think of, trying to find a right answer.

There wasn't one.

Whatever he said would be wrong, and then? Then he'd be punished.

Slate turned away, walking to the bookshelves lining the wall behind the desk. He pulled a tome off the shelf and then, grasping the handle hidden beneath, shoved the entire contraption to the side.

Behind it was a wall of tools, the smallest of three in the manor, and the only one to be hidden. Recessed lights ramped on, glinting off metal and leather and rubber.

"See anything you like?" Slate asked.

"Maybe," the slave said, and Slate barely prevented himself from flinching. He turned slowly. The man was *right* behind him.

No, Slate amended. Not behind him, *beside* him.

"What's this?" the man asked, reaching out and taking a metal cylinder off the shelf.

"An ice lock," Slate answered, remembering to keep his voice level. The cylinder went to pieces in the slave's hands.

"The ice holds it together," the slave said, turning it over. "Clever. Not much good to us tonight, though."

He put it back on the shelf as casually as if it'd been a paperback, instead picking up a thin carbon fiber rod. Slate watched his face, and what he saw *appeared* to be . . . genuine curiosity.

Was the slave stupid? Was that it?

Any other slave in his position would still be waiting in front of the desk, stone still and desperately trying to follow whatever instructions they thought their master was *implying*. Slate had played this game with dozens of different people, and they all played it the same way.

"Does this work?" the man asked, fingering the flat, S-shaped bead at the end of the rod.

"If it's used properly," Slate answered. "What's your name?"

"Micah, sir," the man answered, flexing the rod experimentally. "May I try it?"

The question threw Slate, though he recovered before it showed in his body language. Was Micah looking *forward* to this? Or just resigning himself to the inevitable?

The mild anticipation on his face gave nothing away. It could've been real. It could've just been Arabelle's training.

"No." Slate held his hand out for the rod. "I'll do it. Take your clothes off."

Micah didn't hesitate, stripping his shirt and pants off with the same practiced moves from the auction. The persona of the perfectly trained submissive slipped effortlessly back over his features.

Slate turned the rod over in his hands, watching.

Micah's breath came slow and smooth, the firm muscles of his chest and belly rising and falling in tandem. The hair on his torso was perfectly even, in a way that suggested someone had spent a lot of money on lasers at some point. His chest was bare, but a dark path led down his belly to a diamond of pubic hair. His forearms and thighs hadn't been touched.

There was a balance to him, Slate thought, circling him slowly. A careful cultivation of masculine and feminine in equal parts.

It wasn't how *Slate* would have done it, but he couldn't argue with results.

He set the rod down on the desk and went back to the bookshelf, selecting a length of white cotton rope.

"You could have picked a better activity," he said, releasing the bundle and folding it into lengths in his hands. "This is going to hurt, a lot. So I'll let you cheat."

Silence from Micah—but his breath hitched, almost imperceptibly. What was interesting, Slate noticed, was that it hitched not on *hurt*, but on *cheat*.

It wasn't the pain the slave was worried about. It was the suggestion that he couldn't handle it.

Interesting, Slate thought, looping the center of the rope around Micah's throat. The ends fell down his back, past his crossed forearms, brushing his ass on the way to the floor. Slate made quick work knotting the harness, winching Micah's arms back tight and leaving his front and sides framed in a series of diamonds.

Almost as an afterthought, he retrieved a white silk blindfold from the bookshelf, knotting it loosely over Micah's eyes. Then he stood back to admire his handiwork.

The harness was a hair too tight, pulling Micah's arms sharply back, forcing his chest out. He'd be losing sensation below the elbow soon. He had fifteen, maybe twenty minutes before the medic in the staff quarters would be fixing up nerve damage. Then again, that was why Slate *had* a medic.

Fingering the carbon fiber rod, Slate switched his focus, drawing out the slithering lines that connected this man to the world.

This was always his favorite part. Most owners enjoyed the sight of the barcodes, but Slate saw so much more. Unlike the tangled vines and pathways Slate saw on most people, this man had nearly nothing. His influence coated his body like a soft moss—many people had known him, cared for him over time, but there was nothing left. It was beautiful. Tantalizing.

But then, just below his navel, outlined in the rope, there was . . . the nothing. The very obvious, visible, almost *palpable* space of nothing.

Cautiously, Slate reached out, trailing his knuckles through it. It felt like nothing—or rather, it felt like he was simply stroking the thin path of hair leading to Micah's cock.

Micah shivered lightly and then, incredibly, began to harden.

That was a neat trick.

Slate swatted the rod along the middle of his belly, leaving a long red line. At the end, a perfectly formed *S* instantly began to redden. Micah hissed, flinching away before resuming his stance.

Slate hit him again, twice, lines perfectly parallel to the first. Micah let out a small moan, flexing and then releasing the muscles of his stomach, trying to lessen the sting. It wouldn't work.

"I don't want you going to the medic for this," Slate said, laying three quick *S*'s into the center of the three rope diamonds up Micah's left side. "These will bruise. The bruises will last. You're not to have them removed, is that understood?"

"Yes," Micah said, the word becoming a hiss of pain as Slate repeated the three strikes on the right side.

Somewhat surprisingly, he was still mostly hard.

Slate considered swatting him on the cock, leaving a thin angry line right across the place where the head met the shaft. The thought had his own cock pressing against the inside of his slacks. He *could*. That was what owning this particular contract meant. He could lay a ladder of those lines all the way down to Micah's balls and there was nothing Micah could do—

He shuddered, palming himself roughly. Temperance was key. He'd get there, but he had to work up to it.

Slow and steady, Slate thought, twisting the *S* off the end of the rod. To his delight, Micah stayed half-hard as Slate laid a branching, leisurely collection of crosshatches across his ass and shoulders. The last one, straight across his lower back, came down too hard and drew blood. Micah hissed sharply, beginning to tremble as he reflexively tried to curl in on himself. The ropes wouldn't let him. A bead of sweat rolled down the small of his back, turning red where it crossed the rod's mark.

And he *still* hadn't gone soft.

"Where would you like the last of them?" Slate asked, watching, palming himself leisurely through his pants.

Micah took a deep breath, then exhaled. He'd be considering now. The obvious answer was the shoulders; they were easily the least sensitive place available. But begging for the easy way out was *boring*, and Slate had already shown his displeasure for boring answers.

Then the next obvious thought: Where would be the most *interesting* place to request them? Somewhere horrible—his balls, his hands, his face. Maybe a hole whipping?

But that was a gamble. The worst answers were still obvious, which meant they were still boring. Micah could be asking for a week in agony, without buying himself anything.

No, the trick was in finding the middle ground.

Slate suspected that was what Micah was doing now: playing at enjoying it—but not *too* much—while he tried to determine whether Slate wanted an enthusiastic masochist or simply someone to hurt.

"Hurry up and choose," Slate said, laying another line right above the bleeding one.

"*Nn*—" Micah whispered, and for one glorious second Slate thought he might get to teach the lesson about what happened when slaves told him *no*. His hard cock ached at the thought.

But it wasn't to be.

"Thighs," Micah said definitively. "Please. Sir."

Excellent, Slate thought, grinning to himself. A middle ground answer *indeed*; Micah had in fact given four different answers—back, front, inner, and the tender skin below the iliac crest. A choice that put the decision back in Slate's hands, and a *please* on top of it, just to pretend he hadn't.

Well played.

Slate took hold of the rope twisted between Micah's shoulder blades and pushed him forward, against the edge of the desk.

"Get your knee up," Slate instructed, and Micah complied immediately. He struggled to keep his balance without the use of his arms, but within a couple of seconds, he had one knee up on the wood surface. He had to lean forward a bit to keep from falling back. Slate liked the look of him like that—slightly unbalanced. Spread out. Vulnerable.

"Move one inch," Slate said in a low voice, "and I'll tie you down and leave you for the cleaning crew. Understood?"

"Yes, sir," Micah said quietly. His hair fell across his face, a dark contrast to the white blindfold, the white rope across his shoulders and throat.

Slate let go of the rope, letting his fingers trail down Micah's side, over the curve of his ass, and across the outside of his thigh. Micah's skin was soft, warm, and smelled, ever so slightly, of vanilla.

Slate took a step back and proceeded to lay ten parallel lines down the outside of Micah's raised thigh. Two broke the skin. The slave barely had time to finish his gasping inhale before Slate was on him, shoving him face down onto the desk. Slate tossed the rod aside, focusing on his fly instead. He wasn't going to bother undressing for this.

Micah's hole was already wet—of course it was, he would have prepared; Slate hadn't called him up here for *conversation*—but it wouldn't have mattered if he wasn't. Slate wasn't in the habit of coddling people for their mistakes. He pushed in, hard and deep, and Micah made a low, pained sound. But he didn't move.

The contortion would be hurting him already, but he didn't move. Didn't try.

And *oh*, that was good, Slate thought. He withdrew slightly and pushed in again, relishing the tight heat of the man he'd bought. He took hold of the rope across Micah's back, the slave's short, startled gasp almost sending him over the edge.

Instead, he shoved Micah's shoulders down with one hand, and with the other, he twisted the rope, pulling down and back. Instantly, it strung taut across Micah's throat, cutting off his air.

Now, Slate thought, leaning back to admire the view. *Now we see how well you're trained.*

He moved slowly, fucking into Micah almost casually as the slave's air ran out. He could feel Micah's muscles tensing beneath him, *around* him, as the slave tried to keep his body from moving.

His breath wasn't completely cut off. Just enough to give the experience of suffocating. Most people could stand it ten seconds. A couple had lasted thirty. At twenty-eight, Micah made a valiant attempt to stand up. He was strong—even stronger than he looked, which with his physique was saying something—but not strong enough to throw off Slate's weight. Not without his arms.

Slate leaned down, using his body to pin Micah's. The hand not holding the rope settled around Micah's silent throat, fingers tightening. Beneath him, Micah bucked and writhed, bound hands scrabbling uselessly against Slate's chest.

"Don't make me tie you down," Slate chided, and for one *insane* second, Micah actually went still.

He's trying that *hard*, Slate thought, and then Micah pushed back against him, taking Slate's cock to the root, grinding into Slate's hips, and Slate realized he wasn't going to last. He let go of the rope and rose off Micah, still holding him down by the shoulders as he fucked into him for real, hard and fast. Micah gasped desperately, still fighting to breathe against Slate's weight, and Slate came with a groan.

The striped plane of skin between Micah's shoulders was beckoning, pillow-soft, and Slate almost let his forehead rest on it. Then Micah took another shuddering breath, and Slate was back to his senses. He pulled back, stooping to pick Micah's discarded shirt off the ground. He cleaned himself off, then went to untie his slave.

The rope left red marks, far more temporary than the welts and bruises from the rod, but still contributing nicely to the overall effect.

Micah looked absolutely ruined. Slate surveilled his handiwork approvingly.

"Will there be anything else? Sir?" Micah asked, his voice rough.

"Take this down to laundry for me," Slate said, pressing the soiled shirt into Micah's hands.

"Yes, sir."

Slate shivered at the sound of his voice, the rasp that accented the bruises so nicely, letting everyone know what Micah had been through. What he'd been *bought for*.

Carefully, Micah pulled on his pants and limped from the room.

CHAPTER THREE

∞

*L*eft. Right. Inhale. Exhale.
Left. Right. Inhale. Exhale.
Left, right, inhale, exhale.

The instructions began to flow into a cadence, giving Micah something to focus on as he made his way down the darkened hallway. Each breath felt like swallowing sandpaper, each step twinged. He could feel his heart beating in the stripes the cane had left, and his fingers were beginning to tingle as blood flow returned.

Overall, he'd rate this a six out of ten. No broken bones, no head trauma. Most of the marks on his skin were bruises, and even the broken skin wasn't deep enough to risk blood on the carpet.

Carol met him at the top of the stairs, indifferently taking in the damage. He kept his face down, not meeting her eyes. Carol was an indent, and he *could* look her in the eye, but he'd found that in general it was better to keep his head down.

"How was it?" she asked.

Micah considered his answer. "I got him what he needed."

There was a rasp in his voice that would probably be there for a few days. Carol didn't comment. Instead, she reached for the shirt bundled in his arms.

"I'm supposed to take it to laundry," Micah protested.

"Suit yourself. Here," she said, taking the shirt out of his hand and dropping two white pills in its place.

Micah froze. "It's Tylenol," Carol said. "Take it, get some sleep, and take it easy tomorrow. He's not letting you see the medic, right?"

"How'd you guess?" Micah took both pills at once, swallowing them dry.

"You're not even close to the first." There wasn't pity in her voice, and Micah didn't expect any. There wasn't room for it in a place like this. She could pity the marks on his body, he could pity the years she'd spend here when he was long gone. A net zero. Better not to bother.

"The marks will stay clearer if you don't do anything strenuous tomorrow," Carol said, handing him the shirt back. "He likes that."

"Thanks," Micah said, dipping his head.

He contemplated her words as he made his way downstairs. She was offering him a day off, not that it counted for much. He was in hospitality—if someone called for him, he'd have to go, bruises or no. And if no one wanted him, then his duties didn't exactly amount to much.

But he appreciated the sentiment.

Carol was head of household, but as a barcoded indent, she wasn't in a position much better than him. Someone on the outside cared enough to vouch for her, that was all. It didn't buy anything in here.

Reaching the bottom of the stairs, he relaxed slightly. The honeycomb of facilities that made up the slave quarters were always marginally safer than the upper levels, mostly because owners *never* came down here. He still held to his presentation, keeping his posture straight and his eyes down. At this point, it was first nature rather than second.

It was quiet this time of night. Most people were in the common area, or in their bunks. The small laundry room was deserted. Two of the washers had laundry sitting wet and, after a moment of consideration, Micah switched them over.

He didn't need to. It wasn't his job. He'd even gotten in trouble for it once—not here, but with a former owner. The house had a relatively small staff, but they were well cared for, and the maid had scolded the hell out of him for making her look bad. In retrospect, he didn't blame her for being possessive of the placement.

Here, though, it didn't seem to matter so much who did what, as long as everything got done *right*.

So he switched them over, then stripped out of his soiled clothes and left them in the hamper with the others.

The far wall had the cubbies where clean clothes and linens were stored, and Micah dug through a bin for one of the clean XL T-shirts.

The showers were two doors down the hall, so Micah didn't bother dressing before heading over. He carried the clothes with him, leaving them on the bench by his locker.

It was a misnomer, really. "His locker." It didn't lock, and it wasn't his. The things inside it weren't his, either. They were the toiletry items assigned to him, subject to change if it was determined he needed to look or smell differently. Right now, the interior was fairly empty. Slate didn't care for makeup, and Micah's hair didn't need more than a standard black elastic to keep it out of his face. That left soap, shampoo, and conditioner, all the same French brand name, all the same rich honeyed vanilla scent.

Micah liked it. Vanilla was good in the winter. It was a warm smell. One of his former owners had been in favor of strong peppermint for the holiday season. Fortunately, Micah had only spent one winter with her before being sold on in the autumn.

He gathered up the bottles and headed for the showers.

Surprisingly, the ones here had stalls. The stalls didn't have *doors*, but they did at least have walls. Someone was in the first, a woman, judging by her ankles, and Micah didn't look at her as he headed for the cubicle in the back corner.

Bracing himself, he turned the water on.

The maximum temperature could best be described as *lukewarm*, but at least the pressure was good. The idea was to keep them from dawdling—which made sense, as long as the water didn't dribble out too weakly to properly rinse.

Not being able to get conditioner all the way out was the *worst*.

Turning into the spray, he let the water fill his mouth, taking several swallows before dipping his head to wet his hair. The cool water felt good on his throat, even as it stung the small wounds on his back and thigh.

Taking a breath, Micah looked down at himself.

It wasn't as bad as it felt. The little stick had hurt like hell, leaving marks that were dark but thin. The marks from the ropes were already fading, and that helped a lot.

And for all the soreness of his body, he knew he'd borne it well. He'd lost control for just a second at the end—oxygen deprivation was one of those things that couldn't be ignored forever—but for the most part, he'd done a good job. Slate seemed relatively easy. He wanted a metered, *reasonable* reaction to his treatment. It was difficult to have *no* reaction, but almost worse had been the owner who couldn't bring himself to deliver more than a playful swat but still wanted Micah to sob and howl and beg. That had been . . . challenging, to say the least.

But Slate had seemed pleased with his performance, for the most part.

Micah's face flushed red, remembering the slap, the admonishment for the wanton way he'd gone about it at first. He'd miscalculated there; his new owner wasn't looking for a mutually enjoyable romp with a slut. The impressive *wall* of bondage toys had made that evident. But Micah's second gamble had paid off, because Slate wasn't looking for a rape fantasy, either. He didn't want to force himself on someone unwilling. Micah needed to pretend he *liked* it.

Micah could fake that. It *was* a bit of a challenge, getting hard when he wasn't interested, but he'd had enough practice to pull it off reliably now. Even in the middle of worse things than Slate had done.

Micah smiled to himself, a bit of the anxiety slipping off his shoulders. He knew what his new owner wanted, and he could do it. He *knew* he could. He'd done well. His owner was happy with him.

It was going to be fine.

Micah finished washing quickly, cleaning the blood and come from his body the same way he had a hundred times before. Drying off, he caught his reflection in the mirror.

The *S* pattern up his side was remarkably clear. Gently fingering the welt, Micah felt something warm settle in his belly.

It wasn't the first initial on his body—Arabelle's signature *A* was *tattooed* on him, after all, and that was a hell of a lot more serious than a stupid bruise. But that was more of a maker's mark.

This . . . this felt more like a mark of ownership. Which it was, in a way. Slate *did* own him. But still . . .

Getting dressed, Micah found himself smiling as he brushed against the darkening letters.

After all, people only wrote their names on things they *wanted*.

CHAPTER FOUR

∞

April 2012

"No outsiders," Slate said, not looking at the interloper accompanying his guest.

Jeremiah Locke blinked. "He's a bodyguard."

Slate tried, and failed, to apply the response to the statement. He didn't open the door further. "No. Outsiders."

"You don't need a fucking bodyguard, you pretentious dipshit!" came a voice from inside, and Slate closed his eyes, taking a deep breath through his nose. The voice belonged to Lucas Coffey. At barely twenty-eight, he was more than ten years Slate's junior and acted half that. He was impulsive, asinine, unintelligent, and the owner of the largest collection of magical texts in the northern hemisphere. Slate couldn't figure out how he did it. Most books *he'd* tracked down were owned by people who wouldn't give them up for love or money. Coffey had very few personal virtues, but as a collector he was unrivaled.

"I'm going to have him assassinated," Locke said in a quiet, almost cheerful voice. "As soon as the election's over. See if I don't."

"I'll plead the fifth," Slate replied in a monotone. "Your man can wait in the staff area. I'll call someone to look after him."

The man in question might have objected to being lumped in with *staff*, but Locke waved him off before he got the chance.

"I'm not being paranoid, you know," Locke said, stepping into the meeting room. Slate closed the door behind him. "I've gotten three credible threats on my life since the campaign began. If I didn't trust your warding, I'd have declined the invite."

"Your lover works in law enforcement," Slate said, re-examining the bundle of connections expanding from Locke's body to make sure the statement was still true. "If the resources of their agency can't keep you safe, I don't think one guard with a stun gun is going to tip the balance in your favor."

"That's not public knowledge," Locke hissed, glancing around to make sure no one was within earshot.

"I didn't plan to change that," Slate answered, resisting the urge to take a step back. He didn't know who the lover *was*, for one thing. Just that they existed. That connection, as much as his political ambitions, made Locke one of Slate's more valuable allies. He had no intentions of making any enemies, especially not in the name of spreading gossip.

"See that you don't," Locke said in a low voice, before a mask of congeniality fell over his features and he went over to greet the others.

There were five of them tonight, out of a rotating group of perhaps twenty. They were all carefully chosen—ostensibly by one another, though Slate knew better. The connections in this room formed a perfect roulette curve, one only he knew the full extent of. He'd invited the first three on the pretense of a card game, then proposed the idea of a magical order as though it had occurred to him on the spot. The three had suggested others—exactly the others Slate had predicted. They, in turn, brought their own connections.

And so it went.

Slate looked around the well-lit dining room. The center of the room had been cleared—it was where they'd do their magic. Around the outside were bookshelves, his own meager attempt at building a magical library. At one end of the room was the table set with the supper that his guests had theoretically been invited to. At the other, the backlit bar that they'd actually gathered around.

"All right, what are we doing tonight?" Coffey asked. There was a cut-crystal glass in his hand, almost completely filled with a large spherical ice cube.

"We should try the alchemy again," Locke said immediately. "Just a few ounces of gold apiece, and we'd be able to—"

The group erupted in groans. Of the six of them, Locke was the only one still interested in ways to generate assets. For his part, Slate's income grew too fast to make alchemy a worthwhile hourly pursuit.

"I had to throw my suit out after last time," Coffey complained. "The smell of sulfur wouldn't come out."

"I think the alchemy fused the stink with the fibers," the man beside him added. That was Ryan Stewart, an architect from the West Coast. Tall, broad-shouldered, very much Slate's type if it weren't for the roiling bouquet of connections bursting from every inch of his body.

Stewart's work with elemental magic was unparalleled. When he was nine years old, a wildfire had torn across his town, leaving a line of damage half a mile wide. It hadn't burned Stewart's house, if you believed the legend, because he'd taken his sidewalk chalk and simply asked it not to.

As an adult, the houses he designed did not burn. They did not flood, they did not blow away, they did not collapse when the ground shook. The warding was built into the walls, the tiles, and even the landscaping of his *extremely* eclectic designs. And until someone figured out how to separate his functional decisions from his artistic ones, he could write his own checks.

"What do *you* suggest, then?" Locke asked, a little bitterly. Slate frowned. Locke was souring further on the other members with each meeting. He wouldn't cut ties with any of them—no, a politician didn't burn bridges over something as petty as open disrespect—but he might stop attending.

Perhaps there would be a campaign contribution in Slate's future. That would smooth things over for a few more months.

Or maybe he should stop bothering with the gatherings altogether, Slate thought tiredly, looking over the assembled group. He was reluctant to give up the idea as a whole. He'd hoped that maybe magic could help him find something in a world that otherwise felt as compelling as a crayon drawing. It had been a simple matter to find connections that would put the world's magical resources in his hands, and the result was . . . well. It was less than spectacular.

"I think we should try learning to fly," Coffey suggested, and Slate's laugh was hidden under another cacophony of groans.

"You and your superpowers." That was Mark Mercia, the oldest of the group by at least a decade. His long gray hair called to mind a wizened mage, and not by accident. Mercia had a weekly show expounding on exciting new magical breakthroughs, peddling youth and vitality to America's middle class for six easy payments of only $19.95. Most of it was bullshit, which wasn't uncommon among those who sold magic. What made Mercia special was the ability to sell magic that was *transparent* bullshit. A liar could fool any man once. A con man could fool him twice. Mercia was still fooling people after thirty years, and Slate *deeply* wanted to know how.

"What do you expect from the baby of the group?" Locke muttered, and Coffey lifted a glass to him, making a face.

"I think we should have familiars." The voice was quiet, but Slate would know it anywhere.

Christopher Plant was standing back from the others, his empty hands shoved deep into his pockets. He was Slate's age, but his posture, combined with a small frame, made him look younger. Noticing that people were staring at him, he hesitated to elaborate.

"What?" Slate asked, gesturing at him to continue.

"Familiars," Christopher said again, a little louder. "Mages used to have them. Magical creatures who would bolster their powers, teach them arcane magicks . . . you know. Familiars."

The room was quiet for a moment, and then Mercia laughed.

"Okay *Merlin*," Coffey said. "And what kind of magical creature are you looking to summon?"

"If you're lonely, you can just *buy* a cat," someone sniped.

"How do you propose we do it?" Slate asked. Unlike the others, his comment wasn't sarcastic. Christopher flushed red in a way Slate found slightly appealing, adjusted his wire-rimmed glasses, then pulled the strap of his messenger bag over his shoulder.

He opened the bag and, at first, Slate thought it was empty. *Too* empty, somehow. But then Christopher reached inside and pulled out a book. Old, leather bound, remarkable enough to have its own web of connections.

And one of those connections, Slate couldn't see.

It was the same not-see pooling in the belly of his newest acquisition, the slave he'd picked up barely a month ago. Micah.

It couldn't be a coincidence.

He tried to keep his face neutral as Christopher opened the book, holding it out for the others to see. "It says that they tried to open doorways, portals to other realms, and that sometimes, when successful, creatures would come through."

"Those are *stories*," Mercia began, but the others were less dismissive now.

"Sounds incredibly dangerous," Stewart muttered.

"How would you even begin building a binding spell for a completely unknown creature?" Locke asked, but his voice was speculative rather than disparaging.

"It doesn't mention any binding spells," Christopher admitted. "Apparently they found the creatures to be generally amiable and cooperative."

"Think I can trade my wife for one?" Mercia asked, and Locke guffawed.

"Can I see that?" Slate asked, gesturing for the book. Christopher handed it over, seemingly happy to have *someone* take his suggestion seriously.

The tome was open to an old, hand-drawn illustration of a circular doorway. The place it led to was only darkness, but from the crosshatched shadows emerged a number of chimeric creatures: tigers with hands, people with the snouts of bears, even a large fish whose mode of ambulation wasn't made evident by the drawing.

Slate refocused his eyes, examining the book's energy. The connections thrummed. Christopher, obviously. A number of people who Christopher had outbid, who still coveted it. Weak threads to prior owners, one of whom had stolen it from another before selling it on.

And the dark one, the empty connection, the not-there that led . . . nowhere.

Slate focused harder.

Not nowhere. A not-somewhere. A not-somewhere hidden in the earth, buried beneath a building in the forest that felt . . . like . . .

"Let me see," Coffey said, grabbing it from his hands. Slate barely noticed. He was picturing a hunting lodge, an inn, somewhere he knew . . .

For some reason all he could think of was a business he owned in upstate New York. A twenty-room bed-and-breakfast in . . . Rome? Sparta? Something like that. He stayed in it three times a year while traveling and the rest of the time it ran at a tidy loss that his accountant assured him was beneficial to his taxes.

Why would the book ever have been *there*?

"These are just stories," Coffey said, flipping through the brittle pages. "Fairy tales."

"I think there's some truth to them," Christopher protested, and Slate nodded.

"I can see something there," he said. "But I'm not sure what."

"I can feel something too," Christopher said. "Something different."

Slate watched the book being passed around, and pondered. If Christopher felt something, that was promising.

Of the six of them, Christopher was the least obvious addition to the group. He made his money in stock trades, unassisted by magic in any way that anyone could see.

Well. Anyone *else*.

Christopher had a Gift, one that thrummed through every connection he made. In terms of raw power, there were few who came close to matching him. Slate knew this, though he wasn't entirely sure that Christopher did. He'd certainly never mentioned it.

That alone would have made him a worthy addition, but that wasn't the real reason Slate had invited him. Christopher didn't have Mercia's fame or Locke's influence or Coffey's manic need to collect things. No, Christopher was a member of the club, primarily, because he was the only person Slate actually wanted to spend time around.

"Well look, there's a summoning spell," Mercia said, landing on a page of instructions.

"That's for a water spirit," Stewart said, reading it sideways. "Not an overly difficult summoning, but it's not going to be much use to you once you have it."

"Let's try it," Coffey said immediately. He checked the enthusiasm of the group. "Unless anyone else has a better idea?"

No one did, and so the spell ingredients were quickly assembled—spring water in crystal goblets brought up from the kitchen, single points of quartz aligned in a starburst, and in the center, a large glass salad bowl half filled with salted water.

Stewart inscribed the warding on the bowl in grease pen, copying the book's instructions with only a few minor alterations. He insisted that they were an improvement, and the others took his word for it.

The water in the bowl began to ripple as they chanted, magic harmonizing like a violin bow drawn across the rim. Within a few seconds, a crystal-clear but recognizably humanoid form rose from the rolling surface, peering around at the men. It cocked its head in a show of surprisingly identifiable confusion, and let out a quick burst of chittering noises.

The chant came to an end, and quiet spread over the room. The thing chittered again.

"Is that . . . it?" Locke asked, and Stewart scowled.

"Yes, that's it. I told you, it's just a water spirit. We have captured a water spirit in a bowl of water. Now you can ask it where to dig a well, which is pretty much the only thing they're good for. Huzzah?"

"Dibs," Coffey said.

Slate frowned at him. "Dibs?"

"Yes, dibs, I call dibs on keeping her. Ryan, if I pick up that bowl, she'll move with it, right?"

"Until you spill it trying to back down the driveway, sure," Stewart answered. "Can we eat?"

"Help yourself," Slate said, gesturing to the spread on the table. He was still interested in the water spirit. To be specific, he was interested in how interested *Christopher* was. Christopher had reached out toward the tiny creature, his finger meeting its hand in a rough facsimile of a handshake.

"Hello," he said, giving it a smile. It chittered back at him.

Coffey crouched down beside him, poking it experimentally in the belly. It immediately grabbed his finger, holding on tight while vigorously biting him.

"Shit!" he shouted, yanking his hand back. The spirit didn't let go fast enough, and was yanked outside the boundary of the bowl's warding. It splattered to the floor in a harmless puddle. Coffey wrinkled his nose. "So much for amiable and cooperative."

"She felt threatened," Christopher said accusingly.

"Boo-hoo," Coffey snapped back. Then, "They're not venomous, are they?"

"Not unless you're sensitive to intravenous *water*," Stewart said from the table.

"Whatever. I could probably summon another one, now that I've done it once," Coffey said, shrugging. He walked back over to the book, using his phone to snap a photo of the relevant page.

"Would you mind if I copied some pages, as well?" Slate asked Christopher.

"Of course! The more the merrier." Christopher's voice rose as he tried to reclaim his audience from the bar. "It's really a fascinating narrative, in between all the spells."

"Hmm," Slate agreed, picking up the text. Leaving his guests, he slipped out the door, examining the book as he walked down the corridor toward the foyer. If this were a movie, a magical thriller, it would fall open and reveal a mage the spitting image of Micah, the not-link sprouting cleanly from the center of the page. But that would be too easy. Instead, the link seemed to come from the book as a whole, and it led . . . well. Not to the basement where Micah surely was, at this time of night.

Nor to the lodge in Troy (*Yes, that was it, Troy. Troy, New York.*) that Slate had originally thought of. No, the connection had changed.

Slate stopped before reaching the foyer. He closed his eyes, picturing a map beneath the book. The not-link was there, stygian blue against his eyelids. It crept, twisted, grew, heading north and east toward . . . Boston?

He scowled, opened his eyes, and stepped into the foyer. Locke's bodyguard was there, and Slate gestured to him, letting him know that he could rejoin his employer now. The man set off down the hallway without a word.

Slate's head of household, Carol, was waiting by the stairs to the slave quarters. Carefully, Slate handed her the book.

"I want a physical copy of every page in that book, as fast as you can do it," he said. "Send up the dinner service and three hospitality slaves, I don't care what gender." He hesitated. "And Micah."

CHAPTER FIVE

∞

S late sat at his desk the next morning, diligently trying to read. Against his best hopes, Christopher had let him borrow the actual book for the week, in exchange for a hastily-made physical copy, half the book's purchase price and, at Christopher's hesitant and almost *shy* request, a room and the use of Micah for the night.

The slave still bore a few healing cuts from an evening with Slate a week ago, and they'd enthralled Christopher all evening. Of course he'd *known* that Slate owned slaves—as did Coffey and Stewart, for that matter—but Slate supposed it was different to actually see them in practice. *Thrilling*, was a word Slate would use.

Slate had been thrilled at first too. For years, he'd learned to take more and more from the people he bought, to push the envelope into ever more dangerous territory. He'd felt sure that he'd be caught, and each new purchase carried the heady rush of *surely* being the last he could get away with. Someone would invite the wrong friend, downgrade the wrong indent, do some damage that couldn't be undone, and the house of cards would come tumbling down.

It never did.

Slate leaned back, letting his fingers run through Micah's hair. The slave was currently kneeling beside Slate's chair, his expression its normal carefully maintained neutral. It didn't change when Slate took him by the chin, forcing his face up and to the side. By the looks of him, Micah's night with Christopher hadn't involved anything too terribly strenuous. The bruises around his throat were a week old, but there might have been other marks hidden beneath his light cotton shirt. Slate hadn't done an inspection. Micah could still move under his own power—anything else was cosmetic and could be dealt with as such.

Releasing him, Slate gave up on the book's meandering narrative. He shut the tome, focusing instead on the not-connection seeping from the cover.

"You're coming with me," he informed Micah without looking over. The slave nodded. "To Boston. Carol's having bags packed."

Micah nodded again, not offering an opinion on this development. He was, if nothing else, well trained.

It was a three-hour drive. Slate sat in the back of the town car, engaged in his reading. Micah sat across from him, on the rear-facing bench, watching peacefully out the window.

When Slate had envisioned the trip, he'd thought Micah would kneel on the floor, maybe spend a couple of hours being an obedient little cockwarmer . . . but the thought of a Massachusetts pothole put a shuddering end to that fantasy. It continued distracting him, though, as he tried to focus on the indenturement record in front of him. Usually, he didn't bother reading them—but usually, they weren't such a mystery.

Micah Sawyer.

Onboarded young and securely a good decade ago, trained as personal security as well as hospitality, Arabelle's signature, a collection of owners who kept him for nominal periods of time. No names Slate recognized as being particularly important. No connection to magic at all, as far as Slate could tell.

He set the file aside, leaning back in his seat. He hadn't brought the man not to use him.

"What did Plant want?" he asked.

Micah looked away from the window, dropping his eyes to the ground. "Are you asking specifically?" the slave asked. Slate hummed. Micah dutifully recited off the events of his evening. "He asked me for my limits, I reassured him I was at his disposal. He asked me for a blowjob, which I gave him. He tried to tip me, which I turned down, of course, and then we took a shower and he asked me to sleep beside him, which I did."

Slate wrinkled his nose. "That's *it*?"

And damned if Micah's cheeks didn't color slightly.

"That's the short version, sir. I can go into more detail, if you're looking for—"

"No."

Micah nodded and said nothing.

Seemed almost like a waste, Slate thought, to have someone with Micah's skills for a whole night and to ask for nothing but a plain and simple dick sucking . . . then again, it was rather in Christopher's character to have a world-class escort at his disposal and still request a *snuggle*. Maybe he'd have to have Christopher around again, show him some of the more interesting things that could be done with a slave like Micah. There was an appeal to the scenario that settled low in Slate's belly, even if it would be somewhat *tamer* than his usual interludes.

"Did you get off?" Slate asked, partially out of curiosity, mostly as a segue into the events he had planned for the rest of the trip.

"No, sir," Micah said slowly. There was caution in his voice that sent a shiver of excitement down Slate's back.

"Didn't touch yourself afterward?" Slate pressed, knowing the answer. "Thinking about it?"

"No," Micah repeated, more firmly this time.

"Hmm," Slate answered noncommittally, not giving Micah any clue what he thought about that. "I want you to do it now."

Micah didn't question it, just raised his hips, pushing his pants down around his thighs. His cock was already thickening by the time he took hold of it. His shirt rucked up, showing a crescent of the not-energy above the perfect *v* of his pubic hair. He exhaled slowly.

"You like being watched?" Slate asked, resting his arms along the back of the seat. "Putting on a good show?"

"I like orders that are easy to follow." Micah was flirting, his voice husky as he deftly avoided giving a real answer.

"I'd like to see Christopher fucking your mouth someday," Slate said. "I want you to hint at it next time he's using you."

"Another easy order," Micah said, a little breathless.

Slate smirked at his slave. This one was *quick*. The indecision of a wrong answer, and the unknown consequences, had left more than one of Slate's previous acquisitions little better than mutes. It didn't help; their unwillingness to engage displeased him just as much as a wrong answer, if not more.

Or maybe Micah just hadn't seen enough, wasn't frightened enough yet.

"Don't make a mess," Slate ordered, and picked up his book. He watched the not-energy flowing off it, ahead and slightly to the right of their current bearing. It terminated in something that gave Slate the *impression* of Boston, though he couldn't get much more than that. He could have put it on the map—but then he'd have an address and still need to drive there. This way was more interesting.

The mystery put something warm in his chest. He wasn't used to mystery. He was the man with the answers. Having *questions* was a refreshing change of pace.

If he focused, he could track every other connection the book had. He could connect it to past owners as well as everyone who *wanted* to own it. He could push further, following threads of association as many degrees as he chose to. Connections between people were the most interesting, but people had connections to things, to places, to plants and animals, to *everything*. Every single thing that existed or had ever existed was part of a massive tapestry of interconnected threads, and Slate, given time and perseverance, could see *all* of it. Could step back from the loom and see the whole tangled mess for what it was.

That was an exaggeration. He'd never focused anywhere near long enough to pull *all of creation* within his scope. He didn't need to. Not when every part looked the same.

Micah's breath got slightly more audible. Slate noticed, but didn't acknowledge him. By now, Micah would be trying to figure out whether he was allowed to come, and if so, where exactly he was supposed to do it without "making a mess."

The obvious answer was to ask—but Micah was too smart for that. *Do not interrupt* was the first thing hospitality slaves were taught. All else stemmed from the self-evident truth that their needs came *second*.

Micah's quickening breath was a textbook perfect way to attract Slate's attention without overtly having done so. Micah would be hoping for another order, or maybe just a comment, giving him some idea about what to do. A gracious owner would recognize this and clarify.

Slate was not a gracious owner.

Micah's punishment already sat, waiting, in a duffel on the floor. The slave couldn't delay forever, and sure enough, only a few more minutes went by before he couldn't hold it back, coming into the curve of his hand with a muffled whimper.

Without hesitating, Micah raised his hand to his mouth, licking the mess off his fingers. Slate had to admit, he wouldn't have thought of that. It was a clever interpretation of the orders Micah had been given . . . though it wouldn't save him.

"I told you not to make a mess," Slate said, disapproval clear in his voice. "If I wanted you to come, I would have said so."

"I misunderstood," Micah said quietly, staring at the ground.

Slate hid his satisfaction. He suspected that Micah could, on occasion, enjoy his punishments a little too much. Slate suspected he had a masochistic streak, but those had a tendency to diminish sharply in the moment of clarity that immediately followed orgasm. So, that was where Slate would work.

"Your problem is that you focus too much on yourself," Slate said, inventing the criticism off the top of his head. He reached down and picked up the duffel. "I don't mind that you like your job. But you need to learn the hazards of focusing on your own cock."

"Yes, sir," Micah said, sounding perfectly miserable. "Sorry."

"Don't be sorry," Slate said, lifting a coil of rope from the bag. The car had anchor points hidden within the upholstery, and it wasn't long before lengths of rope pulled Micah's knees wide apart. The waistband of his pants dug into his spread thighs, adding to his discomfort. But the bag wasn't empty yet.

"Put these on," Slate instructed, and watched as Micah buckled leather cuffs around his own wrists. Tight, but not too tight.

"Good," Slate told him, and then held out a bar gag and two small, nondescript pills. One blue, one white. "Now these."

Micah hesitated, and with any other slave, Slate might have expected a protest, but then Micah reached for the pills, swallowing them dry. His fingers spread just the slightest distance too far when he reached back for the gag, verifying, without being asked, that he hadn't palmed the pills. The hair stood up on the back of Slate's neck. He *loved* a professional.

The hood slid easily over Micah's head and buckled tight around his throat, cutting off the light and most of the sound. A short length of rope hung from a ring on the back, and Slate quickly threaded this through the wrist cuffs before tying it off on the headrest.

Satisfied, he sat back and surveyed his handiwork. Micah's body was held on display for him, prevented from covering himself at all. Immediately, Slate realized he'd made a mistake. Leaning forward, he took the collar of Micah's shirt in both hands and yanked, tearing the thin fabric easily in half, all the way down to the hem. Micah flinched at the sound.

It added to the effect, Slate thought. The torn, ruined shirt was a striking visual metaphor. It was one thing to have a slave strip and another to have their clothing simply *destroyed*. For all Micah knew, these were the last clothes he'd ever be given.

And now Micah waited, breathing fast and trying to control it, his body spread out and vulnerable to whatever it was that Slate would choose to do to him. And Slate could do anything—after all, Micah was *his*. His to watch, and enjoy, and use.

The exotic mystery of the not-aura lay across Micah's belly, rising and falling as he breathed.

There was one last step, one whose importance Slate considered explaining, before he remembered that Micah could barely hear him beneath the hood. And so, silently, Slate snapped a metal cage closed over Micah's soft cock. Micah flinched again as the tiny, pointed nubs on the inner surface poked into his flesh.

It seemed pointless, putting a cage on a man who'd just gotten off. Micah would probably be confused right at the moment. In another five minutes, though, the blue pill would begin kicking in. Micah's skin would tingle, his body would overheat, and his cock would begin a valiant battle against the studded metal enclosing it. He'd writhe against his bonds, trying desperately to get some friction, anything to relieve the *need* building in his body.

The realization of his predicament would be hindered slightly by the white pill. Micah would already be feeling the effects of that one. Right now, it would feel like mild confusion, but in a few minutes, it would put Micah half into a dream. His mind would invent explanation after explanation for what was happening to him, punctuated by moments of lucidity, making it impossible to know how long it had been or, more importantly, how long might still be left.

To put it simply, it would feel as though he had gone insane.

"You want to think about your dick?" Slate said, leaning forward to speak in Micah's ear. Micah groaned into the gag. "Have fun."

CHAPTER
SIX

O n the outskirts of Boston, Slate got into the front seat. Micah had been reduced to begging incoherently, and it was making it difficult to give directions.

Between the not-connection's compass point and the car's map, Slate was able to figure out where he was headed. He directed the driver visually, following the dark thread as best as he could.

The car rolled to a stop outside a used bookstore, and Slate tried not to be disappointed.

He'd expected a residence, a person or people whose ancient works would create the kind of anti-energy suddenly populating his vicinity. Someone who knew what they were doing, who could give him answers about what he was dealing with. Someone who knew what he *didn't*.

Instead, he found himself on a broken concrete sidewalk, outside a shop with a cardboard *Open* sign hanging lopsided in the door. The display window had a collection of sun-bleached mass-market paperbacks, partially obscured by the chipped paint of a liberal political slogan.

The book's dark tendril pulsed onward. Whatever the not-connection was to, it was *definitely* in there.

He pushed the door open and went inside. A bell jingled, summoning an older woman in a patchwork denim dress. Her gray hair was dyed a vibrant shade of pink, and for one heart-stopping moment, Slate thought that the path led to *her*. Then she moved, and the tendril didn't move with her. It passed intangibly through her body before vanishing into the wall behind her.

"Looking for anything in particular?" she asked, giving him a warm smile.

He returned it. "Just browsing."

"All right." She seemed to notice the book in his arms. "We're not doing buybacks right now, hon. First week of the month only."

"My mistake," he said graciously, not dropping the smile. She nodded once, then disappeared into the stacks. He went to the left, following the direction of the not-energy.

The building was a firetrap and a fucking maze. Every inch of shelf space was packed with books, books stacked on books with no rhyme or reason he could find. He went up and down the same shelf twice, trying to find where the compass point went after disappearing through the solid paper barrier. He finally noticed a small door, half blocked by cardboard boxes of books.

A paper label on the door read *Employees Only*, so at least he was unlikely to be disturbed as he searched. Quietly, he pushed the door open, and gingerly stepped over the box barrier.

Immediately, he knew he was in the right place. The energy of the entire *room* was off. He felt like he was walking across gossamer, ready to tear at any moment, plunging him, this shop, the whole fucking *city* into the unknown. He didn't need to consult with Christopher's book anymore. He could see what he had come for—a water damaged cardboard box, sitting unassumingly on a low shelf.

He hauled it out and rummaged through the contents, setting leather-bound tomes of magic carelessly on the floor as he delved deeper. And then, halfway to the bottom, there it was.

The book was heavy, and old, and had a sticky writhing aura so thick that Slate could barely see through it. He stood up, cracking the spine as he opened the book.

The centerfold was an illustration of a doorway, through which there was nothing to be seen but emptiness. *Real* emptiness, so much darker than black ink on paper—

"What are you doing in here?"

"What do you want for this book?" Slate asked, without looking away from it. The blackness beckoned from the centerfold of the door-book—the pylinomicon. In the doorway, the pink-haired woman put her hands on her hips.

"These aren't for sale. They're my husband's, he got them from his grandfather and—"

"*What. Do you want. For this book?*" Slate said, louder, turning toward her.

She looked shocked, then crossed her arms. "It's not for sale. They're heirlooms, and my husband—"

"I'll give you twenty thousand dollars," Slate said, his voice flat. Too flat, he realized belatedly. He saw her eyes widen, then narrow.

"I think you should leave."

"Fifty thousand," Slate said. Reasonably, he felt. "There really is an easy way and a hard way to do this."

"Are you crazy?" she snapped. "Get out of here, or I'm calling the police."

She turned to walk away. Slate snatched up Christopher's book and followed her. He adjusted his focus, watching her connections as she moved.

There were lots—family, customers, neighbors, all of them friendly but not particularly strong. An amiable sort, then.

He reached the counter seconds after she did, snatching the phone out of her hand before she had a chance to dial.

"Name a price," he started to tell her, but was cut off when she reached below the register and came up with a baseball bat.

His blood thrilled. He'd misjudged her character. It was rare, but it happened. Very slowly, he laid the books on the counter.

"You have two seconds," she said, her voice harder than her aesthetic would indicate possible. "One."

Her connections fanned around her like a halo, the one dark strand taunting him. He was so close, *so* close, hung up because he couldn't buy a book *from a bookstore.*

"Two," the woman said, and swung the bat at him. It was a slow swing, and he caught it easily, holding it with both hands. Having lost the opportunity to *avoid* a violent altercation, Slate translated his energies into winning it. Time seemed to expand, his heart beating faster, and he was able to see, even *savor*, the confusion and fear on her wrinkled face as he shoved her down. She hit the ground hard and he was already there, coming down on top of her, straddling her, the bat like an iron bar across her windpipe. She shoved at him, clawing at his arms, but it was no use, she was pinned like a butterfly wing. All he had to do was press . . . a little . . . *harder*.

"I'm taking the book," he told her, watching her face turn red. Her hands beat helplessly against his forearms. "You will receive your money within the week. All right?"

He gave her just enough slack to breathe. She nodded vigorously, and he shifted the bat to her collarbones. She let out a cough, her body shuddering beneath his. It occurred to him that he could kill her—the shop was empty, he'd told no one he was coming. He shifted, his half-interested cock pressing agreeably against her soft belly. She whimpered.

"If I need to come back here, I'm going to fuck you up," he said evenly, looking down into her red-rimmed eyes. He searched her connections for something he could use. "I'm going to fuck up your store, I'm going to fuck up your husband, I'm going to fuck up the teenager your husband's fucking. Understood?"

Her face blanched, the ghost-white letting him know he'd hit a nerve. Perfect.

He stood, leaving her whimpering on the floor as he made his way back to his car, books under his arm.

Micah's whimpering misery grew less entertaining on the ride to Troy, which was fine, because Slate's new acquisition had him transfixed.

He had to actively focus on the new book to keep the energy from obscuring his ability to read it. It was challenging, bordering on actually *difficult*, and Slate loved it.

Christopher's book was a story with smatterings of practical magic included almost as footnotes, but this.

This.

Slate stared at the drawing of the doorway, at the empty blackness that seemed to roil beneath it. What did that *mean*? The door couldn't go nowhere, there had to be *something* there, but *what*?

The pylinomicon's aura faded back into view as his mind wandered. The connections—there had to be hundreds of them—

shone from the book in a thick, unnatural darkness, and then . . . vanished. Picking up Christopher's book, one strand re-solidified, connecting the two tomes. But the moment Slate set it down, the connection vanished.

Reaching across the back seat, Slate pressed his palm to Micah's trembling belly. The slave was hot, his body glistening with sweat, and on any other day Slate would have found that unavoidably distracting. But today, he was only interested in the connection between Micah's darkness and the pylinomicon.

There wasn't one. Whatever connected Micah to all this, it wasn't either book.

Interesting.

Slate was still missing a piece. Maybe piece*s*.

He refocused on the book, trying to decipher it as best as he could. It was written in a combination of Old English, Latin, and Greek. Like any self-respecting magical scholar, Slate could read these, passably—but it made for slow going, to say the least. He'd barely finished with the first few pages by the time they got to Troy.

He wasn't sure why Christopher's book had given him such a strong feel for this place. For most of the way here, he'd worried he was imagining it—that he was assigning familiarity to a location that could have been anywhere. That suspicion went away the moment the Mercedes pulled onto the property, and tendrils *burst* from the pylinomicon.

Slate glanced at Micah, who appeared to be semi-conscious again beneath his hood. His not-connection hadn't changed.

Another piece, still not Micah's.

Interesting.

Slate climbed out of the car, taking in his surroundings. The forest surrounding the inn was in its full spring attire, leaves bright and birds singing. The place really was beautiful, which was good, because Slate suspected he was about to be spending a *lot* more time here.

The bellboy greeted him politely, even reverently, and Slate returned the greeting. He'd called ahead, of course, so he would be the only guest in the building tonight. Slate gave the boy a hundred, to help compensate, and told him to take the luggage up to the master suite. The driver would take care of Micah.

For his part, Slate was following the connections—not just one, but dozens of them now—leading into the building. He expected them to stop in the atrium, but rather than tying to something there, the connections went . . . down.

Slate frowned and turned to the indent at the desk.

"How do I get downstairs?"

"Your room is on the second floor, sir," she answered brightly.

He waited, silently, for her to realize her error. She did, and the flash of fear across her features reminded him of the woman at the bookshop.

Gods, but he'd had a good day.

"There's a service stairway down that hall," she said, pointing. "Or you can access the ballroom via the elevator."

"Thank you, miss," he said, and headed for the stairs.

The lower level wasn't anything to write home about. A couple of store rooms, kitchens, and of course, the ballroom. It was nondescript, mass produced metal chairs stacked in a corner, thick curtains covering the wallpaper. The far wall was mostly glass, doors leading to a patio and a scenic mountain overlook. The perfect place for a local bank's annual company teambuilding conference. It would have been completely unremarkable, *except* for the thick strands of not-connection which flowed uniformly to the center of the room, and then stopped dead.

Slate circled the cessation point several times, watching the strands. They didn't rotate evenly in a circle around a central location. Instead, they sometimes seemed to veer *around* something, before turning back and approaching the vanishing point from an angle that never changed.

Almost, Slate thought, *like there's a doorway.*

A doorway that could only be entered from one side.

He set the books down on the ground and shrugged out of his suit coat. Rolling his shirt up to the elbow, he stepped closer. The strands of connection flowed easily through his body on their way to the door. Slowly, he reached his hand out. His fingertips paused at the energy's apex, and then, with a deep breath, he reached further.

Nothing happened. Absolutely nothing.

He took a few steps forward, his whole body moving past the place where the energy stopped. Nothing. He was not transported to a magical far side, nor was he obliterated by the physics of an otherworldly wormhole.

He realized his heart was going incredibly fast, and he laughed, pressing his hand to his chest. He wasn't sure what he had been expecting to find here. *Absolutely nothing* would have been the logical answer. What were the chances of anything being here at all?

He frowned, considering.

What *were* the chances? He was one of a thousand who could get access to Christopher's book—and probably the *only* one who could use it to find the pylinomicon.

So what were the chances that, from all the land on the entire planet, he also just *happened* to own the land where the door was?

Maybe there had been some clue, more subtle than with Micah? Some semiconscious attraction that had told him he needed to own this?

No. He'd bought the place sight unseen on a recommendation from his accountant, who was, easily, the least magical being on the face of the Earth.

The chances of coincidence were vanishingly small, and there was even more to it than that.

The inn was built on a slope, as a split level. Before its construction, the place he was standing now had been *underground*. It had been excavated to this level years before Slate had ever heard of it, but who else could have known to do that? To his knowledge, he was the only person alive who had figured out how to see influential magic the way he could. Nobody who could see what he saw was designing midrange bed and breakfasts. They certainly weren't excavating invisible doorways and then leaving.

Slate put his hands in his pockets and circled the vanishing point again. The conclusion he was arriving at wasn't possible. That wasn't how his magic worked. He could see connections because he knew the magic. He could utilize resources because he was intelligent. But as he'd been explaining to clients for most of his adult life, he could not see *the future.*

But when all alternatives have been exhausted, the only explanation remaining, no matter how improbable, must be the truth.

And the only explanation remaining was: the energy led here because he was *going to build* a gateway here.

Slate stood in the middle of the empty ballroom, hands on his hips, and grinned.

"I'm eating in," Slate said, when the girl from the front desk came to ask. There was a small restaurant on the mezzanine overlooking the atrium, but with only one guest, it wouldn't be running unless he told it to. "Bring up whatever's fresh."

She nodded and left without asking any further questions. Good.

Slate went back to his work. There was a small table in his room, and at the moment, it was mostly taken up by his books and his laptop. Every other inch of space was covered by note paper. His laptop was open to a translation site, but each unknown word had to be entered manually. Optical character recognition software wasn't quite to the point of recognizing calligraphy made with a quill.

That was all right. Doing the translation himself gave him a better understanding of the text, and he had *nothing* but time.

On the bed, Micah let out a quiet moan. Slate didn't look over. The slave had been mostly incoherent ever since the driver had carried him inside. Slate's toys—the hood, the cuffs, the studded cage—had all been put neatly away in his duffel, and Micah had been stripped down to his pants and left on the bed. The blue pill had worn off ages ago, but Slate was going to need to work on the dosing in the white one, because it had been six hours and Micah was only just now beginning to blink his way back to reality.

Slate went back to the book, adding another untranslatable word to the list. They were popping up with alarming frequency. He would need to find someone who actually *spoke* this language, to find out if they were misspelled or simply too archaic for a modern dictionary.

"Nnn?" Micah said, and Slate put his hands behind his head, stretching out his neck.

He could take a break.

"Finally awake?" he asked, turning away from the desk. Micah was sitting up, blinking around the room in confusion. He ran his hands through his hair, then stared at them.

"*Micah*," Slate said, louder, and Micah snapped to slightly-unsteady attention.

Slate gestured to the floor directly in front of his chair and, to his surprise, Micah seemed to understand immediately. Slate gave it 50/50 he'd collapse the moment he tried to stand on his own, but he didn't. Micah crossed the room in four unsteady steps, then sank to his knees in a motion that could almost be described as graceful.

"Have you learned your lesson?" Slate asked him. Micah nodded, not taking his eyes off the floor. Slate frowned. "Use your voice."

"Yes, sir," Micah said weakly.

Slate reached out and took a handful of the man's long hair, pulling until the slave was forced to look up at him. His eyes were a startling greenish brown, and almost as wide as the bookseller's.

"What have you learned today?"

"It's the . . . the punishment . . ." Micah said, his words slurring together. "You're ready . . . ready for . . ." He blinked, then closed his eyes, forehead furrowing as he concentrated. "What I did . . . leads to . . . to punishment."

"And so you'll be very careful not to need punishment in the future, yes?"

"No . . ." Micah frowned, shook his head. "Yes. Sorry. Yes. Sir."

Slate gave him a small smile. Micah didn't know how right he was.

"And you feel better now?" Slate prompted. Micah nodded. Slate let go of his hair, smoothing it back away from his face. "Good. Here's what you're going to do. You're going to go get yourself a glass of water, and then you're going to come back here and wait until I'm ready to have my cock sucked. Then you're going to go next door and thank the driver for his hard work today. There's a room key for you by the door, and I don't want to see you again until you're bringing me breakfast, understood?"

The chances that Micah would correctly remember four directions in a row was pretty low, but like he'd said. His actions lead to punishment.

"Yes, sir," Micah said, rising unsteadily to his feet. "Thank you for . . . for the discipline, sir. I'll try to do better."

Slate didn't doubt it in the least.

CHAPTER SEVEN

∞

Lights. Bright lights.

The hallway was overwhelming, and Micah resisted the urge to cover his eyes as he walked toward the driver's door.

He wondered what time it was. It felt like the middle of the night, but for all he knew, it was three in the afternoon.

Micah was, to put it bluntly, not a fan of drugs. He knew that people were more amusing, and more easily amused, while under their influence, but he wasn't here to be amused. He had a job to do.

His job was to lie. Lie sweetly, and lie well. And he couldn't do that when he didn't even know what was happening.

He reached the door and gave it two short knocks, wincing at the sound.

It wasn't just the drugs. He was failing this placement. This was probably the worst punishment so far, but it seemed like he was screwing up *every* time his owner summoned him.

Micah squeezed his eyes shut, willing tears not to come. Not now.

Heavy footsteps on the other side of the door, and then the driver was leaning against the open doorframe, frowning at him.

"What's he want?"

"S'posed to thank you for your work today," Micah said. The driver's room was dark, illuminated by one tasteful bedside lamp, and Micah desperately wanted to be inside.

The driver's eyebrows rose. "Seriously? Like . . .?" He gestured vaguely between the two of them, and Micah tried to scrape his wits together. Every performance deserved his best. Or at least, the best he could do.

"Whatever you want," he answered, giving the man a sultry grin. The driver's face might have been comical if Micah weren't so fucking tired.

"Yeah, uh," the driver said, backing up and holding the door open. "Come on in."

Micah headed inside. Acting on a suspicion, he put a little extra sway in his hips as he did. "Where do you want me?"

"Uh," the driver said, and only continued when Micah gave him a reassuring smile. "I'm usually, uh, not into guys, you know?" Micah had heard this one before. His owners' window-shopping friends, who somehow always ended up wanting a sample.

"But . . ." the driver continued. "You're supposed to be like . . . really good, right?"

There it was.

"That's what I've been told," Micah answered. "You can turn out the lights, if you like."

The driver went red, shaking his head. "Oh, no, you don't have to . . . Do you mind?"

"Of course not," Micah answered, putting a knowing laugh into the statement. The driver relaxed.

The darkness made it easier, actually. Micah was used to working in the dark. He relaxed too, falling into autopilot, letting his body go through the motions of seduction.

There was stubble on his cheeks, but there wasn't much he could do about that except not let it chafe against the driver's thighs. The man's hands were tight in Micah's hair, pulling a little too hard, but the pain was sharpening him, waking him up.

Micah had the idea that there was something about today he was supposed to remember, some massive realization that he needed to hold on to . . . but he was high, so who the fuck knew. *Every* realization felt groundbreaking when you were that trashed.

It was something about Slate's duffel bag.

Micah didn't have lube, but the driver was groaning without showing any indication of letting go of his hair, so it was probably fine. Micah backed off, the same way he'd done for Christopher the night before, drawing the experience out. Nobody was going to accuse *him* of rushing through it.

For the first time since he'd gotten in the car that morning, Micah relaxed, letting himself fall into an easy rhythm. He was edging the guy a bit, bringing him close and then withdrawing, letting his body do the work while his mind wandered.

The duffel bag had already been in the car. And that was important because . . . because it was in the car. It was in the car because Slate had brought it. And Slate had brought it because . . .

Micah's heart sank, and there was the lightest scrape of teeth as he lost the rhythm.

The driver shouted like Micah had bitten him, but he bucked deeper even as his nails dug into Micah's nape. Micah filed that away.

Slate had brought the duffel, Micah realized, because he *knew* Micah was going to screw up. Micah had been pretending to enjoy the various little torments Slate came up with . . . but that had been wrong.

A tiny rebellious voice shouted that it wasn't Micah's *fault*, he did his *best*, Slate was the one who didn't give him anything to work with—but Micah stifled it. His job was to anticipate. He shouldn't need to be baby-stepped through every basic task. He should have learned what his owner would want. He should have paid more attention.

Micah gave the driver a hint of teeth again, then had to slow almost to a stop before he pushed the man over the edge. Good trick. If only Slate was as easily learned.

There was something in that protest, though, something in Slate's lack of communication—

The epiphany came rushing back, the last two and a half months of punishments as Micah tried and failed to meet Slate's standards. He somehow managed to fail, over and over and over—

Because punishing him was the point.

Micah could have fucking cried with relief. He let it out in a moan that reverberated through his throat and into the head of the driver's cock.

That was too much, and the man tipped over the edge at last. Micah waited patiently for him to finish twitching, then gently withdrew. He knelt in the dark, silent, while the driver worked his way through the aftershocks.

In his head, Micah went through the last weeks, tallying up the elaborate punishments that Slate had put together for such seemingly mundane infractions, and it all made sense. Micah hadn't been fucking up. He *hadn't*.

Slate was making up excuses to punish him because the punishment was what Slate enjoyed.

So all Micah had to do was be good at taking punishment.

If he'd been alone, Micah would have laughed. But he wasn't, so he settled for a grin that couldn't be seen in the dark.

The light clicked on, and Micah schooled his features back into a vaguely satisfied neutral.

The driver had pulled a blanket over his groin, and was considering him nervously.

"Um, should I . . .?"

Adorable.

"Not unless you want to," Micah said, with a knowing laugh. "I can take care of myself."

There was nothing to take care of, but there was no reason to share that. Micah hadn't undressed; for a client uninterested in men, there was usually no point.

"Oh. Okay. Um . . ."

"I have the room next door," Micah said, rising off the bed with a languid shift of his weight. "If you think of anything else?"

"Yeah," the guy laughed in agreement. With a wink, Micah headed for the door, and the keycard he'd left beside it.

The hallway didn't seem as bright this time, and his own room was blessedly dark. He didn't turn on the nightstand lamp, just collapsed onto the bed like his strings had been cut . . . and immediately realized he wouldn't be able to sleep.

There was no one else there. No other staff in the bunk beside him, ready to wake him up if there was a knock at the door and he didn't hear it.

He lay there in the darkness, staring at the ceiling, listening to the fan and trying not to hear things. There weren't footsteps outside his door. No one was coming down the hall. No one was knocking—

He sat straight up, unsure whether he'd been asleep or not. He thought he'd heard something outside.

He had to check.

He leaned against the doorframe as he opened the door, projecting expectant confidence to . . . the empty hallway.

Sighing, he closed the door again, resting his forehead against the cool wood.

He wished he could go downstairs. There would be staff quarters in the basement, filled with the quiet susurrations of voices, the borrowed vigilance only found in numbers.

But this place wasn't like Slate's home. The workers at a place like this would be indents, probably not even lifers, and they . . . tended not to mingle with people like Micah, if anybody could help it. There was a respectability to be found in the knowledge that their time here was temporary. That they had people, and lives, to go back home to when their limited contracts were over.

No, he would only make things awkward, if there even *was* an extra bunk for him. And anyway, Slate had told him to be here, so —

Micah froze, listening. He pressed an ear to the door, holding his breath.

He'd thought he'd heard a footstep.

The sound didn't repeat.

He could hear his heart beating in the silence between his cheek and the door. The hallway was utterly silent.

What was he expecting, anyway? That Slate was tip-toeing silently down the hall, trying to sneak up on him so he could punish him for—

Yes, Micah realized. Yes, that was exactly what he was expecting.

He let out a long breath. In that scenario, sleeping through a knock was the best thing he could do. Let Slate catch him sleeping on the job so that he could implement whatever stress position he already had planned for the ride home tomorrow. Put like that, there was no avoiding it, really. He might as well go back to bed and get some rest . . .

Micah was halfway back to bed when he remembered the driver. He groaned, rolling his eyes to the ceiling.

The driver, the one who was usually only interested in women, but who had heard Micah's type were *really good*.

The driver who he'd left with an open-ended invitation.

Micah had absolutely no doubt that he wasn't the only one wresting with indecision right now. In the room next door, the driver was arguing with himself over whether it *counted* if it was someone like Micah. Micah, who wasn't a man so much as a professional, and who would never, ever, tell *anyone* what had happened.

The chances of him making it as far as knocking on Micah's door were a solid three out of five hundred. But not zero.

Micah groaned, digging his palms into his eyes. He couldn't excuse that as provoking an owner who wanted him to fail. If the driver knocked, and Micah didn't answer, that would be an *actual* problem, not a manufactured one.

Sighing, Micah turned on the light. It was too bright, and it stung his eyes . . . but it might keep him awake.

Micah glared resentfully at the door—and there, bolted beside the peephole, was his salvation.

He switched the light back off and cracked the door in the darkness. He swung the security bar over and let the door swing shut on it.

It didn't latch.

Micah exhaled, feeling suddenly very heavy. He stumbled back over to the bed, half-diving into the blankets in his eagerness to get off his feet.

The door wasn't shut. It wouldn't lock. If he didn't hear a knock, the person could just *come in*. He hadn't locked himself in, he repeated, a mantra that followed him down into sleep. He hadn't.

He hadn't.

He would *never*.

CHAPTER EIGHT

∞

December 2012

"This is a once-in-a-lifetime opportunity for discovery," Slate said over the noise of the Saturnalia revelers. "Think about it. Who knows what could be on the far side? It could be *anything*."

"Could be absolute garbage," Arabelle intoned. She waved down a passing waitress, taking a drink she definitely hadn't ordered. Slate could only imagine the slave's fate when she arrived at the table with her tray one glass short. Arabelle didn't watch her go. "Could be nothing."

"But it would be *exclusive access* to that nothing," Slate said.

Arabelle raised an eyebrow.

Slate hadn't really expected that to work, but you never knew with the New York crowd. He raised his hands. "Fine, fine. I'll admit that the yearning for scientific exploration has limited draw in our circles. I think I've tapped that well. So let's talk about it as an investment."

"An investment in *what*? You don't know where the gateway leads to."

"Oh, but we might," Slate said, leaning forward and steepling his fingers. "I think someone may have opened it before. They were able to summon magical assistance from a spirit realm."

"Familiars," Arabelle replied, her voice thick with incredulity. "You want me to sell my clients on *familiars*."

"I'm not talking about cats and toads," Slate said, picking up his drink with practiced nonchalance. "I'm talking about fae."

Arabelle sighed, leaning back against the velvet loveseat. Her dress was just transparent enough to reveal the sparkling diamonds in her nipple rings. Her dark eyes regarded him from behind a jeweled venetian mask. "I've known you a long time, Adam. I'd be in jail if it weren't for your advice, and so would half the people here. So I value your judgment. Really, I do. But if people hear you're talking about *pet fae* . . ." She shook her head.

"Plant's in," Slate said, and Arabelle laughed.

"Of course he is. Anybody sane?"

"Mercia. Coffey. Cumberland. Bastille."

"*Bastille?*"

"Bastille," Slate confirmed, nodding. "She was one of the first." A slight exaggeration, but it was close enough to the truth.

"How did you get Bastille?"

"I'm asking you to picture this," Slate said, leaning forward. He didn't feel like shouting, and the party was loud. Saturnalia was a big holiday for the kind of debauchery that Slate's social circle enjoyed. "It's a long shot, but just let yourself imagine. I'm not talking about a dwarf you keep in your kitchen to do the sweeping. We have slaves for that. We have *indents* for that. I'm talking about a creature of ethereal beauty, unimaginable magic, and useful intelligence, but still *just a creature.*"

Arabelle's eyes narrowed as she made the connection. *Creature* wasn't an empty noun; it was a legal term. Humans had civil rights. Creatures, by definition, didn't.

"You're talking about abandoning the slave trade altogether."

"We wouldn't need it," Slate confirmed. "We could take this market out into the open."

"The bleeding hearts would crucify us," Arabelle protested. At a nearby poker table, a chorus of cheers and protests as something highly controversial happened. Somewhere behind him, a slave slipped, crying out in pain. Slate resisted the urge to turn and see which one it was.

"Let them try," he said instead. "We put creatures to work for the American public, and by the time congress drags its bloated corpse into the discussion, half of industry could be running on labor *we sold.*"

"Speak of the devil," Locke said, dropping onto the couch beside Arabelle. "What are we failing to fix fast enough now?"

"Fae labor," Arabelle said.

Locke laughed. "Oh. Yeah, we could drag our heels on that for decades. Or it could become the hot-button issue for the presidential election and it's fixed in six months. Then what?"

"Exactly," Slate said. "Then what? What have we gambled, exactly? A finger prick? Most people won't even need to participate in person; those that show up have wasted, what? A couple hours?"

They could die, of course, if the magic went badly enough . . . but that wasn't part of the sales pitch.

"They could test the blood, figure out who it was," Locke protested, and Slate rolled his eyes.

"'They' *who*? They're gonna prosecute us for magic that was legal when we did it? *Especially* once they start seeing names?" He gestured around at the other partygoers, the games, the slaves on display. "Take away the political contributions of this room alone, and the government would be burning office furniture for warmth."

"You're exaggerating," Locke said.

"But not by much."

The drama at the poker table concluded, and a man that Slate didn't recognize stood up, a fistful of metal poker chips held aloft. Goaded on by cheers, he went to the nearest slave and dropped them into the basket she held in one outstretched arm. Almost immediately, her shoulder began to tremble from exertion. Behind the silver of her mask, her eyes were closed in concentration.

"Oh, she's done for," Arabelle said, sitting up, her attention rapt.

The slaves were dressed in sheer, revealing roman garb, fitting with the theme of the night. They stood about the perimeter of the room, their tattooed arms held out to the sides. In each hand was a woven basket festooned with flowers. Each arm was decorated with four metal circlets, tight enough to hold taper candles upright.

As Slate watched, the slave's trembling caused her candle to spill, hot wax dripping over her arm. She whimpered in pain.

"She wouldn't have made it anyway," Locke said. "That's what Whitehall gets for fronting a woman."

"I don't think she was intended to succeed," Slate mused. He'd already switched focus, examining the web of connections between the slave and the men at the table. "Who's the man putting chips in her basket?"

"Dalton," Arabelle and Locke said together.

"*That's* Dalton?" Slate asked, turning to get a better look. "I thought he was older."

"He has a team in Turkey that's making huge strides in cosmetic surgery," Arabelle said. "The mask probably helps too."

"Ah, that's it," Slate said, searching down the tendrils of connection. Dalton dropped a second handful of chips into the slave's other basket.

For the first time, Slate allowed himself to glance at Micah.

The slaves' faces were all covered by silver masks with the aspects of animals, but Slate would know Micah anywhere. The sheer drape of clothing did little to hide the familiar lines of his body. If that weren't enough, the black-magic mark on his belly shone like a beacon.

The female slave's arms dropped, extinguishing her candles, and she cried out as the wax splashed over her arms. The baskets she dropped fell only a few inches; they hung from thin ropes that stretched to the ceiling, looped through a pulley, and returned to vanish beneath the folds of her skirt. She moaned and rose up on her toes as the hook in her ass suddenly took the baskets' full weight.

Shouts and jeers from the table as Dalton pushed her dress off her shoulders, examining his prize. As the last person to put a chip in her basket, he'd won her contract.

Slate watched as the connection between Whitehall and Dalton grew thicker. Not what he'd have expected from a man who'd just lost valuable property to another.

"Whitehall intended her to take a fall," he said, realizing. "Dalton gets a gift, and Whitehall gets taken out of the running early."

"Cheating," Locke muttered.

"She wouldn't have lasted anyway," Arabelle said. "The baskets are weighted at setup. Freedom was never in reach."

It wasn't real *freedom*, of course. Freeing of slaves was a Saturnalia tradition, but in those days, slaves had been a little easier to come by. These slaves could win a week off—*if* they could keep a candle lit until midnight.

"I meant *you*," Locke said, gesturing at Slate. "How is anybody supposed to play fairly against a guy who can see every piece?"

"I don't play," Slate said absently. He was trying to imagine how anyone played fairly *without* seeing every piece.

This game wasn't just about whether a slave was given away or kept. If that were the case, every guest would simply volunteer their strongest man.

The party was, ostensibly, a fundraiser for . . . Slate couldn't remember. Some charity. Suicide prevention maybe. At the end of the night, chips would be tallied up, and the sponsor of the extinguished slave holding the most would be responsible for a donation of the sum total.

Put up a weak slave, and you were likely to lose them. Put up a strong slave, and run the risk of paying for the whole party.

Micah, Slate figured, could hold twice his market value. He was pretty enough, but nothing that was going to make anyone reckless, especially with weaker slaves to bet on.

But nobody here was spending tokens because they were good-hearted. Mostly the opposite. Every token in a rival's basket put *them* closer to losing. Losing their slave, or losing the whole game. Half the money dropped tonight would be spent on spite. A large drop like Dalton's was rare—most slaves would go down by a thousand cuts.

Fortunately for him, Slate had very few enemies.

"You can look around the room and see how everybody feels about everybody; you can tell who's gonna get dumped on," Locke complained.

"But I can't tell what they're willing to pay," Slate explained, suddenly tired. "Or when. Or which token will be the last straw. I've told you—"

"You can't tell the future, yeah, yeah," Locke parroted, waving his hand dismissively. "So you're telling me you run the same risk of losing as anyone else. You couldn't tell which of yours could hold out longest."

"Of course I can," Slate answered, gesturing to Micah. "I only have two at the moment, and the other's a willowy little femme. I don't need to see the future to make that call."

"So you're relying on luck," Arabelle said, finishing her drink.

"'Tis the season," Slate agreed. "You trained him; do you think I made a good bet?"

"I think that man would stand through a hurricane if he thought there was a head pat in it for him."

Slate laughed, his attention still on his slave. If there were any tokens in his baskets at all, it didn't show. Micah stood with his chin raised, eyes closed, mouth moving silently as if he were murmuring a mantra to himself. His body was so still, his candles hadn't even dripped.

Slate had to shift slightly, remembering the night before. He'd put another bruised *S* on the inside of Micah's left thigh, a sore little reminder of who he belonged to. Slate had no doubt Micah could feel it now.

"A friendly wager, then?" Locke said. "Call it a test of your strategizing. If your man goes down before mine, you pay me the sum it took to drop him. If mine goes first, I'll buy into this magic gateway bullshit you're peddling."

"Which one's yours?" Slate asked.

Locke gestured to a man across the room. His strategy was immediately clear—the man wasn't particularly strong, or handsome for that matter. Locke didn't have enough enemies to collect tokens from bad blood, nor was the man likely to hold out *terribly* long. He would drop easily with a small number of tokens. Locke had written him off as the cost of entry, his focus on making sure he wasn't left holding the pot.

From a simple comparison of strength, the wager was obviously weighted in Micah's favor, which meant Locke was stupid, drunk, or hiding something.

Slate looked back to Micah, the silent motion of his mouth, the planes of his body beneath his clothes. It would be a shame to lose him, even if it *was* only until the next time he went up for auction.

"I want first refusal," Slate said to Locke.

"If I win him? Of course."

"A wager, then," Slate said, extending his hand. Locke shook it, smiling, the picture of congeniality.

"Then if you'll excuse me, I have my own strategy to deploy," Locke said, rising and heading for another game table.

"That was stupid," Arabelle told him once Locke was out of earshot. "He has a lot of friends. That's the only way he gets by around here."

"You're telling *me* he's well-connected," Slate said, raising an eyebrow at her. "*Me.*"

"Are you telling me he's *not*?" Arabelle countered. "Because unless you have a secret reason for wanting to lose, the only other explanation is that, somehow, you don't know."

As if to illustrate her point, a man rose from Locke's table, dropping a few tokens into Micah's basket. They clinked lightly against the bottom. Micah didn't react.

"What do you see?" Arabelle asked.

"Nothing that would help me here," Slate answered honestly. "Everyone here knows, or at least knows *of*, everyone else. Lots of people like each other, lots of people dislike each other. Some people are particularly well-liked, some are particularly disdained; Locke is neither."

"And you?" Arabelle asked.

"I can see people who may be open to an alliance with him *if it was suggested*," Slate continued, brushing past the question. "Look, he's talking to Campbell. They're friends, the sort to maybe do each other a favor now and again. But Campbell is equally friendly with two other people at the same table. Maybe he's already committed to another wager. More likely, he's interested in the brunette by the door. Every time anyone puts a sum in her basket, he'll add a token of his own, afterward, hoping it's the straw."

"You said you can't see the future," Arabelle said accusingly.

"But I am occasionally familiar with the past, especially regarding events I observed personally," Slate said, still watching Locke. "I can extrapolate."

"Well excuse me for breathing, then," Arabelle snarked, lifting her empty glass toward a passing server. Immediately, the glass was replaced by a full one. "Gods, what the fuck is this vodka?"

"Probably a seven-hundred-year-old niche vintage," Slate said, wrinkling his nose at his own glass. "Didn't you know? Our host is a *collector*. Coffey's tastes run toward the rare, expensive, and good. In that order."

"Ugh," Arabelle said, taking a drink anyway. Someone else got up from Locke's table and dropped a couple of tokens into Micah's other basket. It was enough to make his arm tremble, and hot wax dripped over his bicep. He kept his eyes closed.

Slate frowned. He might actually need to get involved in this.

"Incredible, isn't he?" Arabelle asked, gesturing to Micah. "I won't say I have favorites, but I was particularly proud of that one. Took to his training like he was born for it. A flowering vine in a sea of mandrakes."

"If you want him back, now's your chance," Slate said, rising from his seat. "Pardon me."

She waved him back and, somewhat reluctantly, Slate allowed her to kiss him on the cheek before he left. Someone else was already taking his seat.

He scanned the tables for his best advantage, and then found it. A moment later he was dropping into a chair beside Christopher.

"We can get Locke if I win a wager," he said bluntly.

"He'd bring in Hearst and Cunningham," Christopher picked up immediately, excitement making his voice a shade too loud.

"At the very least, yes," Slate answered, reaching out and tipping Christopher's slipping cards back to vertical. "He bet me that my slave would go down before his, and now he's orchestrating a coordinated offensive."

"Which one is his?" Christopher asked, looking around.

"It's your turn," Slate reminded him. Christopher checked his cards and threw some tokens into the middle of the table, never taking his attention off Slate. Slate gestured toward Locke's slave, then toward Micah.

"Well, at least you won't need *much* help," Christopher said, having compared the two. "Have a seat, we'll get you dealt in. Everyone, this is my friend Adam."

"Slate," Slate clarified. He was already at least passing acquaintances with everyone at the table, but let Christopher do the introductions anyway. Unlike Locke, Christopher *was* particularly well-liked. He gave Slate a winning smile as he won the round, elbowing him playfully in a way that left them, by mutual arrangement, closer together.

Christopher swept the tokens toward himself, quickly stacking a large percentage into two piles.

"One for Hearst, one for Cunningham," he said, pushing the piles toward another man. "Henry, you've had good luck tonight— care to try some of it on that slave over there? My friend's trying to win a bet."

Henry picked up the two piles of tokens, carrying them over to Locke's slave and dumping one pile unceremoniously into each basket. The sudden weight caused the slave's arm to jerk, spilling hot wax over his wrist. The dripping heat set off a domino effect of flinches and overcorrections, and by the time it was done, the man's arms were at a decidedly visible angle. He was letting at least part of the baskets' weight rest on the ropes, and he shifted in discomfort as that translated into the hook inside him.

"That was nice of you," Slate told Christopher. He was acutely aware of the way Christopher's knee pressed against his. It wasn't unpleasant. "I thought you might be in the market for a slave."

"Not that one," Christopher answered casually, not looking over. "Come on, play."

Winning wasn't an option. Slate knew that. Everyone here knew he could see things they couldn't, and although his sight gave him no *actual* advantage, anyone he bested would sullenly begin to speculate. So Slate played badly, quickly losing the small stack of tokens he'd received at the door. He lost most of them to Henry in the first round, and watched in satisfaction as they were gambled on Locke's slave again. The man's trembling arms were held at an even steeper angle now, causing wax to pour liberally off the candles as soon as it melted. With each passing minute, the exposed wicks lengthened, the flames burned higher, and the wax ran off faster. The slave's own body was simply another cog in a mechanism acting against him at every turn.

Slate checked his watch, pushing down the swell of arousal he couldn't do anything with right at the moment.

Thirty minutes to midnight. At this rate, even if Locke's slave managed to hold, his candles would gutter out long before the bell tolled.

Slate lost the rest of his tokens slowly over the next two rounds, betting conservatively but for much longer than his extremely poor hand could justify. Christopher bought him in for a third round, despite his protests, and he lost that too. Having nothing left to gamble, he made his excuses and left, heading back to where Arabelle was still lounging on her duvet. He settled into one of the couches beside her.

"Admiring your handiwork?"

"Only three of them are mine," she said, surveying the line of slaves. Slate refocused, checking their energy. A few had thin tethers to people in the room, owners hoping not to lose them or gamblers hoping to acquire them, but for the most part, nothing. They stood silent, mimicking statues, inanimate but for subtle shifts as they tried in vain to lessen their discomfort.

Slate found it beautiful. Compelling.

The men and women gambling, his people, existed in a frantic dance. They were constantly trying to exert ownership over each other with money or blackmail or bargains, winning some and losing others, but always caught in a massive, complex tangle of influence. Slate made his money and most of his allies by carefully tugging on those strands. The others saw him as a spider, overseeing a web of his own creation, but in truth, he was trapped just as thoroughly as they were.

The slaves were free of all that. Micah stood with his arms outstretched, candlelight flickering off the sweat beading on his skin, his whole life narrowed to a single problem that would be over in half an hour, one way or another.

Slate didn't *envy* him. But he did find it glorious to behold.

There was a cry to their side as Locke's slave dropped his baskets, a muscle cramp or simple exhaustion taking him out of the running. Henry received a round of applause from the table Slate had just left, while Locke's table erupted in good-natured jeering. Several of the connections at that table shifted in a way Slate wasn't able to explain. Christopher gave him a wave and an enthusiastic thumbs-up. Slate returned it, a little awkwardly.

Having Micah off the chopping block gave him a sense of relief disproportionate to the situation. There was never a real chance of losing him, and Slate could always have bought Micah back in six months when Locke tired of him. Nonetheless, the relief remained.

"How much did Locke get them to drop on Micah?" he asked Arabelle. "Should I be worried?"

"At least a million," Arabelle said. "Maybe two."

Micah had stopped his mantra, and there were tremors in his shoulders as he adjusted his stance.

"That'll probably take the pot, then," Slate sighed, knowing it wouldn't, but annoyed that Locke had gotten so close.

"It's Micah or one other," Arabelle agreed. Slate raised an eyebrow, and Arabelle gestured. There was a particularly handsome young man in the corner who was, apparently, much stronger than he looked. He should have reached his limit and gone down early, but instead, he was proving to be an unlucky combination of gorgeous and resilient.

Slate switched focus, and was surprised to find a genuine thread of *affection* stretching to where the slave's owner sat beside Locke.

"Oh," Slate said, sitting up straight. There was another game he had to play. "Damn. Do you have your entry tokens? Let me buy them off you."

"Take them," Arabelle said, already holding the handful out. She didn't have a purse, and the cut of her dress left very little to the imagination. He considered asking, then decided against it. He took them from her hand, checking his watch. There were fifteen minutes to midnight. Not enough time to try to raise more. He could *buy* more . . . but that felt like it would lessen the win, somehow.

He strode across the room with intent, heading for the beautiful slave. The man was clearly on his last leg. His arms were canted, the candles dripping slowly but steadily down his arms. Slate gave it 50/50 he'd be able to hold out, assuming nothing changed.

Slate circled the slave once, admiring the way the thin gossamer of his robes clung to the sweat on his exhausted body. Returning to face the man, Slate lifted his chin with one knuckle, staring into his eyes.

"I think I'm going to enjoy you," Slate murmured. It was too quiet for anyone else in the room to hear, but the man's eyes widened slightly. Slate held his gaze as he dropped Arabelle's tokens, one by one, into the baskets.

Barely a minute after Slate walked away, the slave's baskets dropped suddenly enough that he almost lost his balance. Slate winced at the thought.

He glanced back over to Locke's table, giving his friend a small nod when their eyes met. Locke looked a little on edge, and why wouldn't he? His *real* wager hadn't played out yet.

The shift in the connections after Locke's slave went down hadn't made sense to Slate at first. The bet was between Slate and Locke, so no one else's loyalties should have been involved . . . but it had been a *bad* bet. Locke stood to gain very little. He'd sacrificed his slave and put himself at higher risk of carrying the pot by drawing attention to a slave who would otherwise have finished solidly in the middle of the running.

But that had been the point.

It was never about Locke; it was about *Cunningham*, Locke's confidante and the owner of the deceptively strong beauty Slate had just won. Cunningham was textbook upper management, lots of grand concepts, very few practical plans. Of course he wouldn't have thought to actually *vet* the slave he planned to put up. He must have realized the man's strength too late and panicked, looking to take the room's attention off his pretty little offering. Locke had orchestrated the bet with Slate as a favor to Cunningham, using Slate to divert two entire tables away from a slave who was, by all other metrics, an obvious first choice.

And Slate had helped, putting Micah in the crosshairs.

It might have worked if Slate hadn't realized what had happened. Without his little contribution, Cunningham's slave may well have lasted out the night, like Micah would.

Sighing, Slate crossed the room, standing before his slave with arms crossed.

"Look at me," he said evenly, and Micah's eyes opened immediately, focusing on Slate's collarbone. Close enough.

"You have five minutes left," Slate said, watching the breath catch in Micah's chest. The man was right to be worried. Limits usually meant counting, and Micah rarely enjoyed the things he counted off. "At some point in those five minutes, you're going to get a significant number of additional tokens. I need you to hold. Do you understand me?"

Micah nodded, his gaze on the floor.

"Tell me you understand," Slate said.

"I need to hold," Micah said, his voice so thin it was nearly a whisper. "There's more coming."

"It is going to be a *problem* for me if you don't."

"I'll hold, sir," Micah said, and there was a bit more determination behind it now.

"I believe you will," Slate said, stepping closer. He brushed a lock of Micah's damp hair out of his eyes, cupping his jaw and stroking his thumb along Micah's cheek. "You've been so good for me tonight. It's just a little longer."

Micah nuzzled slightly, almost imperceptibly, into his hand, and Slate's worries evaporated. Of course Micah wasn't at risk, and never had been. Around the bruised *S* on his inner thigh was an etched spell, giving him the power to do anything he was commanded to. It wasn't without cost, of course. Micah had been in agony from the moment he'd been given the order to hold, and the pain had only increased as the night went on. By now, he probably felt as though his muscles were shredding, sinews tearing loose from bone with each passing second. But his body could not fail without his intentional permission. The magic would not allow it.

The only way the baskets would drop was if Micah chose, deliberately, to disobey.

"I hope you're still mine at midnight," Slate said, just loud enough for Micah to hear, "I'd like you in my bed, come morning."

Micah stared at him like he was the only man in the world, and Slate wondered why he'd worried.

CHAPTER NINE

∞

June 2013

"What do you mean you aren't *coming*?" Slate hissed into his phone. The response, crackling with distance, was almost buried under the sound of crashing waves.

"I said I'm not going to fucking *be* there," Coffey said. "You're in a hunting cabin with a bunch of assholes. I'm in Cabo with two girls who aren't my age *collectively*. Do the fucking math."

Slate scowled and considered protesting. The inn hadn't been a "cabin" *before* he'd renovated. He'd added fifteen suites to cover the expansion of the lower floor. There were slave quarters down there now, and warded cells with iron and banding embedded in the concrete. Whatever came through that door, they'd be ready for it.

"You said you were in," Slate said instead.

"And I got you the vials, didn't I? How many do you have now, a couple hundred? And how many are from me?"

"Eighty," Slate admitted.

"And who put up the slave to be the catalyst?"

"You."

"Good. I'm a venture capitalist, not a fucking carpenter. Call me when it's built."

The line disconnected. Slate closed his eyes, focusing on not hurling his phone against the rough stone of the lobby's massive fireplace. He did not need people changing things on him *now*.

"We're fine," he said to no one in particular. "It's fine."

And it was true. Coffey was no one special, really. Neither was Locke, who at least had the excuse of attending a fucking *senate hearing*. They'd been some of the first on board when Christopher had proposed this project, and it was disappointing that they'd jump ship now . . . but Slate had needed them for their social networks, not their company. That part was over now. And *most* of the people involved would be represented by their vials rather than their person. There were perhaps a hundred and fifty vials of blood, representing a hundred and fifty spellcasters, less than thirty of whom would be making an appearance tonight.

Slate shoved his phone into his pocket and headed downstairs. There was still a bit of construction dust, some of the cell doors weren't installed yet, but what project was ever *completely* finished? He had the important part done.

Taking a deep breath, he stepped into the ballroom.

It was shrouded in darkness, thick curtains blocking out the solstice sunset. Most of the room was occupied by a massive spell circle, carefully laid down in mirrored paint.

Christopher was standing in the corner, his notes and books spread out across an altar. He was scribbling furiously into two different notebooks while, around him, hooded figures set small glass vials on the perimeter of a massive spell circle.

"Do you think the cloaks are a bit much?" Slate asked.

Christopher didn't look up from his calculations. "Mercia insisted. Look at this sigil. Is this an enata or an egnitus? I can't tell if this is an additional stroke or just poor penmanship."

"It's an enata," Slate said, reading over his shoulder. "Egnitum are only used to bind living beings; connections between spaces and times are governed by enatas."

"Right, right, right," Christopher muttered. "I knew that. I did."

"I know you do," Slate reassured him. "Half the people we're going to have here tonight haven't even seen the pylinomicon, and don't want to." He picked up one of Christopher's notebooks and checked over it. "I didn't ask for your help because I think you're stupid."

Christopher's face flushed, and Slate tried not to find the effect endearing. Christopher flipped a book over, his fingers running across the text on the back. "I'm half-convinced this entire *idea* is stupid. That we're going to rip open a black hole, destroy the world."

"We'd certainly be dressed for it," Slate said, gesturing to the cloaked figures around them. "Care to help me with my vial? I haven't done it yet."

"Oh! Sure. Yes. Do you have . . . ?"

Slate pulled a paper envelope from his coat, emptying the contents onto the table. Coffey and Locke had declined to give their own blood, and had expressed confusion about why the others *would*. Slate found this position unbearably cowardly. To do this magic required *audacity*. Spirit. To do it by proxy would defeat the point.

Slate refocused on his task. On TV, magicians did their spells by slicing their palms open, blood splattering dramatically from fists clenched in determination. It made a striking visual, but that was simply . . . not how magic worked. Blood magic *in particular* was known for the efficiency with which any small part granted the spellcaster the power of the whole.

So, in reality, Slate used an alcohol wipe to clean the tip of his ring finger, and pricked it with a sterile lancet. Blood welled up, and Christopher took his hand, his touch lingering as he squeezed a few drops into a glass vial. The sigils inscribed on the outside flashed a deep, luminous crimson, then went dark.

"I give this piece, this inseparable part, in accordance with the whole," Slate recited. "May my will be done."

Christopher's hands cupped the vial and he whispered something, creating the binding with his own magic. The deep red of the sigils faded, leaving a plain glass vial. Slate plucked it from Christopher's hands and went to set it on the perimeter of the circle. Immediately, he lost track of it amongst the others. He could feel his heart beating so fast it was a wonder the vial wasn't strobing.

"That should be enough," he remarked, half to himself, looking around the darkened room. There were easily more than enough vials, and the magical power they represented was . . . well it was a bit daunting, to say the least.

Each one of them had a not-link, a thick taproot that slithered across the floor to the center of the room. The floor was a starburst of emptiness, reflected back at him by the mirrored paint they'd used to make the ikons.

"Only a few hours until midnight," Christopher said, adjusting his glasses. He picked up Slate's book, flipping back through the pages like he was going to find something they hadn't noticed in the last year. "People will be arriving soon."

"The help will keep them out of the circle," Slate said. "Beyond that, they aren't a concern until the spell proper. We really only *need* four—one at each compass point, to center the energy. Everyone beyond that is added security."

"Everyone but . . . the slave," Christopher said hesitantly.

"Yes," Slate answered. He'd almost forgotten. "He's being prepared by some of Mercia's people. I'm sure it's going to be irretrievably gaudy."

Christopher covered his mouth to hide a snort of laughter.

"Shall we go check?" Slate asked, already knowing the answer.

Christopher shook his head, sobering quickly. "No, I don't need to . . . No."

"It's safe," Slate reassured him for the hundredth time. "I've been watching him for months; he's an island, no one will *ever care*—"

"I know," Christopher interrupted, looking up at him. "I know. But I don't need to look him in the eye. All right?"

Slate nodded, and Christopher went back to flipping through pages.

In the year it'd taken to plan this, Christopher had been mildly hesitant to discuss the topic of the catalyst. The blood gave them power, plenty of it, but the kind of magic they were attempting would need . . . rather more than the sum of those parts. In the same way that potting clay was not loam, the magic of life simply was not the magic of death.

And Christopher had always moved carefully around the subject of slaves as a whole. He had none of his own, though he'd taken advantage of Micah's services a dozen more times over the last year. Despite the ample opportunities, Slate never joined them. Christopher had a tendency to stammer when broaching the subject, which Slate found delightfully charming. Micah's recounting of the night's innocent fumblings brought more joy than participation likely could have. The requests came often enough that Slate had offered to buy Christopher one as a gift—but Christopher had only gone red and politely but firmly refused. His line apparently lay somewhere between using them and being responsible for them.

But what they were doing tonight was bigger than one slave's life. Bigger than anything that could possibly befall one man, Slate thought, as he greeted the first of the arrivals and began to usher them downstairs. They were going to create a gateway to another realm. Another dimension. They were potentially going to make contact with something that had never been to this plane before. And, as Christopher had pointed out, never *conceived* of such a place as here.

Slate had been spellbound by the idea of something new. But Christopher could talk for hours about what it meant to *be* something new.

Stewart brought two new friends who needed vials made. The staff moved like clockwork, bringing out drinks and finger foods. Mercia arrived and began bullying people into their robes. As the clock inched closer to midnight, Slate had to admit that the effect was striking.

They stood in a ring around the spell circle, no one stepping over the painted barrier. It was perfectly safe . . . but few of them knew the magic well enough to know that. They were here to witness more than participate. Slate made his polite greetings, formal introductions of the few attendees who didn't already know each other, and then slipped back into the corner where Christopher was waiting.

"You have to stop staring at that book," Slate said, nudging Christopher out of the way and closing it. "People will think we aren't prepared."

"I'm still worried we missed something."

"We absolutely did not," Slate said firmly. "We know it backward and forward, and everything is going to be fine."

"I wish I had your faith."

"You *have* my faith," Slate said. He inhaled, hoping his offer would come across as intended. "That's why I want you to lead this."

Christopher stared at him, eyes wide. "Why?"

Slate considered telling him. Telling him that he had a Gift and the amount of raw power he had access to far outstripped anything Slate could summon up on his best day. Considered telling him it was purely pragmatic, that they had the best chance of success by putting their strongest mage on the forefront. Slate considered lying.

"Because I believe you can do it," he said instead. "Because—"

He didn't get any further than that, because Christopher leaned in and kissed him. A quick press of the lips, over before Slate could react.

It wasn't . . . *un*expected.

In the excitement of the night, it was difficult for something so small to make a difference—but it did. Slate felt his hair stand on end as a shiver went down his spine. This changed things, and he found himself uncharacteristically eager to find out how.

"When this is over—" Christopher started to say, but his words were drowned out by noise from the crowd. Smatterings of applause broke out as Mercia's men brought out the slave that Coffey had contributed.

The man was a work of art. The attendants lifted a cloak off his shoulders, revealing a body that was tanned and descarred, lean with muscle that had been expertly cultivated. Kohl surrounded his dark eyes, and the artful tousling of his hair was held in place with gel.

Around his throat, wrists, and ankles were the bands that Slate and Christopher had designed. The sigils on the bands would capture the magic contained in the transition from life to death, amplify it, and echo it back into the spell.

In theory.

Slate took a breath. He wanted to put everything on pause for a moment, to turn back to Christopher and address what had just happened, but . . . they didn't have time. The stars waited for no one. He risked one glance back. "Here goes nothing."

The attendants escorted the slave to the center of the room, each holding an arm to keep him steady. Slate couldn't remember the exact recipe for what he'd been injected with, but it did involve a healthy dose of ketamine. Still, the slave kept form admirably well as he found the center, turned, and knelt.

"He won't feel anything," Slate said quietly. Christopher was standing close enough that Slate could hear his quickened breath. "He's barely aware of his surroundings, and the spell will kill him instantly. No pain, no fear."

Christopher nodded mutely, still staring at the sacrifice. The slave's back was decorated with a pair of intricately detailed wings, rising from the bottom of his rib cage and spilling down his arms. They flickered as he moved, candle light reflecting off the mirrored body paint. Beside him, Slate felt Christopher stiffen, but they didn't have time for doubt. It was time to go.

"Thank you all for coming to bear witness," Slate said, his voice booming in the silent room. "Those of you on the perimeter, your job is to hold it. If you cannot do this, your job is to step back now. Once we begin, there is no stopping. Is this understood?"

No one stepped back. The slave's attendants scurried away, leaving their charge alone, kneeling in the center of the circle. Slate reached out, placing his hand on the small of Christopher's back in a way that he hoped felt reassuring. Together, the two of them stepped forward, completing the circle.

And then Christopher began to speak, long words that echoed too much for the space they occupied. Those on the edges repeated their mantra, filling the spaces where Christopher needed to breathe.

The echoes fractured, building off each other like ripples in a pond, reverberating in a dull roar that Slate could feel in his teeth.

Around the perimeter, the glass vials began to glow like carnival lights, clicking on one after another. There was a crash as one of them shattered, sending shards of sparkling crystal flying across the marble floor. It was joined by another, then two more.

Christopher didn't stop, keeping the spell up as fifteen or more of the vials exploded.

Slate felt like screaming.

A broken vial meant the blood had been stolen. A year's worth of work was endangered because someone had given them stolen blood, a part with no connection to the will of the whole.

Stupid, stupid, people were so fucking *stupid*—did they think he'd put the time into cultivating this entire network because it hadn't occurred to him to simply *steal*—

In the center of the circle, the slave's face snapped upward with an audible crack. His back arched impossibly, his eyes going wide as they stared at the ceiling. Slate glanced to Christopher, fearing his reaction, but Christopher's eyes were closed. He continued reciting the spell without so much as a pause. Slate turned his attention back to the center of the circle.

Very slowly, the slave began to rise, and Slate shifted, prepared to catch him if he managed to run, but the slave's motion was too smooth. It was less like he was standing, and more like he was being pulled to his feet. He reached his full height and then continued, toes dangling inches above the floor, his body hanging limp from his upturned face. He spun, slowly, as if hanging from a twisted rope. A sparkle ran across the etchings on the silver bands, and Slate realized that the man was already dead.

Something twinged in Slate's belly. He wasn't an *innocent* man, but this was the first time he'd ever caused someone's death.

The slave's mouth opened as if to speak, and tendrils began to climb out. Dark, empty not-vines poured from his throat in waves, wrapping themselves around him like some invisible predator. The woman to Slate's right gasped, and he glanced around the room, realizing that the others in the circle could see these.

The slave's skin began to crawl, and then blood splattered the floor as more tendrils burst to the surface. In a matter of seconds, the slave's entire body was engulfed, only the glow of the silver bands visible beneath the writhing mass. Slate's hands balled into fists as he willed himself not to be sick.

The ball of tendrils widened, flattened, and solidified, and the body was nowhere to be seen as a matte black frame formed around what was, undeniably, a *door*.

Slate's heart hammered in his chest. It was fucking *working*.

He tried not to feel too much relief. He glanced at Christopher, only to see the other man watching him back, face hard even as he kept up his spell. Slate grinned reassuringly.

The surviving vials of blood went dark as one, their essence feeding into the doorway, solidifying it, making it stable. An icy cold settled into Slate's bones, and then dissipated. It might have been the spell taking some of the life force offered—or simply the knowledge that if anything went wrong from here, they were dead. They were all dead.

Christopher finished his chant, and the room went silent enough that Slate could hear blood rushing in his ears.

The dark portal held, stabilized by the lives of the people who had called it open. There had always been a chance—a slim chance, but a chance—that they'd miscalculated, that the breach between planes couldn't be buttressed with the blood's power. There had been a chance that it would burn through them like kindling and collapse back into nothing.

But they hadn't miscalculated. The spell was self-sustaining, keeping itself open with an imperceptible draw on each participant.

The night was half a success. The door was open. Slate beamed triumphantly at Christopher, but the other man was still intent on his task. Now it was time to see what he would call through it.

Christopher knelt, pressing his hands to the mirrored sigils on the floor. At his touch, they flashed bright and began, slowly, to move. They flowed across the floor like water, combining and recombining until they'd formed interlocking circles, turning clockwise and counterclockwise in alternating rings. The room filled with hushed murmuring, and the people on the far side of the circle began to make their way around to the front.

In the darkness beyond the doorway, something began to move. Slate peered at it, trying to make out the shape of their visitor. It was a shadow among shadows, coming closer and clearer until finally, anticlimactically, the body of the slave was vomited out onto the floor.

Slate frowned. That wasn't right. The spell should have brought forth something *else*. What was it doing giving them back the same body they'd used to build the gate?

It lay there in the silence, motionless, shredded, bleeding passively onto the shining sigils moving beneath it.

And then it jerked. A single crack, one of the arms flopping bonelessly to the side.

That was impossible. The man was dead. His death was the catalyst needed to open the gateway, he *couldn't* be alive, or—

Another crack and the body shuddered to its side. Beside him, Slate heard Christopher gag.

"Is he—"

"No. No, this is—"

The body spasmed, muscles going shock-tight with a wet tearing sound that lasted longer than Slate would have thought possible.

"Oh gods," Christopher moaned. Slate didn't look over; his eyes were fixed on the body.

"What's moving him?" he asked, half to himself.

He wracked his brain, going over the spell backward and forward. It should have reached through the gateway to the other side, pulling through the first living creature it found, and—

The body let out a hollow scream, and Slate's bones went ice cold as the gateway redoubled its need for power. Slate's chest tightened; he couldn't get enough air. The woman beside him gasped and went down. Christopher jerked in pain, his hand pressed to his throat.

Slate shifted focus, and there it was.

The slave was dead, but his body lay cloaked in a thick blanket of not-energy, trickling back through the gateway.

"It's inside the body," Slate rasped, stepping forward. Around him, people were pushing their cloaks off, sinking to their knees, pulling at their clothing like that would help them.

Slate stayed up, focusing on pulling in air, slow and steady as he strode across the circle.

Whatever thing they'd pulled through, it was inside the body of the slave, possessing it and using its magic for its own ends.

Realization dawned. It was trying to close the gate.

Slate dropped to his knees and rolled the body onto its back, his vision going dark at the edges as he scoured his brain for anything he could do. The body seized, coughing up wet strands of congealing gore, and Slate held it down. A rib snapped, bursting through the skin, splattering hot blood across his face. His body screamed for air, and he held back a need to vomit. He had to *think*. He considered shoving the body back through the doorway—but it could attack the portal just as easily from the other side.

Slate's head was getting fuzzy. He tried to remember what magic might protect them, but it was all he could do to keep breathing the thickened air.

A faint susurration drew his attention, and he looked toward the gateway. The edges of the frame were dissolving, trickles of black sand forming piles on the marble floor.

"Move," said a hoarse voice beside him, and then Christopher was pushing him to the side. Christopher straddled the slave, blood smearing the insides of his thighs as he took hold of the metal collar.

And then he began speaking again, his voice a grating rasp rather than the strong baritone he'd used a moment ago. Slate only caught every other word, his ears beginning to ring now, but the metal on the collar was changing, shifting, the sigils fading and then reforming into something new.

Slate began to shiver, the heartbeat in his ears coming slower as Christopher placed further demands on the blood's already overtaxed power. Christopher was trying to build a binding spell, but they didn't have enough power to hold the gate *and* the creature—

He was going to die, Slate realized. And the last thing he was going to see was Christopher doing the same.

Christopher's hand pressed against the slave's bloody chest, murmuring the incantation to bind the blood into his spell, and that was when Slate saw his plan.

The creature inhabited a body it didn't own, tying its power to blood it couldn't claim.

Its life force could be used without permission.

Slate's vision blurred, watching Christopher weave the slave's blood into the spell as a whole. The creature's life force would join theirs in protecting and maintaining the stability of the gate. The creature inside wouldn't be able to attack further, not without hurting itself the same way it was hurting them. It was brilliant, and it was horrible.

And it was theoretical. If it didn't work . . . no one in this room would be alive to find out.

"He's not going to stop," Christopher said breathlessly. Slate could hear the shivering in his voice.

It was still trying to close the gate, Slate realized, gaping down at the writhing corpse. Whatever this creature was, it was apparently willing to die for this goal. "Does it have the power to override the rest of us?"

"He won't when I'm done with this," Christopher said. "Drawing the blood will bind him."

"What?" Slate asked numbly. "What does that mean?" Black spots swarmed over his vision, and in a minute the slave's body wasn't going to have any blood *left*—

"*Stop!*" Christopher demanded, his hands curling into claws, nails raking down the creature's flayed chest. It would have been a scream if he'd had the air. Instead, the hoarse whisper boomed with power that Slate *felt* rather than heard.

The slave's bangles flashed a brilliant silver, and the warmth flooded back into the room. The air relaxed, no longer resisting his inhale. Around him, Slate could hear people gasping. He might have been one of them. He looked up at Christopher.

Christopher was staring, horrified, at the thing in front of them.

The sigils engraved onto the collar had changed. Reading them, Slate's heart sank. It was a simple binding spell, the kind used to control animals or low-level elementals. This creature had the intelligence and will to identify the gateway and *attack* it. Christopher would drain his own life force to nothing, trying to power such a spell—

Slate tried to focus, tried to think of some way to alter the sigils. If he could add his own life force to the spell, perhaps they could overcome the creature together?

Before he could force his buzzing thoughts into focus, he saw the rest of the sigils, and understood what Christopher had done. He'd used the creature's *own* life force for this, as well, forcing it to power its own binding.

A sick thrill went through Slate at the thought, a dark pleasure he found himself wary of even as it pooled rich and hot in his belly. To *do* that to any creature with will . . . it was unnatural, even *blasphemous*. Those weren't words Slate usually put much stock in, but Christopher . . .

Christopher stared at the creature, then at his own bloody hands, and then was violently sick onto the stone floor. Slate reached out, not sure what he intended to do. The moment his bloody fingers brushed Christopher's shoulder, Christopher jerked away. He looked back at Slate with a combination of disgust and horror, and Slate's heart sank.

He switched focus, disappointed but not unsurprised to see Christopher's connections disintegrating one by one. Wherever he went from here, he was never going to speak of this night, or to these people, ever again.

And whatever had been between them, it was over now.

Slate saw all of this from far away. Saw Christopher rise, unsteadily, and vanish into the crowd. Slate couldn't scrape together the wherewithal to call him back. His head pounded.

He looked back at the body. There was a thing, in the body, and that thing had tried to kill him. Had very nearly succeeded. It was dangerous.

Slate knew that, in some faraway part of his mind that he had set aside for when it was once again time to know things.

His ears were ringing. There was blood on his hands, wet and sticky. Someone beside him was talking.

He needed to leave.

He reached for his handkerchief, but there was blood on that too. He cleaned his hands as best as he could, and shoved the bloody cloth back into his pocket.

The body at his feet moved, gasped. Kohl-lined eyes went wide.

The thing tried to breathe, and there was a whistling noise as air seeped into his lungs through holes in his chest. As Slate watched, the lacerations began to zip shut, one after another, leaving scars that soon faded to nothing.

Someone gasped. More talking.

The sick curve of the creature's arm began to straighten as the fragments of its bones pulled back together. It took a breath that sounded like a breath.

"Why are you alive?" Slate asked it. It didn't seem to hear him. Slowly he leaned down, looking straight into those dark, unseeing eyes. The not-energy of the portal squirmed over its face like maggots.

There was a hand on his shoulder, holding him back from an action he hadn't fully decided to take yet. He pushed it away.

The creature screamed then, folding in on itself in agony. It tried to rise, failed, tried again. It ended up on its side, panting, the skin on its back smoking as the silver paintings began to glow. The thing screamed again, a horrible desperate keening as the flesh bubbled and burned, turning black and tearing open.

The scream petered out because it couldn't stop long enough to inhale, and a silver lance broke through from the inside. Another tendril, Slate thought, but no. Too solid for that, too straight.

It was a feather, he realized, as more shoved their way through the creature's ruined back. Feathers three feet long, rising from inside the creature like blades, blood splattering off their tips as they twitched and fluttered. The creature collapsed, lying on its belly, panting desperately, its face pressed against the bloody floor. The feathers kept coming, hundreds of them, spread over sprouting appendages fully the size of a second pair of arms.

Silently, Slate stepped forward and touched one of the feathers. He half expected to cut himself on a sharp edge, but they were soft. He stroked it once and then, taking hold of the base, wrenched it free. The creature let out a choked sob but didn't move.

Slate turned the feather over in his hands, watching the face reflected in the surface.

The feather went dark. It began at the tip of the quill where he held it, oily blackness spreading up the shaft and across the vanes like tarnish.

A murmuring drew his attention back to the creature. The same tarnish was overtaking the wings themselves, bright silver dulling and fading into a featureless black. Someone else stepped forward, plucking a silver feather before the tarnish could reach it—but it was too late. It turned black in the man's hand, the same as Slate's.

There was silence as the gathered crowd stared down at the shuddering, bleeding creature on the ground.

"Well, fuck," someone said.

Slate couldn't have phrased it better.

There was blood on his hands.

"Get up," he said. He nudged it with his foot, and it let out a moan.

"*Now*," Slate clarified. A couple of people glanced at him. He was so tired. His skin was sticky with gore. A part of him was screaming to go after Christopher, to apologize, to explain—

But another, larger part knew it was useless.

The creature didn't move.

"Fucking useless," Slate grumbled, then turned to the crowd, searching for a face he could trust. He found Stewart close to the back, and pushed his way over to the man.

"Cut it with whatever you can find," he said without preamble. Stewart gave him a hollow look. "By drawing its blood, you take ownership of its binding and can command it. Do you understand?"

"But you—"

"*Do you understand*?" Slate hissed. The air in the room was sour, he didn't want to be here. Stewart nodded silently. "Good. I have things to attend to. The plan hasn't changed. When everyone's done gawking, lock it up. The staff can handle getting everyone to their rooms. I will be back tomorrow."

"Wait, but what do I—"

"Tomorrow," Slate repeated, in a tone that brooked no argument. Stewart nodded, and Slate stalked away.

He had to get the blood off his hands.

CHAPTER TEN

∞

He didn't remember calling his driver or getting in his car. There was a suite prepared for him here in Troy—his bags had already been sent upstairs—but he didn't care. He wanted to go home. He needed to be home for this. He realized he was wiping his hands on his handkerchief, but there was already blood on it. There was blood on his clothes. He would need to—

He winced at the sound of bones cracking. A crimson shadow, creeping slowly across the marble. The air turning to mud in his lungs—

The whole scene had been slightly more . . . visceral than he'd expected. Messier.

He couldn't imagine how Mercia must feel, all that pomp and circumstance, and the *wings*—

Carol was staring at him. He couldn't remember getting out of the car.

"I would like a bath drawn," Slate said, and because she seemed a bit rattled, "Please."

"Of course, sir. Is there anything else? Are you . . . hurt at all?"

"It's not my blood," Slate reassured her, giving her a smile. Other circumstances might have warranted a familiar but professional pat on the shoulder, but Slate had blood on his hands.

He turned and walked a few steps into the foyer, then paused and turned back to Carol.

"Have Micah sent up."

She nodded, and Slate went upstairs. He didn't look at himself in the mirror as he removed his cuff links, leaving them on the dresser. He stripped out of his clothes, not bothering to inspect them for stains. They were unsalvageable, and he didn't intend to wear them again. He dropped them into a pile. If they stained the carpet, fuck it. He'd buy a new one.

The door to the bathroom opened in a billow of steam, and the maid froze in the process of stepping out.

"Oh," she said softly.

"What the fuck are you staring at."

"You have . . ."

He crossed the room in two strides, shoving her against the wall with a thud. She tried to step forward and he shoved her back again, hard enough that her head slammed against the wall with a *crack*.

"I asked what the fuck you were *staring* at," he said, and she cowered. He pushed her again, crowding her against the wall with his body.

"Sir?" Micah asked, his voice soft. "You called for me?"

Slate turned to where Micah was standing by the hall door, waiting with his arms crossed behind his back, his face down.

If Micah had tried to intervene, Slate realized, this would have gone very badly for him, very quickly. But he hadn't. He'd simply stood and waited.

Slate took a step back, running a hand through his hair. The maid didn't move. There was blood on her uniform.

"You're dismissed," he told her, and she didn't wait for him to change his mind. She didn't even pick up the laundry, just walked past it, past Micah, and out the door. Slate headed toward the steam. His head was pounding.

The bathroom smelled of cedarwood, the tiles warm beneath his feet. The water in the bath was hot, bordering on too hot, and Slate stepped in without waiting for Micah.

The slave appeared a moment later, shutting the door behind him to keep the warmth in. He glanced nervously at the water filling the bath. Slate could see him struggling with the situation, and while that was, normally, part of the fun, Slate didn't have the energy this morning.

"Get a cloth. There's blood in my hair."

Slate sank into the water, letting it close over his face for barely a second before the lack of air startled him back to the surface. Micah was waiting, sitting on the tiled edge of the tub, regarding him with something like concern.

"It's in my hair," Slate explained again, leaning against the back of the tub and closing his eyes. "Get it off."

He listened as Micah dipped a cloth into the water and wrung it out. A moment later, a warm, damp corner was dabbing along the edge of his hairline.

The blood had dried during the drive, and it would have made more sense to shower at the inn. Change his clothes there, get a couple of hours of sleep, come home in the morning—

But no, there would be things to do in the morning. Days' worth of things, if not weeks.

A hundred people were going to want a summary of what had happened, and he wasn't exactly sure how to—

The washcloth brushed over his cheek, warm pressure scrubbing at the dried gore. Micah was trying to strike a balance between what would feel good and what would accomplish the goal he'd been given.

"I think I got all of it," he said after a minute. And then, "Should I call a doctor?"

"I'm not hurt."

"I understand. But . . . someone else? Is?"

Slate opened his eyes, looking coldly up at Micah. *But* was a word that strayed dangerously close to *no*.

Micah paled under his gaze. "I only meant—"

"The source of this blood is beyond the help of medical attention," Slate said.

Micah nodded. "Understood."

"You're not going to ask me again."

"Yes, sir. Do you want the cloth? For your— For anything else?"

Slate took it without answering, remembering the stains on his hands. The blood had dried in the cuticles, and they sat there in silence for a minute while he dealt with that.

The washcloth would probably be ruined, but that was fine.

"I want these thrown away," he said, handing the rag back to Micah. "The whole set. I want a different color."

"I'll relay that, sir," Micah said, going to drop it into the trash.

Slate dipped beneath the water again, this time managing to hold his breath for three full seconds before becoming convinced he was about to die.

He surfaced and shunted the knowledge of his discomfort to the back of his mind before he could get frustrated about it.

Micah returned to the edge of the bath, sitting in a facsimile of the waiting pose.

"Things didn't go well tonight," Slate said simply. Of course that would mean nothing to Micah, who had no idea where Slate had been, but who had *probably* figured out at least *that* much on his own.

Micah didn't reply, just sat, waiting, for his instructions.

Slate considered punishing him for it, demanding that the slave *anticipate* his needs, not just sit there and—

Instead, he found himself reaching forward, turning Micah's face toward him. The slave didn't meet his eyes.

Slate kissed him.

He wasn't sure he'd ever done it before. In the middle of fucking, maybe, there had been a press of mouths and a promise of teeth. But not this.

This was sweet, almost chaste, in a way that reminded him of—

Slate grabbed the front of Micah's shirt, pulling him into the bath fully clothed. Micah came down straddling him, his uniform immediately sticking to his skin. Slate pushed his hands beneath the cotton shirt, needing to touch, suddenly; needing to hold on to something that was *here*—

He nipped at Micah's lip, and Micah opened for him, and Slate didn't think about whether Christopher had kissed Micah like this, whether they'd gone fast or slow, what it was about *this slave* that Christopher kept returning to.

They broke apart long enough for Micah to strip his shirt over his head. The pants were trickier, and Micah ended up tearing them as he settled back over Slate's hips, and for *once* the slave wasn't hard for him. Fuck it, it didn't matter. He was breathing, and solid, and here, and that was all Slate needed from him right now.

They didn't have lubricant handy, but there was already blood in the water. Slate pushed up hard, burying himself as deep as he could go, Micah's cry of pain muffled against his mouth. Slate swallowed it, biting at Micah's lips the way he never could have bitten at Christopher's. The water was so hot that Micah's body felt cold in comparison, and Slate didn't think about whether it was cold on the other side of that black stone doorway, what it would feel like to be enveloped by *nothing*.

Slate shoved again, taking Micah's gasp into his mouth. One more roll of his hips and Micah got the hint, riding him gently, almost tenderly. He broke the kiss and Slate let him, one hand tangling in Micah's hair when the slave buried his face against Slate's throat. Slate could feel him breathing, moaning softly in time with the rhythmic slap of the water.

It wasn't enough.

Slate rolled them over, pressing Micah against the back of the tub and kissing him again. Micah's legs wrapped around his waist. The angle wasn't good but it didn't fucking matter. There was no point fucking Micah like a lover, like he was Christopher. Micah wasn't Christopher and was never going to be Christopher.

Christopher would have been appalled by this. He lived in a gentler world than Slate's, and the time to choose differently was past.

Slate buried himself in the slave again, relishing the cry Micah made. He kept his eyes closed and pictured what it would be like to go a little further. He imagined the water closing over Micah's face, the way panic would build on the man's features as his air ran out. Micah would be so *good*, refusing to fight until the last possible second. Slate imagined his face as he realized it was too late.

Water sloshed out of the tub and over the tile, and Slate realized he actually wanted to do it. He wasn't just fantasizing. The seal had been broken. He actually *could* push Micah beneath the water, hold him down through his struggles until—

He stopped, his hands already on Micah's shoulders. Micah's eyes were down, his features a carefully maintained neutral, but his breathing gave him away. He was taking deep breaths and holding them, maximizing the amount of oxygen in his blood. He knew what was about to happen—or at least, he thought he did.

Micah had even managed to get hard, whether in anticipation or just from the feeling of being fucked, Slate didn't know. Didn't care.

For a moment, Slate was sure he was going to do it. Was going to drown the man beneath him, just to see if he was capable.

And then the moment passed.

"I don't have time for you," Slate muttered, withdrawing and standing up.

Confusion crossed Micah's features, and Slate didn't explain.

CHAPTER ELEVEN

∞

S late didn't wake up until two in the afternoon. He had twelve missed calls.

He dropped his phone on the nightstand and rolled onto his back. Beside him, Micah was pretending to sleep.

If this were a normal day, Micah would have gone down to the kitchens and brought back coffee so Slate would have it for his wakeup. This morning, since Slate had passed out at a respectable 5 a.m., Micah had wisely chosen not to do that. But since he hadn't been dismissed, either, he was just here. Waiting.

"I won't be home tonight," Slate said. Micah was immediately at attention. "I need to go back to the inn."

"Understood."

As Slate dressed, it occurred to him that he could take Micah with him. He didn't need to mix him up with the fae they'd summoned, or anything to do with the gateway; Micah could just . . . stay in the suite. In case he was needed.

Slate looked over to where Micah waited, sprawled artfully across the bedspread like a contented tomcat. With the bright sunlight pouring through the windows, Slate could almost forget the fate of the slave from last night.

He decided against bringing Micah with him. Instead, Slate sat alone in the back of the car, staring out the window and thinking. In the light of day, his midnight flight was embarrassingly childish. He had a job to do. He couldn't go half-mad and flee every time it got a little uncomfortable.

The gateway was open, it was stable, and they'd brought a creature through it. He'd done what he'd set out to do. He'd known that

Christopher was unhappy with the sacrifice it would take to make that happen. Slate had assumed that it would be quick, almost *sterile*, and his friend would get over it.

He hadn't foreseen an ending where they succeeded, and somehow still failed.

And he hadn't realized that it would matter so much.

His phone rang, and he let it go to voicemail. It was Coffey, for the third time today, but fuck him. If he wanted an update, he could get on a plane and fucking be where the update was.

The inn was busier than it had been the night before. Every suite was accounted for, and several workers Slate didn't recognize were finishing the slave barracks, which were also full.

Apparently, news of their "acquisition" had spread. To *strangers*.

Slate passed the ballroom and headed for the holding cells.

They were empty.

Slate caught a workman by the shoulder as he passed. "Where's the creature?"

"The angel?"

"The—? Fine. Yes. The angel."

"Down there." The man gestured to a door down the hall. Two rather large guards stood beside it, but they wordlessly moved to the side when Slate approached.

The space inside had been a meeting room, complete with a small kitchenette. Now, it was a bloody horror show. The occupied corpse of the slave lay on the wood conference table, staring blankly up at the ceiling. Two men stood beside it, bloody to the elbows. Slate recognized one as Stewart, but the other was a stranger. He switched focus and was unsurprised to see an array of thick connections to others in the inn.

"Is it alive?" Slate asked without preamble.

The men looked up as though startled to see him. The stranger, Slate realized, was holding a scalpel.

"Adam Slate, I presume?" the stranger said. "I'd shake your hand, but. Well." He raised his bloody palms, and Slate saw he was wearing rubber gloves. Not that it helped with the blood smearing his forearms.

"What are you doing?"

"Science," Stewart answered. "Slate, this is Dr. William Godfrey."

"Charmed," Slate said, giving him a little smile. "What are you doing."

"Taking a crack at a medical marvel," Godfrey answered. "I assume you haven't heard of my work?"

"Can't say I have," Slate said evenly. "Though I appear to be the only person in this building who hasn't."

"I specialize in elective surgeries," Godfrey explained, stripping off his gore-soaked gloves and dropping them in a trash can. "Specifically, surgeries that people elect to have performed on other people."

Pieces clicked into place in Slate's mind. He *had* heard of Godfrey. While the doctor washed his hands in the kitchenette sink, Slate tried to remember who he'd heard *from*. Stewart was the obvious answer, but that didn't seem right. He refocused on Godfrey, checking close links for someone he recognized.

Coffey. That was it.

"A friend of mine has spoken highly of your work," Slate said graciously. Then, "What are you doing?"

"Testing responses to stimuli," Godfrey answered, pulling on a new pair of gloves. "Your shareholders want to know what they've bought, and Stewart put me in charge of figuring it out."

"You were gone," Stewart said, almost apologetically.

Slate had no defense against that. He stepped up to the table, careful not to touch the naked body of the slave. The feathers of his wings were splattered with gore, the bulk of the appendages crushed awkwardly beneath the limp body.

"Is it alive?"

"Oh, yes," Godfrey said, picking up a scalpel. "Watch this."

Without further preamble, he sank the knife into the body's sternum. With practiced ease, he slit the body wide open, down to the pubic bone. Setting the knife aside, he slipped his thumbs into the slit and spread the abdomen wide, skin and muscle parting to remove crawling viscera.

Slate wrinkled his nose. "Is it possessed?"

"Well, yes," Godfrey said. "But this is just peristalsis. The organs are continuing to process whatever food was in his body when he died. It looks weird, but this is what we'd expect from any other vivisection. Now watch. Time?"

Stewart started a timer on his phone, and Godfrey released the sides of the incision. Instantly, the muscle walls began to draw together, each end of the cut sliding closed like a zipper. A moment later, the skin followed suit. In less than a minute, there was nothing remaining but blood on perfectly intact skin.

"Forty-two seconds," Stewart said, stopping the timer. "He's getting marginally faster. Last night it took him forty-five."

"You've been here all night?" Slate asked. "Just cutting it open?"

"Taking measurements, yes," Godfrey said, tapping a small box that lay beside the body's shoulder. "Heart rate's still elevated. Interesting."

"So what can you tell me?" Slate asked, looking at the body's face. Its eyes stared blankly at the ceiling, and there was a trickle of blood coming from its mouth.

"I can tell you he's going to be very useful to *me*, even if he's worthless for your needs," Godfrey said. "What I have here is a perfect training dummy."

"He's warm," Stewart muttered. "So that'll keep at least some of them happy."

"Not to be vulgar, but he's not wrong," Godfrey said, tilting his head in Stewart's direction.

Slate resisted the urge to scowl. He hadn't torn a hole in the universe and reached through just to come out of it with a brain-dead cocksleeve.

"Does it talk?"

Stewart and Godfrey exchanged glances.

"Well . . . not right now," Godfrey said.

"What did it say?" Slate demanded. "Anything about what it was, where it came from?"

"Oh, gods no," Stewart said. "Mostly it just screamed."

"I was getting to that," Godfrey cut in. "I'm working with *extremely* preliminary data, but I think it might be aware of us and what's happening around it." He gestured to where the slave's hand was lying limp atop a bed of feathers. "I've been getting involuntary reactions consistently all night. Pupils dilating, increased heart rate, various reflexes, et cetera. But around 3 a.m., we cut one of the fingers off, and ever since it grew back—"

"It grew back?"

"In about fifteen minutes, yes, and that's another market we can tap into, assuming the magic doesn't render its organs incompatible with those of humans—I'm getting ahead of myself. So we cut a finger off, and ever since then . . ."

Godfrey lifted the hand, his gloves smearing blood across the palm. Very gently, he squeezed it.

It squeezed back.

"What does that mean?" Slate said.

"Using the absolute best-case scenario in which everything goes our way? It means there's something intelligent in there, trying to communicate." Godfrey dropped the hand back onto the bed of black feathers. "Or it's an unconscious reflex and we've managed to turn a semi-competent slave into a doll."

"Does the other hand do it?" Slate asked, looking down at it.

"No."

"Seems like a pretty quick experiment, then," Slate said, mildly annoyed that this had to be explained. "Cut a finger off the other hand, see if you can reproduce the results."

There was a small voice in Slate's head, one that sometimes asked how he'd gotten here. How he'd become a person who stepped back to avoid the blood as Godfrey indifferently sheared the slave's index finger off.

As the finger slowly began to rebuild from the stump, Slate tried to recall the discomfort he knew he used to feel, years ago, at the beginning of all this. Would he have felt bad for the man on the table? Or just felt guilty because he knew he should . . . but didn't?

Maybe it had been as simple as fear of repercussions, a fear of getting caught by some nebulous power for good, one that would hold him accountable for the things that *didn't* bother him.

Slate didn't worry about that anymore.

Deliberately, he remembered the night before, the air vanishing and the ice creeping through his bones as this thing tried to kill him, and he didn't feel quite so bad.

He stepped into the creature's line of sight, switching focus.

He expected to see black tendrils by the dozens, a lifetime's worth of connections stretching back through the gate to whatever life this creature had left behind.

Instead, there was nothing.

Immediately, there were questions to answer.

Slate climbed the stairs to the restaurant's balcony seating, and had barely sat down when Cunningham slid into the chair across from him.

"Locke wants an update."

"And I want breakfast," Slate replied, not bothering to read the menu. The staff here knew his order. "I don't have any information you don't already know."

"Bullshit," Cunningham snapped. "You sold us on 'a portal to slaves of ephemeral beauty,' and instead I got . . . I don't even fucking know what you did last night, but I'm going to be in therapy about it for years. What the *fuck* was that."

"I said there was *potential*," Slate corrected. "I never promised an outcome."

"Then is this it?" Cunningham asked, incredulous. Slate opened his mouth to protest, but Cunningham barreled on. "You built, what. A machine that turns slaves into angels? That's not good return on investment. I thought a shortage of disposable slaves was the problem we were here to fix."

"Do you want your man back? Is that what this is about?" Slate asked abruptly.

Cunningham looked almost *too* taken aback, which Slate filed away. Cunningham's Saturnalia loss wasn't the source of contention here, and Slate knew it, but he was too goddamn tired to argue over promises he'd never made. *Especially* with someone as self-important as Cunningham. "I don't need him. I have more. I'll have him sent back to you; he's not a good enough fuck to make this conversation worth it to me."

"You're an asshole," Cunningham snapped.

"And you're interrupting my breakfast because my unprecedented magical breakthrough didn't produce results that were instant and perfect," Slate shot back. "We have made *one* summoning attempt and retrieved one entity. At this stage in the process, that is a success. The creature you saw last night is not the gestalt of our efforts."

Cunningham scowled. "You're impossible. When's Plant coming back?"

For a long second, Slate wasn't sure how to respond.

"Plant . . . Christopher left last night."

"We all saw, yeah. When's he coming back?"

Slate looked out over the balcony, at the people on the ground floor mingling and socializing. The web of connections here was particularly dense, starbursts of influence meandering through the building and around the grounds outside. The atmosphere was charged, but overall, remarkably calm.

It hadn't occurred to him that anyone might think Christopher was coming back. That anyone who knew him might be laboring under expectation that their gregarious friend was still on board. Not after seeing the expression on his face when he'd walked out last night.

Maybe none of them had ever really known him at all.

"I'm . . . not sure," Slate said carefully.

"Then who does?"

"Probably only Christopher," Slate answered, trying not to sound as hollow as he felt.

"Fuck me," Cunningham grumbled. "Then I wanna see it. The gestalt."

"Be my guest," Slate said tiredly. A waitress with a barcode was approaching with a cup of coffee, and he desperately hoped it was his. "Godfrey has it, not me."

Cunningham left, but Slate had to have the exact same conversation with three more people before he finished his food, made his excuses, and escaped downstairs.

He took the long route to the ballroom, using the service hallway rather than the elevator. The lower floor was bustling with activity. The kitchen wasn't used to operating at their *old* full capacity, let alone this new one.

The staff knew his face, and didn't ask why he was there. Almost everyone around him had a barcode. Slate had staffed the inn with a combination of life-term indents and slaves, all of whom were housed on site. The last thing he needed was for rumors to start spreading in town.

He reached the door to the ballroom, and hesitated before pushing the doors open.

It . . . looked like a ballroom.

While he'd been sleeping, the staff had cleaned the floor, until not a drop of blood or paint remained. The candles were gone and the lights were on, and it could have been any other empty ballroom, except for the doorway in the middle of the floor.

Slate switched his focus, and the doorway remained exactly the same. Peering through it from this direction, he saw nothing but a void of not-energy, shifting like shadows cast in the dark. Slowly he circled it. From the side, he saw nothing but the edge of the frame, dark rough stone eight feet high and a few inches thick. He kept walking, around to the back where there was . . . nothing. Not a frame, not a dark place, nothing.

Taking a deep breath, Slate stepped forward, across the threshold of where he knew the doorway should be. Nothing happened, but when he turned around, the portal was there, in the space he'd just stepped through.

His strings cut, and Slate went to his knees, staring at it. It was real. It was *real*. They'd done it, and it was *real*.

In front of him was a doorway to something utterly beyond human comprehension, the beginning of something humans had barely scratched the surface of, and all he had to figure out was how to reach through. Not only to see what he could pull back. With the right magic, *he* could go through. He could go somewhere *else*.

Enjoying the quiet, Slate went to the back of the room, opened his books, and began to read.

CHAPTER TWELVE

∞

July 2013

Weeks passed uneventfully.

There was always a party on the main floor. People drifted in and out of their rooms at all hours of the day and night, guests leaving the inn and immediately being replaced. It came as somewhat of a surprise; Slate had expected people to mostly go home after the main event. There was nothing to see, other than Godfrey doing medical experiments and Slate reading his books . . . but guests kept showing up. There were *People* here, and people wanted to be where People were.

Slate stood at the edge of the restaurant balcony, watching the crowd in the atrium below him. It was well after midnight, but the festivities were in full swing. Someone had organized a dance, complete with live music. The musicians had barcodes, but they weren't Slate's. Someone else must have brought them. Maybe Mercia. Slate didn't tend to think of that sort of thing.

There was a crash as one of the servers dropped a tray of drinks. Slate looked toward the sound and saw that one of the guests had grabbed a waitress. The man—Slate couldn't recall his name, just the font they used to print it on billboards—was sitting on one of the circular couches in the corner. Broken glass sparkled on the floor as he pulled the woman onto his lap. She gestured at the glass, and he only laughed, rucking up her skirt and getting a hand between her thighs. The others on the couch—two men and a woman, none older than thirty—jeered and goaded him on.

It appeared that Garamond had made his friends jealous, because when a second server appeared to clean up the glass, she was quickly pulled into the debauchery as well. This group wasn't the first to engage in what Slate would classify as "antisocial behavior"—but they were the most overt about it.

So far.

Slate narrowed his eyes, shifting focus.

People were noticing the festivities, and Slate waited for a connection to break. He waited for someone to get disgusted, or at least mildly offended, and leave.

It didn't happen.

That was . . . unexpected. There was, admittedly, a certain amount of outrageous behavior to be counted on when this crowd gathered. People used naked slaves as avant-garde art installations, or had slaves kneel by their feet through dinner, and, of course, there was the thrilling objectification of the auctions and the games . . . but this felt different. Guests didn't usually feel so entitled to the waitstaff, and Slate couldn't remember a time when he'd seen someone fuck a slave outright, right in the middle of a party.

It was a noteworthy development, Slate thought to himself, and went back downstairs to his books.

He'd spent a lot of time with his books, in the weeks since the portal had opened.

He sat in the empty ballroom, listening to the muffled sound of the music from upstairs. It was a wonder that, with so many people, the crowd didn't spill over into the lower level, but it seemed that no one else was really comfortable being down there.

They'd come down when they first arrived, of course, to gawk at what they'd helped accomplish. Some of them even tried to talk about it, asking Slate what it meant and what they could do with it. He found he was bad at explaining, and soon enough, people stopped coming.

Slate fell into a routine.

He woke up, drank a purification tonic to deal with the effects of the night before, and went to work. He'd had the staff set up tables for him in the ballroom, and he'd covered three of them in printouts, notes, and different texts that he'd begged, borrowed, or bought off the people upstairs. He'd stare at the words and diagrams, trying to make the old theories connect in a meaningful way. The staff brought him food, which he ate without tasting.

Then, as the evening got later, he'd attempt to see through the gateway. The strategy differed, slightly, depending on what he'd found or read that day, each attempt altered just enough to give him hope.

And it never worked.

He couldn't open it *fully*, of course—it would be a year before the energies of the earth and sky aligned again—but he should at least be able to *look*.

He'd been over the magic back and forth, forward and back. The logic was sound. His spellwork was beyond reproach. And there was something there to see—Christopher had proven that beyond a shadow of a doubt. Slate just couldn't *see* it.

He made the day's attempts alone, pulling the power he needed from the blood of the gateway, trying to force the shadows into something comprehensible.

But day, after day, after day, he heard nothing but silence, and saw nothing but darkness.

No. Not even darkness. Darkness was the absence of light, and was in that way quantifiable. What he saw had no relation to light: a place that could not be illuminated with a thousand suns because it was, well and truly, *something else*.

He understood this as he looked at it, and then ceased to when he looked away, his mind unwilling to hold on to the reality of what it had failed to see. He understood it as darkness, and understood that in the long term, that was for the best. The nothingness that existed between anywheres was not meant for human ken.

At that point in the evening, he would leave his work on the table, go upstairs, and drink. He would drink until someone offered him something stronger than a drink, and he wasn't really sure what he'd do after that.

At some point, he had some of his slaves brought over. Slate took a bitter satisfaction in having Cunningham's man at his feet as he took his nightly journey toward nescience. The man, Anthony, cast the odd glance at his old master. There was a connection there—one way, of course, but persistent enough to be annoying. Slate pretended not to notice, until one particularly fucked night, when he told Anthony to go suck Cunningham's dick if he missed him so fucking much.

Someone helped him back to his suite after that—maybe Anthony, maybe someone else—whoever it was got a throat-fucking for their trouble. That wasn't odd. Most nights, Slate ended up fucking whoever ended up in his room.

And then he'd sleep for four, maybe six hours, wake up, drink the purification tonic waiting for him on the nightstand, and repeat.

After almost a month of this, Slate was starting to wonder if it was sustainable. The money wasn't going anywhere, and apparently, neither was the revelry, but every day, he cracked the spines on books written by people who had spent lifetimes doing exactly what he was doing now—with nothing to ever show for it. He'd opened a stable gate, which was more than the others had accomplished, but . . .

Fortunately, that was when the angel started talking.

CHAPTER THIRTEEN

∞

August 2013

Godfrey hyped it up for days, his "presentation of the Gestalt." Slate didn't pay much attention. The Gestalt was a success of the past, a first draft, a proof of concept. Slate could summon and bind whatever it was, and that was old news. To put it bluntly, the angel bored him.

At least, it did until he saw it.

The inn was packed, a significant number of the guests finding lodgings elsewhere or simply planning to leave afterward. Outside the atrium's glass walls, a helicopter perched on the manicured grass. Coffey's, as it turned out. Apparently, he'd wrapped up his business in Cabo when he'd heard about what waited for him here.

Slate watched from the balcony, second or third drink in his hand, as people milled around below. He watched Coffey cross to the center of the room, Godfrey at his shoulder.

"Thank you all for coming," Coffey started, his voice carrying clearly through the space. "I know you all had high expectations for what we'd be able to achieve here, and that what you've seen so far might be disappointing."

A murmur of agreement went through the crowd. Slate shifted focus. Almost every person here was connected to Coffey. First degrees, maybe second.

"I'm happy to announce that the good doctor here has made significant progress with the Gestalt since last you saw him. Gentlemen, if you could, please?"

The doors to the main hallway opened, and Slate dropped his train of thought like a hot coal.

The creature that stepped through the gateway was . . . unrecognizable. The last time Slate had seen it, it had been a bloody and barely animate corpse. Now . . . now . . .

The light played across oil-slick colors in the rich black of the creature's wings. The barring on the feathers made a complicated pattern of circles that overlapped and shifted as he moved. His naked skin was a sun-kissed bronze. As he walked slowly, hesitantly, to the center of the room, his movements were as smooth and graceful as a cat's.

He reached Coffey and then, at a gesture, went to his knees. His wings folded almost delicately behind him.

"The body sacrificed to open the gate is now inhabited by a new kind of creature," Godfrey said, addressing the crowd. "We don't have a name for what this is. There's no record of it. But what we *do* know, ladies and gentlemen, is that he can be made docile." A murmur went through the crowd. Connections began to open to the creature— normally a bad sign, but these weren't of a particularly benevolent nature. "The silver bands you see are the manifestation of a binding spell ingeniously manufactured to run off his own, considerable, power."

"May I have a volunteer?" Coffey asked, addressing the crowd. Immediately, someone stepped forward. Even from this distance, Slate recognized Arabelle.

Coffey greeted her by kissing her glove, then handed her a small blade. As Slate watched, the Gestalt stood, lacing his fingers behind his head. At Coffey's instruction, Arabelle used the blade to make a nick in the creature's side. Slate couldn't see, but he expected that it healed quickly.

"Drawing his blood, any amount, allows you to take possession of the binding spell," Coffey explained to the crowd. "After which, he becomes yours to command. As harmless as a kitten." He turned back to Arabelle. "Ask him to do anything you like."

"I'd like a feather," she said immediately.

For a moment, the creature didn't move. Then, one of his wings began to unfold, curling around so that his primaries fanned between his face and Arabelle's. He was trembling so violently that Slate could see it from where he stood.

"Pluck it for me," Arabelle clarified, and within a few seconds, the Gestalt had taken hold of the first covert. He pried it loose with a whimper of pain that went straight to Slate's cock. He leaned forward against the balcony, enthralled.

Arabelle extended a hand, and the Gestalt laid the feather, gently, in her waiting palm. She held it up by the quill, turning it slowly to let it catch the light. It was easily eight inches long, the quill half an inch thick. Satisfied, she tucked it into her hair, where it sparkled beside the jewels holding her auburn tresses in place.

The next part happened very quickly.

The Gestalt moved like lightning, snatching the feather back with a wide motion that slashed towards Coffey's face. Slate saw less than a second of crimson before Coffey cried out, his hands covering his cheek.

"Freeze," Godfrey said, almost calmly, and the Gestalt did, the sharp tip of the quill still protruding from his fist. "Do not move."

"Fuck!" Coffey screamed, clutching at his face. "Fuck, *fuck*—"

Someone in the crowd laughed.

"Fae follow fae rules," Godfrey said, stepping closer to the trembling angel. "You can command them to leave you unharmed, but your commands must be ironclad, even to the trickiest of minds."

The angel stared up at him, features twisted into a mask of hate. Godfrey reached out, brushing a lock of hair almost gently from the creature's face. Someone handed Coffey a handkerchief, and he strode from the room with the cloth pressed to his face. Almost no one watched him go, their attention already back on the angel, eager to see what horrors might be inflicted next. Slate felt confident that he alone had noticed the problem with the kerchief, wadded up to staunch blood that wasn't flowing.

The injury had already healed.

"What was his error?" Godfrey asked the creature.

"He is stupid," the Gestalt hissed back. His voice was rough. "Stupid like you are all stupid. Figure it out."

Slate laughed, taking another swallow of his drink.

Godfrey sighed. "You'll have to be punished for that," the doctor said, his voice dripping with remorse. "Shall we say, an eye for an eye?" Slate didn't swallow, letting the bourbon burn his tongue, wondering if this was going where he thought. Fear flickered across the angel's features, plain even from this distance, and Godfrey gestured. "Go on, then. Put your eye out."

The Gestalt tried not to. It was obvious in the trembling of his hand, the way the whole of his arm went tense. The muscles of his shoulder flexed in tandem, fighting against their own inexorable power as, slowly, the hand holding the feather moved. The Gestalt tried to stay quiet as it rose to the level of his face. He shut his eyes tight, but it didn't help. He let out a whimper as his own hand pushed the quill of the feather deep into the socket of his left eye.

Godfrey's command fulfilled, his arm dropped limply to his side, his whimpers of pain echoing in the silent atrium.

"Very good," Godfrey said, before taking hold of the feather and withdrawing it from the ruined eye. The angel let out a sob. "We'll remember this for next time. Now, a clean one, for Arabelle. She's still waiting."

The command had a hundred interpretations. It was almost embarrassingly vague, and yet, the angel slowly lifted his wing and, with a wince, withdrew a second covert. This he presented to Arabelle, who took it without a word.

The angel watched, tears of blood on his cheeks, as she placed it in her hair.

CHAPTER FOURTEEN

July 2013

S late went home the next day.

He sat in the car for two hours, and thought about calling Christopher.

He didn't know what he'd say. That things had gotten out of hand? Ha.

No, if anything, things had gotten out of hand when they'd done the summoning, when a simple spell had torn a man to shreds right in front of them, and they'd kept going.

But really, the problem was that things *weren't* out of hand. Godfrey apparently knew exactly what he was doing, and he was getting results. The Gestalt was contained and mostly subdued, his attack on Coffey notwithstanding. The gateway was stable, with nearly a year left to figure out how to make it work.

And today, Godfrey had tortured an angel in front of an entire crowd without breaking a single connection. *Not one.*

If anything, the web got stronger. People waited with bated breath for someone else to protest, and no one did. Anticipation shifted easily into an unprecedented confidence.

So it wasn't that things were getting out of hand. They were progressing according to plan. It just wasn't a plan Christopher wanted anything to do with.

The car pulled up to his front door, and Slate got out. He sauntered nonchalantly to the back and opened the trunk. Anthony, gagged and blindfolded, turned his head toward the sound.

"I hope this has given you time to think," Slate said, his voice as harsh as he could make it.

Anthony nodded vigorously, insisting something through the twisted rags in his mouth. It must have been hot in there. His clothes were soaked with sweat. A doorman had approached and was waiting nervously at Slate's shoulder.

Slate stood, regarding his slave. Anthony's behavior over the last few weeks had been irritating, but last night it had spilled over into unacceptable.

"Clean him up," Slate told the doorman, and headed inside. He didn't envy the pins and needles that Anthony was going to have when he was untied. The slave's wrists and ankles had been bound together, so he'd been lying on one shoulder for several hours.

Slate pushed open the door to his office and stopped short.

Micah was standing beside the desk, pouring from a carafe of coffee. He saw Slate in the doorway and set it down, moving easily into form.

"Something happen to the maid?" Slate asked, leaning against the doorframe and crossing his arms.

Micah shook his head quickly. "Sorry, sir. I meant to be finished by now."

Micah was a good liar, but he was still lying. What interested Slate was *why*.

He shifted focus and . . . there it was. The tiniest, most ephemeral connection. Micah had done the maid a favor, something about a member of security.

Micah, who had nothing, had traded something to make this encounter happen.

Why?

Micah wasn't supposed to be up here without being summoned; why would he bother orchestrating such a minor act of disobedience and then get so easily *caught*—

Oh, Slate realized, looking at Micah's downturned face. Of course. To be caught.

Affection bloomed in his chest, and Slate turned around, heading back into the hall where the doorman was still working on unloading the car.

"I want Anthony in my study. Now. I don't care what state he's in."

The doorman nodded, and Slate went back to his office. Micah was exactly where he'd been left. He had his eyes on the ground, his arms crossed behind his back.

"Might as well keep pouring the coffee," Slate said, sitting down at his desk. Micah nodded once, and it almost looked . . . like . . .

"You have a black eye," Slate said. Micah froze, then nodded. Slate swiveled the chair toward him. "Come here."

Micah took two steps and dropped to his knees, sitting back on his heels between Slate's legs. Slate caught his chin, forcing him to look up. There it was—an impressive shiner, the bruises a couple of days along, with a small cut over Micah's cheekbone.

"This isn't from me," Slate said, mostly sure it was true. "And I haven't loaned you out. Explain."

"The security team," Micah said immediately.

Slate blinked. An escape attempt? From *Micah*? "Details," he said. "I'll have the truth one way or another, don't make me nag it out of you."

"They spar, sometimes, in their off hours," Micah said quickly. "And I've been trained in hand to hand. I asked if I could practice with them."

"But you're not *on* the security team," Slate said. He ran the pad of his thumb across Micah's lower lip, before pushing it inside. Micah met him with a wet press of his tongue. "So why?"

Micah exhaled and withdrew, just enough to speak.

"My paperwork says I'm fit for security work. I wanted to practice, in case you . . . You've been gone for weeks, and you took some others, but not . . ." He dropped his chin, and Slate let him. "I thought maybe I was going to be for sale."

Slate smirked, stroking his fingers through Micah's hair. The slave was fishing for information; Slate wasn't going to reward him.

"You thought you'd sell better with a black eye? That's why you're coming to me like this, instead of having the medic take care of it?"

"I went to the medic, and he said . . ." Micah hesitated, like he was unsure. Slate didn't buy it for a moment. He stroked Micah's hair fondly, letting the slave build his narrative. "I still have the marks, sir.

From the last time you were here? I wasn't sure I had permission to heal them yet."

Micah paused, and Slate could practically see his thoughts. In Micah's mind, this was where Slate would say, *Let me see*, and Micah would strip his clothes off, shirt first, then the pants, a feigned blush as he revealed the bruises the cane had left on his skin.

Slate wasn't going to give it to him, as pleased as he was by this scenario Micah had concocted.

"Sir," said a new voice, from the doorway. Anthony. Slate beckoned him in, still playing with Micah's hair.

"I assume you two know each other?" Slate said, without looking to see Anthony nod. He didn't have to assume. He could see. There was no connection there. They may recognize each other, but they were functionally strangers.

He ran his household this way on purpose.

"Isn't he pretty, Micah?" Slate asked, and Micah dutifully checked before he agreed. And Anthony *was* pretty—his blond hair short and artfully tousled, his blue eyes wide and endearing, his full mouth perpetually giving the impression of a shy grin. Under his uniform, he was slender. Like Micah, he was kept fit, but unlike Micah, he wasn't encouraged to build muscle. His barcode was new and crisp. "Anthony's been with us for six months. How about you, Micah? How long ago did I buy you?"

"A year and a half, sir," Micah answered. "Approximately."

"And how many times have I had to discipline you?"

Confusion flickered over Micah's face, but he reined it in. "I haven't been counting, sir."

"Estimate."

Micah closed one eye, his brow furrowing, and then, "Maybe sixty times? I'm sorry, I don't—"

"Good. Show Anthony what happens when one of my staff fucks up."

Micah glanced to Anthony, then stood. Slate leaned back in his chair to watch. Micah pulled his clothes off slowly and carefully, revealing the caning that Slate had given him two weeks prior. It was mostly healed, except the parts where the strokes had overlapped and broken the skin.

When he finished, Slate said nothing, letting the silence drag out. Micah had come here to brag, to show off. He'd tried to take pride in his marks. Slate wasn't going to let him. At least, not yet.

Micah laced his hands behind his neck, a variation of the waiting pose that didn't obscure the view of his back. He was looking at the ground, but his usual confidence was missing. He wasn't doing it to demonstrate form. He was genuinely embarrassed.

"What did you do to earn those?" Slate asked.

"I was presumptuous and selfish," Micah answered immediately, and Slate nodded. He couldn't recall the exact circumstances, but that sounded plausible.

"That's an ongoing issue with you, isn't it?"

"Yes, sir," Micah answered. His voice was hardening now.

"Anthony doesn't have that problem," Slate said. "Do you know what Anthony's problem is?"

Anthony opened his mouth and almost protested but snatched it back before he could get in more trouble.

Micah's eyes flicked in his direction before he answered. "I wouldn't know."

"Anthony thinks this is a game," Slate said, turning away from Micah. "Anthony, can you tell me why Micah was caned?"

"Punishment for being presumptuous," Anthony said, a tone of sullenness edging into his voice. Beside him, Slate felt Micah shift minutely.

Micah knew the answer to this question.

"Wrong," Slate said. "If I wanted to stop him being presumptuous, I could gag him. He looks good in a gag. I'm asking you if you understand the purpose of discipline."

"I . . ." Anthony said, then trailed off into silence.

"Micah?" Slate asked, turning to him.

"Discipline helps us understand our place," Micah answered immediately.

"Good," Slate said, and a small smile appeared on Micah's lips. The thing Slate admired was, Micah didn't just *know* the expected answer. He talked like he really *believed* it. Anthony might be able to parrot this sentiment back later, but he still saw punishment as an external consequence being inflicted on him against his will.

But Micah? Micah had really internalized that his will was irrelevant. He was disciplined because that was his purpose: to be something that Slate could inflict discipline on. Micah had come upstairs today, disobeying and deliberately being caught, specifically in order to be useful in that purpose.

Incredible, Slate thought, looking the man over. Absolutely incredible.

Slate had to know how far it went. He stood and went to the bookshelf, sliding it aside to reveal his tools.

"Anthony, take your clothes off and put your hands on the desk. Do not move them until I give you permission." He listened while the slave complied. "Do you understand what I mean when I say that you think this is a game?"

"No, sir."

Slate turned slowly, staring at him until, paling, Anthony realized his mistake.

"I mean, I don't understand, sir."

"Try again."

Anthony stammered, clearly unsure of what he was being asked for. He didn't have Micah's training, and Slate wondered whether it would be worth it to remedy that.

"Please help us understand, sir," Micah said, and Slate sighed.

"I asked *him*, Micah, you're being presumptuous again."

"Sorry."

"We'll address that later. In the meantime, yes, I will help you understand." Slate removed a thin wooden switch from the shelf, swinging it experimentally through the air with a *whoosh*. "A game is an arrangement between two people, in which they both act according to negotiated rules in order to achieve a goal." He set the switch down and picked up another one, thicker, not as springy. "Your problem, Anthony, is that you think you get to have goals. You don't. There is no arrangement and there are no rules. We are not negotiating."

He set the cane down and crossed the room to behind where Anthony was waiting, half bent over the desk. Anthony didn't try to turn his head. Slate came up close behind him, nudging his foot, indicating that he needed to spread his legs wider. He let his hands rest on the small of Anthony's back, running them up toward his shoulders, enjoying the feel of smooth, warm skin. The remains of broken connections pebbled under his fingers.

He leaned down, one hand resting on the desk, the other coming up to cup the curve of Anthony's throat.

"So when you *suggest to me*," Slate murmured in his ear, "that I trade you for someone whose tastes more closely match mine, it shows a fundamental misunderstanding of your place in the hierarchy." Slate glanced at Micah then. "You don't get input on that. Whether I use you, sell you, or put you in a cell and forget about you, is not something you get to weigh in on."

"I just thought—" Anthony started, and Slate didn't let him finish. He shoved hard, pushing the slave down onto the surface of the desk.

Micah flinched.

There was a small sound outside the door, likely the maid or the doorman overhearing. Slate didn't need to shift focus to know they wouldn't intercede.

"I did not ask you to think," Slate said. "And I did not ask you to talk. Stay right there."

He stood up and left the room. The two of them could stew a few minutes.

The bulk of his toys and tools were stored in the playroom, and that was where he went now. He had something specific in mind, and it didn't take him long to find what he needed.

When he returned, he waited silently outside the door, listening. Micah was silent, but Anthony was talking, about how *Cunningham* was the one who had offered him the contract, and how things were supposed to be *different*. Slate smirked.

Indeed.

It didn't take a genius to figure out what had happened there. Anthony had been involved with Cunningham *romantically*, and one of them (probably Cunningham, but Anthony could be surprisingly submissive sometimes) had pushed the idea of lifetime indenturement. Legal ownership, to add a little gravitas to the games they played.

Slate pushed the door open, and Anthony went silent. He was still bent over the desk, the pose putting his ass nicely on display. It was enough that Slate almost abandoned his plan in favor of simply fucking him and calling it a day. But then, he could never pass up an opportunity to teach a lesson. And this was a *good* lesson.

Micah was staring at the items Slate had carried in. Anthony could see Micah getting nervous but didn't dare turn around. He wasn't *that* untrained.

"Hands behind your back," Slate said, and Anthony complied. Slate fastened them together with a pair of leather cuffs. "Good, now open your mouth."

He did the good deed of letting Anthony see the gag before it went on. It was black leather that would cover the bottom half of his face like a muzzle. The silicone cock affixed to the inside slid easily into Anthony's waiting mouth. It pushed deep into his throat as Slate began buckling the mask tight. Anthony gagged, his body bucking involuntarily back against Slate's clothed cock. He quickly got it under control, so his training apparently wasn't a total waste.

"That should help you remember your place in this conversation," Slate said. He was looking forward to this. He'd had dozens of slaves, but he'd never been anyone's *initiation*. It had always seemed like too much of a risk.

But things . . . well. Things were changing now, weren't they?

"Micah, do you know why I chose you for the Saturnalia event?"

"I don't, sir," Micah said, shifting his weight slowly.

"Because you're strong, and you're obedient, and you're not pretty enough to make anyone irrational. I told you not to drop your baskets, and you were able to follow that order." Slate nonchalantly picked up a small bottle, drizzling the contents over Anthony's lower back. "Do you know what would happen if I put up someone with the opposite characteristics?"

Micah was very still, calculating his answer.

"They would . . . fail?"

"Precisely, they would fail. Everyone runs the risk, of course, but there are strategies, and getting out early is an easy one to spot." Slate ran his finger through the slick fluid, drawing nonsense shapes on Anthony's back. It ran slowly downward, toward his ass. "So, assuming Cunningham is an asshole, which he is, but isn't stupid, which he isn't, why would he put up a slave like Anthony?"

In the following silence, Slate slid one slippery finger down Anthony's ass, barely ghosting over his hole. Anthony flinched.

"Answer me, Micah," Slate ordered.

"He expected to lose," Micah said quietly.

Anthony had gone very still.

"Look at that, it took Micah fifteen seconds, and you haven't figured it out in six months," Slate said, picking up a plug that he'd carefully kept out of Anthony's eyesight. He set it down now, right in front of the slave's face, and Anthony's eyes widened. It was big—probably too big, but what better to drive a point home?

Anthony said something muffled, shuffling back a little, pressing into Slate's unmoving body. Slate caught him by the straps of the gag, hauling him back into place.

"Hold him, please," he said, gesturing to Micah. Micah complied immediately, coming around and holding Anthony's shoulders down against the desk. Anthony mumbled something else as Slate began dripping lubricant over the tip of the clear plug. It wasn't a kindness. He just wanted to feel Anthony trembling while he watched.

"I will not be selling you back, for one simple reason," Slate said, watching the fluid slowly drip over the surface. "Cunningham does not *want you*." Slate smiled a little, switching focus to the slave's connections, smug with the proof of his words. "He gave you away." He picked up the plug, running the tip down the furrow of Anthony's ass, until it rested against his hole. "And I don't *care* if your tastes align with mine."

He emphasized the point by pushing, a little too hard, and Anthony jerked against Micah's hold as half the plug vanished inside him at once. He keened into the gag, his hands flexing into desperate fists as Slate continued relentlessly on.

"I want you to remember this, because *this* is what I want from you," Slate said. Only the widest half inch was left outside Anthony's body. The slave was taking deep breaths in through his nose. From the sound of it, he might be starting to cry. "It isn't your job to think, or strategize, or worry about who owns you. You? Are a *fuck hole*."

He pushed the last half inch inside, and Anthony's body immediately closed around the narrow part of the flared base. It still looked massive, the clear resin holding him open without obscuring the view. Slate could see the velvet skin twitching as Anthony breathed, deep and ragged, trying to adjust.

"You can let him go," Slate said, circling around his desk. He sat in his chair, leaning forward so his face was almost level with Anthony's. "I don't want any more bitching out of you."

Anthony's curse was amazingly well pronounced considering how full his mouth was. Slate sighed and leaned back in his chair. Micah was staring at Anthony, rightfully worried about the other slave's outburst.

"I have work to do. Micah, go find an impact toy, I don't care which one."

Micah's face hardened, and he dropped his gaze to the floor. "Yes, sir."

Slate opened his laptop, deliberately not watching while Micah examined his options. His choice was predictable, and Slate had to repress a smile. Micah was a bit of a brat, always goading his way toward a punishment for himself, but he *hated* doling it out to others.

Micah returned with a flogger made of thick leather strands. It was formidable, but unlikely to break the skin. A safe, sane, predictable choice.

"Should I have him count?" Micah asked, and Slate resolved to take him, instead of Anthony, when he went back to the inn. Anthony would have asked, *How many do I have to give him?* and provoked a longer duration. But Micah, Micah put *thought* into his interactions. Micah asked *artfully*.

"No," Slate answered, beginning to type. "I'll tell you when he can be done."

Micah nodded once, then put a gentle hand on Anthony's back, adjusting his stance to keep Anthony's cock and balls out of the line of fire. Anthony's whole body went tense, his forehead pressing against the desk as the first blow landed with a *thwack*.

Slate actually did have work to do, a summary of a project that was already overdue, but he couldn't focus on it. Something was wrong with the setup, though he couldn't quite figure it out. Micah was going a little slower than Slate would have preferred, and wasn't hitting as hard as he could, but that wasn't it.

Anthony whimpered as another blow landed, wrapping ever so slightly around the inside of one thigh. Oh, that was it.

"Turn around," Slate said, gesturing. Both slaves looked at him, unsure of who he was addressing. "Anthony. Turn around."

Carefully, Anthony stood, turning so that Slate could see the angry red of his ass and thighs. The base of the plug was barely visible, nestled up between his cheeks.

"Sit on the edge of the desk and spread your legs."

Anthony let out a little whimper but did what he was told. He hissed as he was forced to put his weight on the plug. Slate could *hear* the question in Micah's hesitant step back.

"Keep going," Slate said. "Throat to thighs. And I want him to see it in the mirror this time next week. Understood?"

Micah swallowed hard, set his jaw, then nodded. Of course he did.

Anthony's whimpers got louder over the next half an hour, as Micah carefully tried to trade force for frequency, hitting hard enough to bruise and then waiting as long as he could before striking again. At one point, Slate almost threatened to make them change places, before he realized that Micah would almost certainly prefer that.

The room settled into a comfortable cadence, Anthony's whimpers fading into background noise as Slate typed. His bound arms trembled as he tried and failed to take weight on them. It was impossible to watch him without remembering the toy keeping his hole open and ready. Thus motivated, Slate finished his summary, sending it and the relevant report to the client who had commissioned them. Eagerly, he came around the desk, surveying Micah's handiwork.

It was lovely.

Anthony was leaning back with his hands together on the desk, stretching his body into an appealing curve. As Slate had ordered, he was red, beginning to bruise, from his collarbones almost all the way to his knees. Distinct reddish purple stripes stood out where the flogger had wrapped around the insides of his thighs. It was clear that Micah had done his best to spare Anthony's cock, but he'd known better than to miss a spot.

"Well done," Slate said, giving him a nod. Anthony had his eyes closed, his chest heaving as he took deep breaths through his nose.

Reaching out, Slate ran his knuckles down Anthony's sides, relishing the hot blush of his skin.

Six hundred dollars. That was what he'd put into Anthony's baskets. Six hundred dollars had bought this slave off the man he loved, and now not even a shred of that connection remained. Slate shivered, his hard cock suddenly demanding satisfaction.

He pushed Anthony back onto the desk, onto his bound arms. Slate hooked a hand beneath each knee, forcing them back, and Anthony held them spread without being asked. The clear base of the plug showed off the soft pink of his stretched hole, surrounded on all sides by the angry red of the flogging. Slate took hold of it, relishing Anthony's sob when he began to pull. In this direction, the taper wasn't in Anthony's favor, and he was immediately forced to stretch around the widest part. He let out a keening wail, but it was such a compelling sight that Slate pushed it back in, fucking him slowly open a couple of times before finally withdrawing the toy.

It left him a little too stretched but far from unusable. His hole was hot and velvet soft when Slate freed his cock and pushed inside. He didn't bother undressing, instead relishing the hissing inhale when the rough fabric of his slacks ground up against Anthony's sore ass. It killed the bare beginning of a hard-on that Anthony had managed to get. He obviously liked a *little* subjugation and pain along with his pleasure, but this was far beyond what he could handle.

"This is perfect," Slate said, resting his hands inside Anthony's knees and pushing them further back. The slave was almost bent in half, and it was doing a wonderful job of making him tighter. The cock gag was still buried in his throat, and one of his shoulders was dangerously torqued. "This is you, *exactly* where you're supposed to be."

Tears shone in Anthony's eyes, and Slate fucked into him ruthlessly, enjoying each exhale he forced out of the man beneath him.

Worth every fucking penny.

Anthony glanced to the side, and Slate didn't need to look to know that Micah was standing there with perfect form, waiting silently while he watched his master fuck someone else. He was probably already planning his next round of misbehavior, hoping for a better reward next time—

The idea hit Slate hard enough that he didn't have time to slow down. He came inside Anthony's hole with a noise between a gasp and a growl.

In the silence that followed, Anthony wouldn't meet his eyes. He kept his head turned, and Slate could have laughed.

"Nothing's *changed*," he said, giving Anthony another slow roll of his hips. "You've been here half a year. Have I *ever* asked your permission? For anything?"

Anthony glared at the far wall, his eyes glistening.

With an exaggerated sigh, Slate pulled out. He wiped himself clean on a piece of discarded clothing, then picked up the plug again. Carefully, he used the tip to collect the smear of come that was escaping Anthony's well-fucked hole. The slave let out a shuddering moan as Slate pushed the plug back inside. The crystal head sparkled like a jewel, half hidden between his cheeks.

"How's your shoulder?" Slate asked casually. Anthony mumbled into his gag.

"Mmm, I bet," Slate said. "You can stand up. Micah, help him get cleaned up."

Slate returned to his seat, enjoying a rare mix of satiation and excitement. He watched silently as Micah gingerly removed the wrist cuffs and gag. Risking a glance at Slate, Micah began rubbing Anthony's numb shoulder, trying to work circulation back into the limb. He helped Anthony up, and reached for his clothes.

"Just one last thing," Slate said, leaning forward. Both slaves froze. "You got worked up, didn't you, Micah?"

"I—" Micah started, but Slate cut him off.

"Don't be shy, Micah, you got hard while flogging him, and you got hard again watching me fuck him. Didn't you."

"Yes," Micah said, beginning to slowly massage the muscles of Anthony's arm again. Anthony stayed very still.

Slate was pretty sure Micah did it on purpose. Somewhere in his training he'd learned that he was supposed to at least *look* like he was enjoying whatever was going on. Slate didn't give a shit either way, but it was a convenient target for pushing Micah's buttons.

The only other explanation was that Micah was a *genuinely* masochistic submissive who enjoyed imagining himself in Anthony's place. Definitely not Slate's, though. Micah could take it like a champ, but when it came to dishing it out, Slate suspected Micah'd rather be caned.

Too bad.

"I'm not going to leave you unsatisfied after you did such a good job for me. Which one do you want?"

Micah's eyes went wide, and Slate smirked.

"Which one, sir?"

"Which hole," Slate clarified, gesturing to Anthony. "Pick one. As a treat."

Micah clenched his eyes, but Anthony was still there when they reopened. The slave was looking a bit peaky. His full lips were pink and swollen from being wrapped around the cock gag so long, and his jaw had to be killing him—but his ass wasn't in good shape either. His eyes met Micah's, pleading.

"I'm all right, sir," Micah said, unable to tear his gaze away from Anthony.

"I'm not asking, Micah," Slate said, his voice hard.

Micah knew better than to answer back. He stepped forward, into Anthony's space. Micah was a good four inches taller, and much broader across the shoulders, making Anthony look almost small as Micah took him into his arms. He lifted Anthony's chin, kissing him tenderly as his hands skirted down over Anthony's naked hips.

Micah put on a good show, cupping Anthony's ass before his fingers delved closer to the plug. Anthony's gentle moan let him know when he'd found it, and Micah quickly withdrew. His damage assessment had told him what Slate already knew: as usual, there was no good choice.

Micah broke the kiss, then followed it with a shorter one, right at the corner of Anthony's mouth. Anthony gave him a small, almost imperceptible nod.

Slate pulled out his cell phone, scrolling through his contacts while Anthony sank to his knees. He was a decent cocksucker, but Micah wasn't exactly small. Anthony compensated with his hand, turning it into a combination handjob, and Slate tutted.

"No slacking, Anthony. Swallow it all, I know you can."

Anthony's brow furrowed and, slowly, he leaned in. Micah regarded him impassively, keeping his face carefully neutral despite his obvious discomfort—though to his credit, he managed to stay hard.

Anthony's fingers tightened on his knees, his body fighting against the gag reflex. He still had half an inch to go when he lost the fight, pulling off with a gasp. He silently pleaded with Micah, like that was going to help him.

"I'm not asking again," Slate said, and something passed between the two slaves. Anthony swallowed Micah back down again, his hands resting lightly on Micah's hips. Micah stroked his brow once, and then buried his fingers in Anthony's hair. His hands were like stone, keeping Anthony from pulling back as he slowly but purposefully began to fuck in deeper.

"Much better," Slate said, raising his phone. Neither slave looked at him as he took the video, making sure that the camera captured Anthony's forming bruises.

Keeping half an eye on the show before him, he sent the video off to Arabelle.

Think you could teach this one a decent technique?

The response came faster than he expected.

Taught the other one, didn't I? I have an opening in August. Usual fee.

Fair warning. He's new. Cunningham put up a virgin indent for the Saturnalia party.

Bastard. Want me to spread that around?

Slate grinned.

Please do.

Micah's breathing was going ragged, his lithe body tensing as he chased his climax. Slate put down his phone to watch. He didn't have Micah come often, but there was beauty in it when he did. Between Micah's artfully tailored body and impeccable submissiveness, it was easy to forget the almost animal *strength* he had.

Anthony pulled back at the last second, but Micah was too far gone. Anthony's face was painted with lines of come as he gasped for the air Micah hadn't allowed him.

Micah took a few deep breaths, then stepped back, sliding easily into the waiting pose.

"Thank you, Anthony, you can go," Slate said, satisfied. Anthony staggered to his feet, predictably going for his clothes before Slate stopped him with a sharp clearing of his throat. Anthony met his eyes as Slate slowly shook his head. Naked and debauched, Anthony turned for the door. The flush on his downturned face was almost bright enough to light his way down the hallway.

"And Anthony?"

The slave stopped with his hand on the doorknob, and didn't turn around.

"In case it doesn't go without saying, you may not go to the medic for those bruises. And you're to wear that plug until I send word otherwise."

"Yes, sir," Anthony said quietly, and limped out of the room. Carol would probably intercept him before he got back to the barracks belowground. Most of the indentured staff were content to look the other way, lest Slate's attention come down on them next, but Carol was invested in, at the very least, the *functionality* of everything under her roof. She'd make sure he got some water and ibuprofen, maybe a couple of extra hours of sleep.

In a gentler woman, Slate might suspect a maternal instinct, a softness or even affection for the people who worked under her care. But Carol, like the rest of the people he employed or owned, didn't form connections. She didn't care about them. She just needed them to work properly.

"Get dressed," Slate said, opening his laptop without looking at Micah. He opened the document where he was working on deciphering the pylinomicon's more creative penmanship.

Micah didn't respond, just redressed with the same feline grace he'd used to strip the clothes off. Slate wondered if Arabelle had taught him to do that. He imagined Micah in front of a mirror, practicing over and over until he got it right.

Slate tapped the desk to the left of his knee, and Micah came to kneel on the floor at his feet. Slate absently stroked the slave's hair as he worked. It was much quieter here, without the sounds of debauched revelry filtering in from the floor above.

"I didn't summon you to the inn when I went," he said quietly. Micah nodded against his knee. Slate thought of the slave who had become the Gestalt's avatar. Of the way the spell had reverberated through the room as his body shredded beneath the magic being wrought. He thought of the Gestalt, the way his hand had trembled as he'd put the quill through his own eye. "I have my reasons," Slate said, putting steel into his voice. "Do not question me again."

Micah nodded and said nothing.

CHAPTER FIFTEEN

September 2013

"I don't think you can win that one," a female voice said at his shoulder. Micah didn't look over. He wasn't particularly invested in Megan's opinion. She wasn't dumb, but she tended not to think things through. It made her a poor conversationalist and a worse card player.

Which wasn't to say she was *wrong*, he admitted, cycling through the cards again. The ace he needed was locked behind a six, and there didn't seem to be anything for it.

Sighing, he swept the cards up and set to righting them.

"You wanna play rummy?" Megan asked.

Micah shrugged. If Megan was talking to him, it was because she wanted something. And that something was . . . most likely sex.

Micah couldn't really complain. It wasn't exactly like he was being run ragged. Slate hadn't been home in a week and probably wouldn't be home for another one. When Anthony had been sent to Arabelle's, Micah thought maybe he'd get a shift at the inn. Instead, Slate had bought somebody new and taken *him*. Micah didn't even know his name.

It wasn't his business, Micah reminded himself for the hundredth time. He'd been told as much in very clear words.

Still. It got boring.

Megan took the seat across from him, watching him shuffle. He was getting pretty good at it. People kept suggesting he should learn to do tricks, but there was no one to teach him.

"You want to make it *interesting*?" Megan asked, and Micah looked up at her through his eyelashes.

Megan didn't need much from him. She wasn't in hospitality, but she still seemed happy to do most of the flirting in any given interaction. Mostly, she just wanted Micah to be receptive to it, which was easy enough. It beat being ignored—or worse yet, *pitied*.

There was a certain sad masochism to strip poker (or strip rummy, as the case may be) when it was played by two people who were both wearing pants, slippers, and a T-shirt. You win or lose *quickly*, without much time for the stakes to rise.

Megan lost in three rounds, and the group by the TV broke out into whistles when she stripped out of her pants. She flipped them an amiable bird, then took Micah's hand and led him toward the showers.

They didn't turn the water on, of course. Sex in a shower was a delicacy reserved for owners and their guests, in the rooms upstairs that were plumbed for hot water. Sex in a shower *stall*, though, was the closest to privacy they were likely to get. Megan liked that he could take her against the wall, holding her full weight as she wrapped her legs around his hips. The stall could handle it. It was stronger than it looked; two months ago, someone on the security team had taken *Micah* against the wall, and it had held just fine.

Micah fucked her hard, panting into the hollow of her throat, counting off the thrusts so he'd know when to shift her weight. It was all sets and reps, the same as the exercise routine he did each day. Her nails dug into his shoulders, and he got the impression that she would like to squeeze harder but knew better. Bruises from training were one thing. Marks from this? Would be something else.

Someone banged on the wall of lockers, startling Micah out of his thoughts.

"Boss is on his way," a man's voice said. Micah couldn't place it. "Driver figures thirty minutes out."

"Thanks," Micah said, loud enough to be heard over the wall. The messenger slapped the locker door again in acknowledgment and went back into the hall.

"Please," Megan whispered. Her lips were against his collarbone, her fingers laced behind his neck. Micah considered. Thirty minutes wasn't a *good* refraction, but it wasn't impossible. If his owner asked for him, asked him to get off, he'd . . . *probably* be able to do it. And if he couldn't . . . well, he wasn't sure what would happen if he couldn't. He never really knew with Slate.

"*Please*," Megan said again, and Micah looked down at her sharply. There was something else in that word. Her downturned face offered no explanation. She was nuzzling her face against his chest, and for a moment, Micah felt almost self-conscious.

Then the moment passed, and she squeezed her thighs around him with a wicked grin. "Send me back to him wet," she whispered, leaning up until her lips brushed his ear.

Micah decided to go for it. It seemed important to her, or at least, more important than the alternative was to him. He did switch it over into a quickie, though, moving fast and erratic. He gave it another ninety seconds and then had to dial it back. Megan wasn't there yet, and he couldn't keep it up forever.

"You seem pretty wet to me," he said, letting his voice drop low. She groaned into his throat, her hand leaving his shoulder to slip between them. He shifted them slightly, giving her room.

"Harder," she ordered, and Micah gave her a rakish grin. He could do that.

"Not gonna last," he groaned, breathlessly, driving up into her hard enough that she slid up the wall an inch. She moaned, clutching at him tighter.

It made it harder to move, but if that was what she needed . . .

Micah closed his eyes, focusing on what he could feel, keeping all the moving parts in sync—he needed not to fuck this up. He wasn't asked for a lot.

He could feel the tension in his arms and shoulders, telling him he couldn't keep her off the ground all day. He ignored that, trying to focus on the good parts. Her breath was warm against his skin. Her moans of pleasure were genuine—this wasn't a show, and she didn't work for him. That was what made heat flush through him, more than the wet heat of her body or the way she shuddered around his cock as she came.

He rocked her through it, then set her down. She didn't ask why he hadn't come, didn't say a word as the two of them cleaned up and re-dressed.

That was fine with him. He didn't really have an answer for her.

Slate didn't call for him.

Micah tried not to be too disappointed.

He got dinner with the others, half-expecting the food to be tinged with the bitter taste of Slate's little white helpers . . . but there was nothing.

Megan wasn't there, though. So maybe Slate had work to do, and that was why he hadn't called for Micah. Or maybe he'd brought the other hospitality slave home and didn't have any use for a second one.

Micah sighed, pushing his food around his plate. He'd been here for a year and seven months. It was completely predictable that Slate was getting bored with him by now. *They always did.* Transience was the nature of hospitality placements, it was just how it was.

Half of him wished Slate would finally get around to selling him already. Tell Micah he was boring and get it over with.

There was clamor in the hallway, signaling a shift change. Micah didn't look up from his food until someone sat down across from him. Then two someones. Then three.

"You coming out with us?" Gino asked, dropping his tray down on the faux wood. "I need you to show me that side plank thing again; I'm fucking it up, I can feel it."

"It's because you hold the stress in your neck," Micah said, not needing an explanation. He'd been working with Gino for two months. He did it *every* time.

"I'm not."

"You definitely are," Micah countered. On Gino's other side, Ralph chuckled. Gino threw a french fry at him.

"So are you coming out with us or not?" Justin asked, ignoring them.

"I can't get too deep into it," Micah said, almost apologetically. They didn't ask why. When Slate was home, Micah was on call. The kind of on call that didn't leave a lot of prep time.

"That's fine," Gino said, around a mouthful of chicken. "We promise to keep you pretty, if you return the favor." He winked.

Micah gave him a sarcastic grin, and Gino laughed. Justin ate his food. He was the one who'd given Micah the black eye, when Micah had asked. Justin had been weird about it for a week or two, but Micah had shown him some of the worse marks Slate gave him, and Justin had gotten over it.

It wasn't like Micah's ongoing bruises were any kind of *secret*, like they were in some other houses. In some places, the medic would come and set Micah right before he was even allowed to leave the bedroom, and everybody pretended they didn't know.

Here, Micah pretty regularly had marks—a limp, a split lip, a ring of bruises around his throat. At least, he did when Slate was home. Bearing them was Micah's job, and he didn't complain about it.

He considered it, sometimes. Turning the mundane irritations of his job into funny stories like the maids or the security team did . . . but down deep, he knew better. His life was different from theirs because he was different from them. That was why they were indentured, while he'd been made into a slave.

So Micah kept his complaints to himself and did his job. And sometimes, doing his job meant getting a black eye to provoke his owner into using him. So he did that.

"Nobody could make you pretty, Gino," Micah said, and there was a twinge of uneasiness in his stomach for the half second before Gino laughed.

The security team were lifers, but in . . . not quite the same way as the others. They had a comradery to them that the rest of the staff tried their best to avoid. A couple of them had talked about serving together . . . but Micah wasn't sure if they'd served their country or time. Even money, the answer was *both*.

They spoke to each other in the form of casual insults. It was easy enough to replicate, but it still left Micah slightly on edge. It was dangerous ground to walk, and he wasn't sure what a misstep would cost him.

Justin and Ralph started arguing about something, clearly picking up a discussion from earlier, and Micah turned his attention back to his food. It wasn't bad here at all. The grilled chicken and french fries were joined by fresh grapes, and broccoli in a delicate cheese sauce— most likely a recipe the kitchen staff were testing out on them.

Micah had gotten there first but finished eating last. The security teams tended to eat food like someone was going to take it away from them, a habit Micah didn't ask about and they didn't explain.

That done, they went outside.

Micah liked being outside. He liked it enough to ignore the constant nagging feeling that it wasn't allowed. It wasn't forbidden. No one here had told him he *couldn't* go outside. And he was just in the side courtyard, with guys from the *security team*, of all people.

They laughed and joked with him, but Micah harbored no illusions; if he slipped away into the woods, they'd bring him back in whatever state they could manage.

Not that he would. But some others might, and that was why the staff weren't typically allowed outside unless they had something specific they needed to do.

Training counted as something specific, Micah reminded himself, as he sat on the manicured grass to stretch.

Gino sat beside him, mimicking his motions, enduring the mockery of his teammates when his attempts fell far short of what Micah was capable of. It wasn't Gino's fault. Micah had been going through the same set of stretches and bodyweight exercises since he was twelve. Gino was trying to get back levels of flexibility that Micah had never lost.

Gino didn't *need* Micah's help. He was in decent shape, especially for a job where a gun, a taser, and a radio were going to carry more than their share of the work. No, Gino copied Micah's routine because Gino wanted to look like Micah did.

And Micah was happy to help him, because he wanted to be able to disarm an opponent like Gino could.

That wasn't quite accurate. Micah could disarm like Gino. He wanted to be able to disarm like *Justin* could, and helping Gino was Micah's ticket into the arena where those lessons were on offer.

Justin wasn't interested in looking like Micah, mostly because he never would. His hands and arms were scored with scars, and though he always sparred with his shirt on, Micah had no doubt that his chest and back were more of the same.

Micah knew the shape of those scars. They came from dropping your guard, from failing to anticipate. They came from blocking wrong or being too slow to block at all.

Micah had had scars like that once, given to him by the same people who'd taught him how to train his body with nothing but determination and its own weight. They were the ones who had taught him to fight, preparing him for a life like Justin's.

A life Micah's looks had spared him from.

Justin's job had been to fight people. Specifically, to *win* fights against people. For owners like Slate, there was money to be made when their slave could win fights.

Micah couldn't win. The best skill he could claim was that he very rarely *lost*.

He could dodge. He could block. By the time they'd changed his training, he hadn't been so much as *nicked* by an opponent's knife in more than two years.

But he hadn't managed to land against anyone else, either.

Micah's cheeks colored, and he pulled himself back into the present. In the real world, he was sitting on the grass with the soles of his feet pressed together, his hands reaching forward as far as he could stretch them. The skin of his arms was pristine, the mistakes of his youth washed away when his owners had deemed them unsightly.

In Justin's case, no one had bothered. His scars didn't interfere with his duties—not the ones on his arms, not the mottled red patch that stretched from his jawline to his temple.

Maybe that scar was why Justin didn't fight anymore. Why he was here, teaching Gino and Micah and Ralph how to spar.

He didn't ask why Micah was already so good.

And Micah didn't tell him.

CHAPTER SIXTEEN

∞

November 2013

S late supposed that, after everything else, he shouldn't really have been surprised that Coffey kept a vampire in his basement.

The creature was bound in a straightjacket lined with silver, hissing at the gathered visitors through a thick layer of plexiglass. Its face was too long, the bones too jutting and cruel to ever be mistaken for human.

Slate stared into its red eyes and took another sip of his drink. People milled around him, taking in the various parts of Coffey's menagerie. Tonight was a grand unveiling, the first time Coffey had deemed it *safe* to allow others into his sanctum.

Since the gateway had opened, the people around Slate had begun revealing increasingly disturbed proclivities to the group. And since the gateway had opened, no one—except for Christopher—had walked away.

"How do you feed it?" someone asked, and Coffey waved noncommittally.

"The staff take care of it. I think the medic gets blood from them. And from the Gestalt, of course."

"It can drink the blood of other creatures?" Slate asked, genuinely curious.

Coffey shook his head. "As far as we can tell, the Gestalt's body parts are human. Once disconnected from his power, they act just like any other body part."

It took Slate a beat to realize what he meant by *disconnected*. The woman wrinkled her nose, stepping away from the two men to feign interest in a different display. There were plenty to choose from.

Apparently, Slate wasn't the only one hiding things underground. Coffey's estate, a beautiful manor on the banks of a placid lake, had a full paranormal menagerie hidden beneath it. The large subfloor was filled with circular cages made of iron or acrylic, and inside each one was a monster.

Or an animal, Slate thought, noticing a leopard curled up in the center of its display. Plenty of normal beasts mixed in with their more paranormal counterparts. Animal, vegetable, or spirit, Coffey seemed less interested in the taxonomy of his specimens and more interested in whether he was legally prohibited from owning them.

"The wings, though," Slate said carefully. "They aren't human. There's magic in them?"

Coffey scowled. Slate was being delicate in his questioning, but they both knew the purpose of his question. An angry red line still crossed Coffey's cheek where the Gestalt had slashed at him with the quill. It had missed his eye by an inch.

The doctors had tried healing it, of course, but by the time they'd gotten to it, the feather's magic had already accelerated his healing, closing the wound. Four months later, Coffey hadn't yet managed to find a descarring method that would touch it.

"We've pulled out enough feathers to stuff a fucking mattress," Coffey muttered, casting around, probably trying to change the subject. "If there's any inherent magic in them, it's nothing we're able to detect or use. Oh, this should look familiar."

Coffey drew Slate's attention to the side, where an acrylic pillar was partially filled with water. Perched delicately on the surface was a familiar figure.

"Is it the same one we summoned?" Slate asked, inspecting the translucent elemental.

"Who knows? They all look the same. Not really important, is it?"

Slate wondered again what *drove* Coffey to amass things in this way. It wasn't a need to collect—collectors cared about the hoards they built, saw value in each scrap and shred they managed to tuck away. Coffey didn't. His joy was found in the acquisition.

It was why he'd snatched up the Gestalt, laying claim to him on the basis that he owned the slave whose body the creature was currently riding. Christopher had been the one to summon it, but gods knew *he* wasn't about to mount an argument. And Slate owned the portal, as far as anyone was concerned, but he had no interest in keeping the thing cloistered in *his* basement. Godfrey was the one most interested in it, and he was more than happy to move his operations into the more *specialized* facilities that Coffey offered him.

It was the Gestalt that Slate had come to see, and it was toward those facilities that Coffey guided them now, stopping here and there to make small talk with the other guests. Maybe *that* was Coffey's drive: to show off. For all his ignorance about what he *had*, he did have detailed and interesting stories about how he'd *gotten* them.

It took the two of them nearly forty minutes of socializing to reach their goal: an unassuming door painted to match the wall around it. It wasn't locked, but a large man stood beside it, perhaps less casually than he appeared. By the time Coffey finished chatting with him and actually opened the door, Slate was almost ready to give up and go home.

Not that any of his homes had much appeal these days. That was why he was here, after all.

Coffey held the door open, and Slate stepped into the darkness. Immediately, motion lights clicked on, spotlights illuminating the figure in the center of the room. This wasn't the room where Godfrey did his work—white, sterile, tools on trays arranged around a stainless steel table. No, this was where they kept the creature when he wasn't in use. A dark cell, designed to display.

The angel was kneeling, his back bent, his palms on the floor. His dark, messy hair fell across his downturned face. His wings were limp at his sides, feathers splayed on the dusty floor. Even in their current state, Slate could see the evidence of magic in them, in the colors that flickered across the interlocking circles on the barred surface.

"He's been ordered not to move," Coffey said, his voice laced with resentment. "He's good at wriggling through loopholes, but that one seems to work."

"He's not breathing," Slate observed, giving the wretched creature a wide berth as he circled it.

"I suspect his heart isn't beating, either," Coffey replied. "It usually does, though it doesn't seem to actually hurt him when it doesn't. Godfrey thinks his body runs off magic."

"What's Godfrey feeding him?" Slate asked.

"He doesn't eat. So . . . nothing, as far as we can tell."

For all Godfrey's experimentation, the Gestalt's naked skin was remarkably unmarred. His hands were perfect, with no evidence of the fingers that had been removed. The only sign of what he'd been through lay in a ladder of short, parallel scars leading up the side of his rib cage.

"His ownership marks," Coffey explained, noting Slate's interest. "They don't heal. Everything else we do to him vanishes like it was never there. Hell, Godfrey tried giving him *tits* once, they just—"

"Spare me," Slate said, wrinkling his nose.

Coffey produced a small pocket knife from somewhere and handed it over. "Mark him, it's the only way to be safe."

Slate quickly crouched and used the blade to make his mark below the others. The Gestalt, true to his orders, did not even flinch. A single drop of blood welled, then broke and rolled down his side as the wound faded shut.

"I have a theory," Slate said, watching it thin into a small white line. "I don't think the feathers are magic at all. I think there's a simpler explanation for why your scar won't heal."

"Do tell," Coffey said dryly.

"Because he chose not to let it," Slate said, regarding the scar he'd left on the angel. "It's why his body does two different things: The first mark on him forms a covenant. He can heal it, but not remove it. But I think, for the others, he has a choice. Heal to scar, or heal as though nothing happened. Am I right?"

The Gestalt was still as a statue, his dark eyes fixed on the ground.

"Answer him," Coffey ordered. "Truthfully."

"I can choose how to heal," the Gestalt rasped as the bands encircling him flashed.

"And you chose to heal the wound you inflicted on my friend," Slate said, standing. "You *chose* to leave the scar, to make it resist our magic."

"Yes," the Gestalt said. His mouth curled into a bitter smile. Coffey raised his hand to his cheek, fingering the red pucker.

"You little *shit*," he snapped, and before Slate could move, Coffey buried his foot in the angel's naked stomach. "You absolute fucking *waste*."

The creature gagged, collapsing onto one elbow before the edict not to move froze him again.

Slate caught Coffey by the sleeve, tilting his head to indicate a retreat. He had more to say, and he wanted to say it where the Gestalt couldn't hear him. This was the conversation he'd come to have. The revelation of the scar had come to him two days ago, at three thirty in the morning, as he stared down at a page he'd read often enough to recite in his dreams.

They left the angel crippled on the floor, stepping back out into a solitary corner of the main menagerie.

"There's a wider implication here," Slate said, his voice low.

"Do you think *he* can remove the scar?" Coffey asked, and waved down a passing slave. The slave was dressed, so to speak, in an elaborate net of leather straps. They were laced into a tray in a way that allowed him to serve drinks despite having his arms bound tightly behind him. It didn't do much for Slate, but he did appreciate the craftsmanship. Coffey took someone's drink, then shooed the man away.

"I severely doubt it," Slate answered, once the slave was out of earshot. "His healing magic wouldn't be any different from a doctor's."

"*Fuck—*"

"I'm more interested in the fact that he was *able* to do it," Slate continued, undeterred. "It means he can work magic on humans. No incantations, no circles, no nothing. He has *inherent magic* and he can use it *on us.*"

"I want another one," Coffey said, and Slate wasn't sure the man was following the conversation properly.

"What's wrong with this one?"

"What's—" Coffey gestured to his face. "Look at me. Look what he did to me."

"You think a second one's going to be better?" Slate asked, raising an eyebrow.

Coffey gave an exaggerated shrug. "This one . . . *you* remember how he was at first. Damn near brain-dead, couldn't get a damn thing out of him. We were cutting fingers off to bring his autonomous motor functions to his attention, and it took him weeks to get any kind of movement, to say nothing of *language*, and the whole time Godfrey was doing experiments with poisons and acids and who knows what the fuck else . . . so he's kinda . . . combative at this point."

"And you think you might have better luck with a softer touch."

"Well, it's worth checking, at least, right?" Coffey said, and there was something desperate in the tone. "The plan was never to make just one."

Slate gave a long exhale. Clearly, he wasn't going to get anywhere with Coffey. Which only left . . .

"I want to talk to him," Slate said. He didn't expect resistance, and he didn't get it.

Coffey only nodded, distracted. "Sure. Whatever you want. But I've got the next couple picked out. Since I know I'm getting them back, now." He gestured to one of the hospitality slaves threading their way through the crowd. "That one, actually."

"Mmm," Slate said, not looking. Coffey waved down a passing guest with a comment, and Slate took the opportunity to edge away, toward the guarded door. Coffey didn't call him back, and the posted man didn't protest as Slate slipped inside.

The Gestalt hadn't moved, of course.

Slate took a moment to admire him. He was a beautiful specimen and had been even as a human. With the addition of the wings, he was a work of art, truly. Not in the way that Micah was a work of art—Micah's body was crafted, honed, made to look the way it did through deliberate effort. This creature . . . this creature simply *was* beautiful. Inherently, the way a sunset was beautiful.

"You can sit up," Slate told him, and the creature actually hesitated before rising. "You may not touch me, with matter or magic. You may do nothing to harm or mark me."

With no sign of stiffness or discomfort, the Gestalt shifted into a cross-legged pose, his hands resting on his knees, his wings folded almost *primly* behind him.

His nakedness didn't seem to bother him at all, as he sat there regarding Slate with reserved curiosity. His dark eyes were a rich brown under the spotlight, clear and bright with no sign of what had happened with Arabelle.

"You're new," the Gestalt said, by way of introduction.

"We've met before," Slate reminded him. "When you arrived here."

"Oh. My eyes didn't work then."

"I would assume not," Slate said, thinking of the dripping carnage that had been ejected from the gateway, new passenger tucked safely inside. "Your body was pretty torn up."

"I fixed it. I can fix it, now," the Gestalt said. Then, wearily, "Are you here for a demonstration?"

"No," Slate answered. He'd seen what he needed to, on that front. "I want to know what you saw."

"My eyes weren't working," the Gestalt repeated, and Slate shook his head.

"Not with your eyes. I want to know what it was like in the *between.*"

He half expected the angel to claim ignorance, to refuse to speak to him, to hurl insults until each bracing syllable was dragged out of him by force. Instead, the creature looked thoughtful.

"It was . . . dark," he said, frowning slightly. "And there was no . . ." He paused, regarding one of his hands closely. He rubbed it vigorously against his naked thigh. "What is this? When you feel this?"

"Heat?" Slate guessed. "Friction?"

The Gestalt shook his head, then repeated the motion on the floor. "No. When you are aware of . . . of realness. Of being interacted with by—" the angel waved his hand through the air "—things that touch."

Slate wondered if the limited vocabulary was a shortcoming of the creature's, or if the man he inhabited had been equally ineloquent. Though, to be fair, the angel did get his point across. The space inside the gateway was dark and empty. It made sense that the place in between realities would not be, in a matter of speaking, a place.

"What about the world you come from?" Slate pressed. "What was it like there?"

The Gestalt peered up at him, seeming, for the first time, to really look. "You're the first to ask."

"I'm not surprised the others don't care. Tell me."

The silver bands flashed but not brightly. The creature wasn't resisting the order.

"I don't know," he said simply.

Slate frowned, lowering himself to the Gestalt's level to get a better look at his face. "You don't remember?"

"I *remember*," the Gestalt said, rubbing one palm against his face. "But I cannot . . . *tell* you."

"Tell me," Slate repeated, a hard edge to his voice. The bands flashed again, even dimmer this time.

"I do not have the *words*," the Gestalt said. He tapped the side of his head. "They are here, inside, but I cannot find what I don't know to look for. It is slow. Tedious. They are arranged in *metaphors*, paths through a labyrinth. I don't know which reference to follow."

"Try," Slate told him, and the bands barely glowed. Slate had come prepared to fight the Gestalt for this information—he hadn't considered that the creature wouldn't be *able* to tell him.

The Gestalt let out a slow exhale. "My home is *bigger* than here. And I am bigger. But I do not take up more space, I am simply more *of* the space. Do you understand?"

Not even a little bit. Slate switched tack. "What does it look like?"

The Gestalt's expression was pained, and Slate cherished it. Not because it was making the creature miserable—but because what must it *be* like, this place so alien that it couldn't even be described?

"It does not *look*. We do not see," the Gestalt said slowly. He raised a hand, watching his fingers as they flexed, then relaxed. "We do not use ourselves to feel. We understand, because we *are*."

Slate let out a slow exhale, trying to imagine.

"I want to go through," Slate told him, deciding against his better instincts to use honesty as his first tactic. The creature only blinked at him, and Slate didn't try to explain the *need* he had, to find something outside of his own, tiny world. To find something that was worth looking at, to see something he didn't instantly understand all too well.

"There are places beyond," the Gestalt said slowly. "There are many others, to be from. But you will not see them. It is dangerous for you. I can make . . ." He rubbed his arm again. "I can make skin have thoughts. But your thoughts *are* skin. You cannot take the skin with you."

"Then I can learn," Slate insisted. "If you can learn to exist here, then I can learn to exist somewhere else."

The Gestalt gave a very practiced, intentional shrug. "Maybe. You know yourself more than I do. I don't think it will be safe for you.

I think that even if you are able to exist, you will be made . . . wrong. By it. But I understand why you would want this. To understand where I come from." He exhaled, then held up his arm, pressing a fingertip to a place above his wrist. "This. You see this place, and then this place?"

Slate leaned in, looking closer. The Gestalt was pointing to a birthmark, a small round patch that was darker than its surroundings.

"The mark?"

The Gestalt nodded. "Yes. That is what I am from. The distance between marks. Between . . ." He paused, looked around, and then pointed to a gradient in the marble tile. "This. I am from this."

It was nonsensical, and it was incredible. Slate could almost hear his heart beating faster as he tried to conceive of it. What lands had grown a creature who believed he existed in the distinction between *colors*?

"You're different," Gestalt said, resting his arms across his knees. "You do not seem angry about what I did to your friend."

"He's an asshole," Slate said, shrugging. "I'm guessing he forbade you from trying to kill or injure him?"

The Gestalt's smile was wicked. "The wound healed as I struck it. Hardly an injury."

"It took me some time to figure out," Slate admitted. "I didn't realize you could perform your magic *on* us, even at a distance."

"None of you did. You are trapped inside skin, and so you assume that I am too. But you are smarter than the others. And so I will tell you a secret." The Gestalt leaned in, lowering his voice. "I can heal the bloodlettings, if ordered to. Remove the marks the others have left on me. All but the one who gives the order. Now, I am shared. I belong to—" He gestured at the line of lacerations down his side. Slate's eyes flicked to his chest, the tiny half-moon scars that had been his first binding. He remembered Christopher's nails digging deep into shredded flesh—

"I can be free of them," the Gestalt was saying. There was an edge to his voice now. "Allow me to heal, and I will belong to only you. I will take you through the nothing between. I will show you the things you wish to see."

"You said it wasn't safe," Slate countered, humoring him.

"It isn't. But I think that you will go either way," the Gestalt said. "I think there is a pull in you that cannot be put down. Maybe I can help." He hesitated then. "Please."

"The doorway is broken," Slate said. Finally, after all of it, his real reason for coming to meet the angel tonight. Almost six months of experimentation and guesswork, and that was the conclusion he'd come to. He wasn't just a terrible magician. The gateway didn't react the way it should because there was something *wrong* with it. "It's open, but when I look to the other side, there's nothing."

The Gestalt peered at him, considering what Slate had told him. "The doorway is closed, then," he said slowly. The satisfaction on his face was almost imperceptible. Almost.

Slate remembered the way the air had gone out of the room, the terrified expression on Christopher's face, the freezing emptiness in his blood as the Gestalt had battered at the gateway. The angel blinked innocently at Slate now, as though the silver bands around his body weren't the only thing that had kept Slate alive that day. Of *course* there was damage. The Gestalt had damaged it.

"Can it be repaired?" Slate asked. "Do you know how to fix it?"

"Maybe," the Gestalt said. "If I am allowed near, I can work my magic on it. The way I work magic on you. Maybe I can fix."

"You can send me through safely?"

The Gestalt exhaled slowly. "I will do what I can."

Slate reached out, his fingers bare millimeters from the scars along the Gestalt's side. He could feel the heat radiating off the creature's body as the Gestalt froze, refusing to recoil. "And you will do this for me if I help you? Free you from them?"

The Gestalt nodded, slowly. "Please." His voice was soft, the desperation beginning to leak through. "You know what they do to me. I am not safe here."

"I know," Slate said. He withdrew, and his knees protested as he stood, leaving the Gestalt on the ground. He switched focus, watching the dark energy roiling around the creature's body. There were two connections now, tethering him to Coffey, who saw him as an object, and Godfrey, who saw him as a hobby. Slate gave him a smile. This creature, who had been dragged across worlds, shoved into a corporeal form and *tortured*, still assumed the best of him. Of *him*.

It was precious.

"The marks stay. You'll help me either way."

The Gestalt's face hardened. "Then you *are* like the others."

"No. The others have the playthings that I *give* them. Now tell me the truth. How do I repair the gateway?"

"*I don't think you can*," the Gestalt sneered back. Slate almost laughed. Truthful, but unhelpful. It was going to be fun playing games with this thing.

"Tell me how *you* would do it," he ordered, and the bands flashed a bright silver.

The Gestalt laughed, a single, bitter sound. "Your language does not have the *beginnings* of what it would take to bind me to that truth. But as a gift . . ." He stared bitterly up at Slate, his face a mask of anger and hate. "I hope you try. I would like you to see the between place."

Slate smirked down at him. He had six months until the solstice. Six months before the year's only opportunity to reach through again.

He had until then to wring the truth out of this tricky beast.

"I'll tell you what I think," he said, changing tack. "And you tell me if I'm close, hmm?"

The Gestalt said nothing. Slate didn't waste a command, just carried on speaking.

"I've been testing it for months now, trying to see what you did when you came through. And the problem I'm having is that the damage is *irregular*. Some days worse, some days better, but always changing over time." Slate paced around the perimeter of the light. The Gestalt turned as slightly as possible but was clearly unwilling to let him out of view. The creature did little to conceal his frown as Slate described what he'd seen within the gateway. "I thought maybe I was measuring wrong, until it occurred to me: what if the damage is inconsistent *because it's still being inflicted*?" Slate stopped before the Gestalt, crouching down again. "What do you think? Am I on to something?"

"I only know some of those words," the Gestalt said. "So this is only a guess, but—" he let a Cheshire grin spread across his face "—it sounds to me like *someone* is still interfering with your plans."

"Someone who can do magic remotely," Slate said, his voice hard.

The Gestalt's grin got wider as he stared defiantly up into the light. "Someone very good at magic," he said. "Better than you. Probably working spells you've never even heard of."

"Stop it," Slate ordered, and the collar flashed brightly. "The magic you're working on the gateway stops, now, and it does not continue."

"Of course!" the Gestalt said, almost sweetly. "I solemnly swear that I'll do no more *magic* against your gateway, ever again."

Slate's eyes narrowed. "So when I look tomorrow, the damage will be consistent? No more fluctuations?"

"Oh, no," the angel said, mock concern falling over his features. "I expect that they'll be as bad as ever. Maybe worse."

"But I told you to stop," Slate protested.

"Then it seems one of the words in your order doesn't apply to the situation in the way you think it does," the Gestalt said, shrugging. "Bad luck."

Slate sighed, fingering Coffey's blade, where it still waited in his pocket. "Then I guess I'll have to figure out which one."

CHAPTER SEVENTEEN

∞

December 2013

Slate almost begged out of the Saturnalia party this year.
Last year, he'd *needed* to attend, needed to build the social connections that would help him open the gate. This year, he had more than ever. The people he'd brought together now drew closer without his help, the webs between them growing thicker and more incestuous with each passing week.

Slate avoided them when possible.

He wasn't opposed to the things they did. He just had no interest in being a spectator. He knew what they were seeking—that sense of control when their slave or creature stared out over an indifferent audience and knew, *knew*, that they were alone . . . there was nothing like it. But Slate didn't need the audience. He could stand alone, and look, and know.

So he didn't need to go. He had absolutely no reason to go. He had work to do.

Except . . . he couldn't stop thinking of last year. A settled sort of satisfaction wrapped the memory, one that had nothing to do with the season.

He almost didn't go.

He put up one of his slaves for the competition, just to stay in good standing. A nondescript man he'd picked up while Anthony was gone and immediately gotten bored with. Slate had more promising candidates at home. Anthony was freshly back from Arabelle's, her signature still healing on his hip, and Micah . . . Slate was well on his way to having Micah trained exactly the way he wanted. Slate had sent all three ahead while he debated whether to go, had dressed them for the occasion and made sure they'd been given an entertainingly significant dose of his preferred mind-altering substance.

He put it in the food. He didn't need to—he could have them eating it out of the palm of his hand, quite literally—but he liked coming at these things from an angle. He liked watching the security feed, the inner war as they considered *not* eating. Anthony spread his food around his plate, trying to minimize the dose, and the other one—Slate had forgotten his name—took three bites, recognized the taste, and dropped his tray in the trash. That was fine. He'd be getting an injection before he went anyway.

But Micah.

Watching the screen, Slate could see the exact moment that Micah recognized the taste. Apprehension flickered across his face, and there was the smallest tremor in his fingers as his fork hovered over his tray. He didn't check to see what the others were doing. He simply schooled his expression, inhaled, and took another bite.

Slate exhaled deeply, taking a moment to picture what the rest of Micah's night was going to be like. The drug wouldn't make him delirious, not like it did at the higher doses Slate had used at first. But it would take his control away. The one thing that anchored Micah through the maelstrom of his life, and it was going to be taken away.

Slate decided to attend the party, after all.

Slate dressed in white for once, getting into the spirit of the thing.

Stewart was hosting, taking the opportunity to show off one of his most recent projects. It was a house, in theory, but it had clearly been built to entertain. It had not one but *eight* ballrooms, arranged in a fashion that Slate didn't understand until he found a map of fire escapes.

Stewart's designs didn't burn down, of course, because he built magic into the very walls. These walls, Slate saw, were rounded, built into a network of concentric circles that he recognized immediately.

Slate wound his way through the crowd. He ignored the card games, not even checking on the nameless slave whose contract he had almost undoubtedly already lost. He had a different show to watch.

He went off in search of his slaves, keeping a drink in his hand so the various serving-slaves would stop trying to offer him one. It seemed like there were more this year, the draped roman costumes sheerer than usual.

Each room had a different theme. He didn't notice until the third one, which was completely dark. It wasn't just that the lights were off. The light *stopped* at the wide, arched doorway. Slate reached his hand out, watching it vanish into the shadows demarcating the threshold. He almost laughed. The other side was warm, humid with the press of bodies. Nothing like the door he spent his days peering into.

Exhaling, he stepped through.

Inside was utter blackness. He opened his eyes wide, but they didn't adjust. There was nothing to adjust *to*. He could hear people moving around him, talking, murmuring, moaning. If he angled just right, he could see a speck of light on the far side of the ballroom. Above the black silhouettes of the revelers, the doorway to the next room shone a brilliant white.

Cautiously, Slate set off toward it.

A hand landed on his elbow, and he turned on instinct, peering into the impenetrable dark. The hand slid slowly, languidly, down his arm, nimble fingers skimming over the back of his hand before plucking his drink from his grasp. Mischievous laughter rippled out of the dark, moving away before Slate could even react.

He switched focus, thinking to follow the person through the crowd—but there was nothing. He couldn't examine what he couldn't see.

He shook his head with a wry smile and continued on. He didn't get five more steps before he brushed against someone on his left. A woman, by the feel of it.

"Pardon me," he started to say, but the woman had turned toward him, one arm wrapping around his waist. Her other hand was on his chest, then his throat, his jaw. Lips pressed against his, soft, but with a hint of teeth. Resting his hands on her hips, Slate realized she was naked—or at the very least, *quite* unclothed. He returned her kiss, raising a hand to card through her hair.

"Stay a while," she murmured, standing on her toes to press the length of her body to his.

"Wish I could," he answered, following the statement with another quick peck. "But I've got somewhere to be."

She made a noise that was accompanied by a dramatic pout—he could hear it in her voice, even if he couldn't see her face.

"Maybe next time," he said, pulling away—and immediately running into someone else. This new someone was already engaged, if the noises were to be believed, and Slate slipped past, holding his hands cautiously out in front of him. The light that had been ahead of him was now slightly to his left, and he corrected course. His hand met someone else's, and the someone quickly laced their fingers together.

Something small and hard was left in his palm when they retreated, and Slate dropped it to the ground.

He hoped Micah wasn't in this room, though he'd never know if he was. Process of elimination was all he had to go on.

Someone came at him from the side, laughing, hands sliding over him as they passed. They didn't try to engage.

The path across the room was a series of similar encounters. It wasn't at all unpleasant, and more than once, he considered staying, as least for a while. There were worse evenings than a slow, anonymous fuck in the dark.

It occurred to him to wonder what the ratio of slaves in this room might be. There was no way to tell, he thought wryly. That was probably part of it, for some of them—being mistaken for a slave, being taken, being *used* . . .

It did nothing for him, and he carried on toward the door, and into the light.

Stepping out of the blackness, he raised a hand to cover his eyes. At first, he thought the room was bright enough to blind him—but it wasn't just bright. It was *white*. The whole room was white, from the matte paint on the walls to the thick carpet underfoot. And it wasn't just white, it was . . . *soft*.

The couches and chaises and sofas scattered throughout the room were all overstuffed, upholstered in velvets and brocades that begged to be touched, stroked, *felt*.

The people reclining in them certainly appeared to be having a good time. The dark room hadn't been an anomaly. As Slate looked around, a good number of the people here were actively engaged in some form of sex, either with slaves or with each other.

He considered switching focus but didn't bother. It didn't matter, really. It was a new development either way.

"Can I get you anything, sir?" a man at his elbow asked, and Slate turned.

The slave was dressed as an angel, though his tunic was scandalously short, and the gold-feathered wings on his back were small enough not to be ungainly.

Slate considered telling him he was looking for someone, but there were hundreds of people here. It was the largest gathering of the year. And Slate had no idea where his slaves might be, what they might be doing . . .

"No," he said, and the slave left him with a little bow.

Slate meandered through the room, taking in the various scenarios. It was clear Stewart was trying to do something with the sequence of rooms—the mundanity of the game room followed by the black room and then this gleaming palace in the clouds—it was probably some kind of statement about death, though Slate would have to see the other rooms to be sure.

The door on the far side of this room was red, and he had a suspicion that the activities there might be somewhat more extreme than the soft and fluffy fondlings that mostly greeted him here.

To his left, a trio of women reclined into an oversized couch, their fingers laced together, skirts draped over the golden wings of the slaves between their legs. Slate wished them a happy Saturnalia as he passed, but if they heard him, they didn't respond.

Slate carried on, toward a head of red hair he thought he recognized. Sure enough, Arabelle turned toward him at his approach, with a cheery "Speak of the devil!"

She was seated at the edge of a large sectional, half draped over the arm, her long legs extended over the loveseat in front of her. Two men sat at a professional distance, giving Slate nods as he approached. Slate returned them, then noticed what the three of them must have been watching.

In front of the couch, Anthony was spread out across a thick, plush fur rug. His eyes were closed, his arms stretched languidly over his head. His body seemed to almost ripple, undulating under the slow thrusts of the man between his legs. The man's back was to Slate, but Slate didn't need to see his face to recognize him.

Micah's breath was husky—it was clear he was close and holding back. How long he'd *been* there, holding that edge, Slate shuddered to think.

Arabelle was saying something, but Slate only had eyes for the men on the ground. Micah's hand was between their bodies, stroking Anthony's cock in time with his slow thrusts. Behind his hand, Anthony's signature flickered in and out of view like sunlight through blowing leaves.

"Just like that," Micah breathed, leaning forward. His hair was half up in braids, but a few loose strands still brushed against Anthony's cheek as he leaned down. "You gonna come for me, baby?"

Anthony let out a noise that was half gasp, half moan, and reached for him. Slate took a step closer, but neither slave had eyes for their audience—only for each other, as Micah leaned down into a soft, tender kiss. Anthony stared up into his eyes, smiling, and Slate could see the edge of Micah's returning grin.

With one last departing kiss, Micah straightened, the muscles in his back flexing as he resumed his earlier ministrations. There was some kind of gold dust on him—subtle, but unmistakable, and it caught the light in bright streaks as he moved.

Slate sat on the couch beside one of the strangers, taking a drink off a passing tray. Luster dust swirled in the amber liquid, giving it the appearance of molten gold. Slate downed it in one swallow.

And then he switched focus.

There was so little space between them, it was difficult to be sure at first. Micah was moving faster now, his breath coming hard through a wide grin. Anthony reached for him again, and rather than leaning down to meet him, Micah pulled him up, shifting his weight until Anthony was atop him. Anthony rode him the last half a dozen strokes, eyes never leaving Micah's face, and then he was coming with a groan. Micah was only a few seconds behind, letting out a breathy moan as he clutched at Anthony's arms.

"Very well done," Arabelle said, with a polite clap.

Micah gave her a wide smile, his breath coming hard, his cheeks flushed, his hands still resting softly on Anthony's thighs . . . and then he saw Slate.

For the first time, hesitation crossed his features. His eyes flicked from Slate, to Anthony, and back. Slate leaned forward, his elbow on his knee, knuckles against his chin, regarding his slave.

This angle made it obvious; there was no connection. The two of them were playing like love-struck puppies, but it was just an act.

But a *good* act.

So good it might have fooled him if he weren't able to switch focus and see for sure.

Arabelle patted her knee and Anthony moved immediately, settling beside her with his cheek on her thigh. Micah snapped out of his confusion and sat up as well. He didn't look at Slate, just melted into a waiting pose, his knees spread and his hands at the small of his back. His softening cock was still wet.

He didn't glance to where Arabelle was petting Anthony's hair.

"He's much better," Slate said, gesturing to Anthony. He turned to Arabelle and ignored Micah for the moment. "You've gotten some of the attitude out of him."

Anthony reddened but didn't say anything.

"I know my business," Arabelle said cheerfully. "Four months is a long time, when it's spent mindfully."

"And they're both yours?" one of the strangers asked Arabelle.

"No, they're Slate's," Arabelle said, stroking the side of Anthony's throat. "I just trained them."

"I don't know what I'd do without her," Slate said. "That one was a hell of a brat when I first got him. But this one . . ." Micah risked a glance at him, and Slate beckoned. Not rising from his knees, Micah shuffled the short distance, until he was kneeling before the couch. Slate hooked one finger under Micah's chin, lifting it until the slave was forced to meet his eyes. There was gold dust on Micah's lids, bringing out the green in his hazel eyes, making his lashes darker in comparison. He was as beautiful as magic could make him, and in those eyes, Slate saw nothing. Not fear, not determination, not lust. Micah was a vessel, waiting to be filled with whatever he was asked to be.

If he was told to fuck Anthony, he would. If Slate needed him to dislike it, he would. If Arabelle needed him to adore it, then he'd do that too. And he'd do it so convincingly that Slate hadn't even realized it was an act.

Slate stroked the side of Micah's face, and Micah nuzzled against his knee.

"He's perfect," Slate said quietly.

CHAPTER EIGHTEEN

∞

January 2014

The one with the light eyes is back again.

When the door opens, I think maybe he is here to help me. I think this too often. It is never true.

He does not look at me as he approaches, his eyes set on the table. It is covered in the sharp man's sharp things. The gray-eyed man does not fear the sharp things. He sets his papers down on top of them, unconcerned even for the safety of his books.

"I have some more questions," he says, and I do not answer. I am bound to answer questions; I have no duty to exchange pleasantries.

The gray-eyed man does not expect this of me. He is not like the stupid one, the one with the scar. The stupid one thinks I will do what he means. The gray-eyed one knows I will only do what he says.

"What am I missing here?" the gray-eyed man says, holding a sheet of paper out to me. I don't answer because I cannot take the paper. There are manacles around my wrists, holding my arms out to the sides. I could break them, but I was long ago ordered not to.

Today, I am not temped to try. I am holding very still.

Noticing, the gray-eyed man takes his paper back. He reads me a line of nonsense. The words reverberate softly. I watch the ripples as they dissipate. Quietly, I hum the reverberation back.

The gray-eyed man does not hear me. He reads me another line.

Another reverberation, a different form.

I hum this one back, and wince as my side erupts in a cacophony of noise.

It is not noise. It is a similar experience to very loud noise, but the air does not move. The flesh cringes from it, and the motion makes the noise worse. The sharp man is doing one of his tests. He brought ropes today, wrapping them ever-tighter around the base of my wings. He wants to see what will happen.

He thinks the wings are magic. I do not correct him.

They are flesh, the way the rest of this avatar is flesh. I built it from ruined scraps, doing the best I could with the information I had. I did not realize that the instructions for the wings were different from the rest. I barely understood what it was I was building, with only a sickening, overwhelming sense of *damage* urging me to try.

The noise I hear now once again sings of damage.

I am still. The noise does not happen when I am still.

"Is that the reverse?" the gray-eyed man asks me. I ask him to repeat the words. I do not need him to, but I would like to prolong his visit. When there are humans in the room, they turn lights on. I like the lights.

The gray-eyed man reads the first reverberation, then the second. He asks if they are the reverse. I assure him that they are. It is not a lie. Being nonsense, the statement is nonfalsifiable.

I do my best work in the midst of maybes.

He is putting together an incantation, one that he hopes will repair the damage I did to his encroachment. The theory behind it is quite clever, actually. I'm not sure I would have thought of it myself.

I answer his questions carefully, putting the most malice and obfuscation into the most irrelevant, mundane of details. I spit my hate at him while feeding him nonsense.

Crafting puzzles for him helps take my mind off the flesh. The flesh is loud today.

The sharp man wants to know how the magic flows through my body. He wants to know the difference between a stilled heart and a tourniquet. I could tell him. I choose not to.

He does not ask. Wisely, he does not trust the answers I give him.

Not like the gray-eyed man. The gray-eyed man believes my answers because he believes he is too clever to be lied to. He is wrong.

I feel the blood try to push into my wings, and I feel it turned away. The wings feel like nothing now, so long as I do not move them. I worry for the state I will find them in when the ropes are loosed.

I worry that the sharp man plans to remove them again.

The heart beats faster. The flesh fears for its own.

"Is it safe?" the gray-eyed man asks me, and I realize I have not been listening. I have been trying to hold still. The flesh moves when it is frightened.

I do not like being flesh. I cannot begrudge the gray-eyed man his quest.

But I will not help him succeed.

He holds the paper out to me, and I stare blankly.

(I maintain that I cannot read. They accept this without question. Stupid.)

Frustrated, the gray-eyed man snatches the paper back. He reads out his nonsense, the reverberations forming a clever melody. I nod approvingly.

"It is safe," I assure him.

"How safe?" he demands. I inhale to speak, and my back erupts in cacophony. I bite my tongue to stop a whimper. I do not wish to inhale again.

"There is *no way*," I say truthfully, "that performing that magic could ever harm or kill a human. Outside its intended target."

Because he *will* kill another human to attempt this magic. The same way he killed the man once built of this flesh.

There is something reprehensibly *incorrect* about this species.

The gray-eyed man searches my face. I stare back at him, not caring if the noise shows.

He likes what he sees and withdraws.

He has more paper.

The noise from my wings is very loud.

It is disgusting that I can feel them and not heal them. I *detest* being locked inside the flesh, subject to the endless, endless, *endless* noise of its needs.

Not for the first time, there is temptation.

I could help the gray-eyed man. I could make a doorway back to my home. I could—

I *cannot*, I tell myself, and the weight of it turns the noise to pain.

Pain is when the noise sounds like despair. It is what I feel now. I fear that it may never stop.

But I will not teach the gray-eyed man the magic he needs. I will not let him bring pain to my people.

He shows me discordant nonsense. I say nothing. He orders me to speak, and I tell him it is wrong. He beats himself against it, and me, for the next hour, dragging each corrected syllable from my reluctant lips. When it is done, he has a simple melody. Any child would be proud.

I tell him the words are correct now. It is not a lie.

His face is smug as he collects his papers, revealing the sharp things waiting for me beneath.

I hate them.

I hate them.

I hate them.

CHAPTER NINETEEN

∞

June 2014

There were significantly fewer people at the second summoning. There was a party upstairs, of course. There was always a party upstairs. But in the ballroom, that quiet, dark, offsetting ballroom? There were eight people, the bare minimum that Slate required to open the gate. He'd only needed eight the first time too, but at least then, people had been curious.

They weren't curious now. They were impatient. They didn't understand why he needed to work a spell he'd already worked, they didn't understand why he'd needed to wait so long, they didn't understand why this was different. He was being slowly buried in the expectations of people who didn't understand.

Coffey brought the first sacrifice out. Mercia was here, upstairs, but he hadn't bothered to engage with theatrics when there wasn't an audience to perform them for. This slave was dressed in a plain blue uniform, cotton shirt and drawstring pants. Silver bands gleamed at her wrists and throat. Her soft shoes squeaked as she dragged her feet along the marble floor. She'd been given the same narcotics as the Gestalt's slave, even though the spell had taken that one with a minimum of pain and fuss.

Slate cast a dark glance to where the angel stood in the corner, waiting. A thick leather muzzle covered the bottom of his face, and his wrists were held behind his back with metal shackles. His wings were restrained too: thin chains laced through grommets that Godfrey had punched through the skin.

He could be ordered not to move, of course, but there was the potential for this scenario to get somewhat volatile.

Slate turned his attention away from the angel and went back to his books. After working on this for a year, he *thought* he knew what the problem was. The angel had described it as *scoring*, as though he'd dug claws into the walls of the gateway as he'd been dragged through. Slate hadn't found a way to make him stop working that magic—the unknown conceptual unknowns of the magic created linguistic shortfalls that Slate didn't know how to overcome. The Gestalt's description was intentionally vague and misleading, but it had given Slate a place to start.

In theory.

In theory, Slate should be able to open a second, smaller gateway within the first, but while the first gateway had come from his side, this second one should be able to open from the far side. The two gateways would work against each other in the void, forming a kind of torus that should hold the gateway open while containing the Gestalt's damage safely within.

Should.

Should.

Not for the first time, Slate wished Christopher were here.

In the year since the last attempt, Slate had heard nothing. Not a call, not a text, not a glimpse. He heard the assorted gossip—so and so had seen his TED talk, he was lecturing at such and such—but nobody present that night had heard a word from him. Nor were they likely to.

"What are we waiting for?" Coffey asked. "I don't have all night."

Slate sighed.

Picking up the book, he headed to the edge of the re-painted spell circle. It was mirrored, just like the year before—all that was missing was the vials of blood. He didn't need the physical representation anymore. He could pull their power directly from the gateway.

Taking a deep breath, he looked at the woman in the center of the circle. He switched focus one last time. Nothing. Definitely nothing.

Unbidden, his brain dredged up the memory of the Gestalt's arrival, the thick, wet sound the corpse had made as it fell from the gateway and onto the marble. The ice in his bones as the gate indifferently sapped the life from his body. The horrifying tearing as the bones of the Gestalt's wings had carved through his skin—

Slate breathed again. He'd borne those memories for a year and was no worse off for it. He could bear some more.

And maybe, like the hedonistic revelries taking place upstairs, it would get easier with time.

He didn't have time to wrestle with this. It was today or wait another year.

Casting one last glance at the doomed woman, Slate began to read.

He carefully noted each change as he read past it, every modification he'd worked into the spell over the months since the Gestalt had been forced to explain the damage he'd done. Slate ran through them in his head, making the energies balance, checking and rechecking his math as the magic flowed easily from his lips.

His blood cooled. Not deadly cold, not the airless cold that came when the gateway pulled more than the blood could give it. Just a chill, so faint it could have come from the air, if he didn't know better.

It was much easier to prepare the gateway when it was already, in a sense, open. Like walking a worn path, rather than cutting his way through underbrush.

The slave in the center of the room tipped her head, like she was listening to something he couldn't hear. Her brow furrowed in concentration . . .

And then silently, calmly, she stepped through the doorway.

Slate kept his eyes on the portal as long as he could, barely glancing at the paper. It wasn't like he didn't have the incantation long since memorized. His blood roared in his ears, or maybe it was the sound of the magic.

She didn't fade away, like someone moving away down a dark hallway. Instead, the moment she passed over the threshold, she simply ceased to be there. Like she had walked through a waterfall, a smooth curtain of black paint.

He waited for something. Anything. Any sign of what had happened to the woman once she'd stepped into the void. He wasn't sure what he expected. Screaming? Flailing? Maybe a fine mist of blood and viscera, venting forth like an exhale from some unknowable beast.

There were only two lines of the spell left to read, and then there was . . . nothing.

The room was quiet, everyone looking toward the stone doorway in rapt fascination.

In theory, her death should form the inner wall of the torus, sealing the damage inside and creating a hole through which Slate could reach. He stepped forward, into the circle, peering into the darkness.

Could he see something there? Just the slightest variation in the black-on-black that had taunted him over the last year?

There was no way to tell whether it had worked, whether the gateway was open, except . . . to try to bring something through.

Slate didn't look at the Gestalt. Didn't need to see those dark, hateful eyes regarding him. Instead, Slate kept his attention on the doorway he'd opened, on what might be waiting to journey from the other side.

Crouching down, Slate activated the circle, beginning the spell that would bring another angel through. The air in the room *twisted*, wind rising in a loud rush.

Something flickered, once, and he was reminded that it wasn't blackness he was seeing. No, that flicker of shadow had been *black*, and it stood out like a spotlight against the colorless void that surrounded it. Slate stepped closer, searching for another flicker. He had to be ready; if this new arrival was as aggressive as the Gestalt had been, he'd only have a few seconds to activate the bands.

The blackness flickered again . . . and vanished, leaving Slate staring into the nothingness that his brain helpfully, inaccurately, interpreted as *dark*.

Nothing happened. To his right, someone else came around to stand at his shoulder, staring along with him.

Absolutely fucking nothing.

"Oh, *shit*," the person—Coffey—said. It took a moment for Slate to see what he'd seen. Slate had been so focused on what he could see *inside* the gate, he'd failed to notice the gate itself, which had begun to bleed.

It wasn't damaged, as far as Slate could tell. The blood wasn't coming from any particular crack in the stone. Instead, the whole surface had begun to weep, like a glass on a hot summer day. Thick, dark blood welled from the stone, trickling in slow, thin rivulets to the floor.

In the corner, the Gestalt began to laugh.

Anger welled up in Slate, a deep rage that made his vision go red. He whirled on the angel, his hands forming into fists at his sides.

"*Shut up!*" he screamed, taking no satisfaction when the laughter instantly stopped. Mirth still danced in the angel's eyes. Slate crossed the room in four strides, shoving the Gestalt against the wall. The laughter was replaced by a look of pain as the angle of his wings changed, yanking at the grommets.

"What did I do wrong?" Slate demanded. "Every single one of those invocations was correct. I did them right. *I know I did.*"

The Gestalt mumbled into his muzzle, almost smug as he did.

"Oh for fuck's sake," Slate said, tearing at the buckle and throwing the gag to the side. "Talk."

"You invoked them wrongly," Gestalt said, wrinkling his nose.

"Tell the fucking *truth*," Slate ordered. "I *know* I said them right."

"You did the magic wrong," the Gestalt insisted.

Slate reached out, taking a handful of the chains strung between the creature's wings. Without warning he twisted, yanking against the raw wounds. Behind him, someone made an approving noise. Coffey, or maybe Godfrey.

The angel made a noise halfway between a groan and a gag as fresh blood began to drip from the grommets.

"I'm *telling* the truth," the Gestalt managed, when Slate released him. "You perceive a deep mystery and you try to compel it by shaking air at it. You shook the air the way you meant to, but the magic laughs."

"You mean the gateway can't be fixed with an incantation?" Slate demanded incredulously. "You said it would work!"

"What I said," the Gestalt said, breathless laughter in his voice, "was 'It is safe.' And it is. Your impotent magic has left you utterly unharmed."

"Why didn't you tell him it couldn't work?" Coffey asked, uselessly, and Slate rolled his eyes, knowing the answer even before it was spoken.

"Because he didn't ask," the Gestalt said. Slate took hold of the lowest chain and yanked. The angel screamed as the grommets pulled free, tearing through skin and muscle on their way out. He staggered, going to one knee, his breath coming heavy as the pain washed over him.

Slate had no sympathy.

A year. He'd wasted a year. He'd wasted the year trying to perfect magic that had never had a chance.

"What magic *will* work?" Slate demanded, and the angel gave him a wide grin.

"Nothing *you're* capable of."

"Bullshit," Coffey said. People were gathering now. "He used this the first time; that's how we got you."

Slate's heart skipped a beat. Coffey was wrong: he *hadn't* opened it the first time. That had been Christopher. Christopher, who had a power Slate couldn't hope to touch.

But the Gestalt was shaking his head.

"You tripped and fell down a path unguarded," he said, and Slate could tell he was struggling to find the words. "It would take you, your books, a thousand years to learn the framework of what you're meddling in, another thousand to understand why you succeeded, and a *million after* to know how you've been confounded."

"*You* fix it, then," Coffey demanded, grabbing the chains. The Gestalt stumbled as he was dragged across the room and shoved face to face with the black sheen of the doorway.

"It works perfectly, for my purposes," the angel said, and Coffey shoved him closer.

"Then maybe we change your purposes," he hissed. "Maybe you *do your best* and if you manage to fix it, you get to survive when I fucking push you through!"

"I would rather die," the Gestalt said, his voice level.

The look on Coffey's face was angry enough to be almost comical. Slate regarded them, switching focus. Coffey, in a suit that cost more than most men would make in their lives, the undulating network of his connections surrounding him like a starburst. And beside him, this slave—no, this *creature*, with his black cotton pants slung low on his thin hips, his feet bare, standing tall and unafraid as he faced his death.

Slate, somewhat to his surprise, found it arousing. The anger and resentment sat in his belly like a burning stone, but it seemed that in some regards, heat was heat.

Slate wondered if the creature could be humiliated, or if he were too inhuman to feel shame. Maybe it was just a matter of how low he could be brought, how much dignity could be stripped from the bound, bleeding—

Slate blinked, switching his focus back to normal vision.

The angel was *still* bleeding. A slow rivulet of dark blood ran from his wing down his side, soaking into his waistband. There was a trail of it across the floor, disappearing into the puddle surrounding the doorway.

"He's not healing," Slate said aloud, interrupting Coffey's litany of threats. The Gestalt didn't react.

"We know," said a voice from nearer the wall. Slate glanced over. He'd almost forgotten the others were there. Well. Some of the others. Some of them had gone upstairs, but Godfrey had apparently stayed around to watch the show. "He's been slowing down."

"And you're telling me this *now*?"

"Didn't know you were interested in my research," Godfrey said, stepping closer. "I usually get the impression you'd rather not have the details."

"And you're usually correct," Slate said. "But what do you mean 'he's slowing down'?"

"I mean the rate of his healing is slowing down," Godfrey said. "A thirty centimeter incision at two centimeter depth took seven point two seconds to heal, this time last year. Yesterday, it was up to twenty-four."

"He's doing it on purpose," Slate said. "He's fucking with you." He turned to the angel, gesturing to the place where the grommet had torn loose. "Heal that. As fast as you can."

"I am," the angel said simply, still staring into the darkness. "My powers are running dry. Did you think I was the only creature in existence who could exist in perpetuity?"

Slate whirled to Godfrey. "What are you doing about this? Can't you . . . I don't know, feed him better or something?"

"Yes, it never occurred to me that a starving creature might need to *eat*," Godfrey snapped. "His power comes from . . ." He gestured widely. "I don't know. *Osmosis.* Whatever power source he used for sustenance back home, it doesn't exist here."

Slate rubbed his face. The anticipation from this morning had utterly dissipated, followed by a quiet, rolling sense of dismay.

The doorway was still closed, and would stay that way for another year, at the minimum. The methods he'd been using to compel the Gestalt were clearly ineffective, and he didn't know why. And to top it all off, the one creature they'd managed to pull through the gate was *dying*.

"It's more concerning to me that he was lying to you," Godfrey said, stroking his chin as he regarded the angel. "I thought we'd gotten that out of him by now."

"I didn't lie," the Gestalt said, and Slate didn't miss the way he pulled, slightly, away.

"You didn't tell the truth either," Godfrey said. He stepped closer, turning the angel with an almost gentle touch on his shoulder. The torn wing came into the light, feathers burnished with drying blood. "You know what that means."

The Gestalt said nothing. The proud stance from a moment ago was gone, replaced by a bitter stoicism.

"How long do you think it will take to heal this time?" Godfrey asked. Slate crossed his arms, listening despite himself. The Gestalt didn't answer.

"Godfrey does debarkings," Coffey explained, seeing Slate's confusion. The Gestalt's face went ever so slightly paler. "I've had like four of mine done. There's no reason slaves need to talk."

"It leaves them with a dull rasp, at the moment," Godfrey said, not taking his eyes off the angel. He reached up, drawing a line down the column of the Gestalt's throat. "But I'm working on it."

Slate could feel the hairs on the back of his neck standing up, though whether in arousal or disgust he wasn't *fully* sure.

The Gestalt looked toward the gate with something like longing as he was led away, leaving Slate alone in the ballroom. It was very quiet, after the noise of the magic. Even the sounds of the party upstairs seemed exceptionally muted.

Slate was exhausted. He slumped, leaning with one hand against the stone doorway, heedless of the blood coating it.

It was gritty with something that wasn't stone.

Slate stared into the nothingness, remembering the way the woman had simply *vanished* as she'd crossed the threshold. What did that feel like? *Could* it feel like anything? Or had her body simply ceased to exist the moment it had passed from the human realm?

He wondered if she'd seen anything before she died. If the doorway had given her the tiniest glimpse of the unknown as payment for what she'd sacrificed. Did the magic recognize the magnitude of what it demanded? Or was it simply a force, churning the universe as thoughtlessly as gravity?

Slate stared into the void, and in his mind's eye, the void stared back.

It didn't escape him that he could answer these questions. He could simply step . . . forward . . . and *know*.

His fingers tightened on the stone, as if anchoring him against the pull of his own intentions.

He didn't have to go . . . *all* the way through. Maybe just—

His hand stilled before he realized what it was doing. The fingertips of his free hand were barely an inch from the inky blackness of the door. He could just . . . he could just . . .

The space narrowed, so slowly as to be almost imperceptible. Inside his own mind, Slate questioned whether this was really happening, watching it as though from outside his own body. The idea that he could *stop* didn't seem entirely accurate.

A single millimeter remained, and then—

The tips of his fingers vanished, as though sliced off by an invisible blade, and pain instantly jolted through him, seizing through his wrist like an electric shock.

Slate yanked his hand back, staring at it in disbelief. At first he thought there was blood—but no, he'd simply cradled the injury in his bloodied hand on instinct.

His fingertips had turned black. Not the empty, lightless black of the doorway, but the ashy purple-black of frostbite. He could feel his heart beating in the surrounding flesh, each pulse screaming agony down his arm.

Fuck, he thought, staring down at them. A disconnected part of his mind noted the clear, straight delineation between damaged and undamaged flesh, while another equally neutral voice suggested that maybe he should seek medical help instead of kneeling here all night, staring at himself.

He hadn't even realized he'd fallen.

He lurched to his feet, trying to think of what he knew about frostbite—if it even *was* frostbite, or some paranormal malady following different rules entirely.

He needed to get to a medic, *immediately*—and it wasn't until he'd staggered into the elevator and pressed the button that he realized he had a better option.

Godfrey. Godfrey was a doctor.

The elevator doors opened and he staggered out, his hand screaming as he jostled it. Most of the people gathered around didn't turn to look—and why would they? Someone had just stepped out of the elevator. No reason for alarm.

The bones of his hand were like molten lead, the fire leaching its way up into his forearm.

He scanned the crowd, looking for the wings that would stand a head above the rest.

There. Across the atrium, headed for the private rooms.

Slate wasn't aware whether he actually vocalized an *excuse me*, or even a *move* as he pushed his way through the crowd, leaving blood on more than one evening gown or suit as he went. His hand was going numb, which was a horrid mix of good and bad news.

"*Godfrey!*" he called out. He still couldn't see the man through the crowd, but chances were, he was with the Gestalt, who had stopped moving. "Fucking *hell!*"

The people nearest him quickly chose to make a path. It widened as he barreled through it, not slowing for those who wouldn't move on their own.

At the end, Godfrey stood with his arms crossed, looking him up and down.

"I only left you for a second," the man said, voice more incredulous than worried. "What happened? Where are you bleeding from?"

"It's not my blood," Slate said, struck with a strange case of déjà vu. Wasn't that what he'd said to Micah, a year ago? "No, it's my hand, it—"

He held his hand up so Godfrey could see the damage for himself. It was perfectly fine.

The fingertips that had been black and cracking a minute ago were now covered in pink, healthy skin. The numbness overtaking his hand was rapidly fading into a neutral lack of pain. And the agony spreading up his wrist was now a mild soreness, no worse than the persistent click he'd had in one knee for years.

He flexed his hand, turning it over like he thought he might find an explanation written on his palm.

Nothing.

"I . . ." he said, but Godfrey just clapped him on the shoulder.

"Been partaking in the party, have you? That didn't take long."

"No, I . . ." Slate couldn't stop staring. Had he somehow managed to heal himself? He didn't have that power. He was sure of it.

Godfrey was grinning at him. Behind his shoulder, the Gestalt was giving him a curious look.

Had the angel healed him?

From all the way across the room?

Why?

"Did you . . .?" Slate started, but Godfrey interrupted him.

"Can't trip sit you tonight, friend. I've got plans. But hey, this one's yours, right? Give him up, Walter."

Walter. Why did that name ring a bell—

Slate turned, slowly, to where Godfrey was tugging on Anthony's shoulder, pulling him off a familiar guest.

Walter *Cunningham.*

"Not to break up the love fest, but your owner needs you tonight," Godfrey said, as Anthony stumbled to his feet. He was dressed for the solstice in high deerskin boots and a short skirt of ivy that left little to the imagination. His bare torso and face had been painstakingly painted with flowers—paint whose smeared patterns made it clear what he'd been up to.

Anthony was staring at him with wide eyes, and there was a blush rising beneath the clematis that climbed across his cheekbones.

"Of course," he stammered. "How can I...?"

He trailed off, glancing back at *Walter* as if waiting for him to say something. A strange emotion twisted deep in Slate's belly, something sharp and hot. He let it leech into a wide smile.

"Don't let me interrupt your evening," he said to Cunningham, ignoring Anthony completely.

"I..." Cunningham said, looking like he'd gotten his hand caught in the cookie jar. "He's, uh..."

"Arabelle knows her business," Slate said, pushing his hands into his pockets, the picture of nonchalance. "Enjoy the new and improved version, I have no use for him tonight."

He turned, trying not to feel the eyes of his guests on him as he strode back toward his suite. In his pocket, he touched his thumb to each of his fingertips, verifying the sensation. There was no pain. No ice crackling through his bones. If anything, his skin felt... warm.

He kept his composure as he walked down the hallway. The sigils carved into his doorframe recognized him, and the door swung open, then shut behind him. The lights rose, illuminating the coverlet, buried under the books he'd been reviewing before the ceremony tonight. Sighing, Slate pushed them aside, sitting heavily on the edge of the bed.

He was somewhat surprised to find his cell phone in his hand. He stared at it, watching himself scroll through contacts, until...

There it was. Plant, Christopher.

Christopher would *love* to know about this.

He could just call. Offer the olive branch. There was no reason he couldn't.

Except Christopher wouldn't answer. Slate was sure of it. And if he did... Slate wasn't sure Christopher wanted to hear anything his former friend had to say.

He stared down at the name on the screen, waiting for his hands to move on their own, to make the decision for him like they had at the gateway.

The screen went dark.

He dropped the phone onto the coverlet, then raised his hand closer to his face, studying it again.

It looked . . . completely normal. No sign of the damage he'd seen in the basement. No magical transformation, no sign of anything having happened at all.

He was fairly certain the Gestalt hadn't healed him—the angel wouldn't have even known *to* heal him.

Maybe the damage was proximal? Or, rather, not damage at all, but a change of state, brought on by exposure to the source, that dissipated as he moved further in time or distance from that contact . . .

Slate lost a good few minutes considering the ramifications of such a possibility . . . but it didn't seem likely.

Lying back on his bed, he let his mind wander, going over the spell, what had happened . . . what had happened after . . . what had happened *after.*

Fuck.

What the fuck had he been thinking?

You were thinking you were out of options, a mean little voice offered, and he sneered—but it wasn't wrong. He had a deadline now—there was no way he was going to get the gateway fixed without the Gestalt, and the Gestalt had an expiration date.

His phone buzzed, and he resisted the urge to throw it across the room. What the *fuck* did someone want now?

It was Godfrey.

How had Godfrey even gotten his fucking number?

Godfrey had sent him a photo. Sighing, Slate opened it.

It was the Gestalt, looking significantly worse for wear. A thick black cloth was knotted around his eyes, and a thick trickle of blood ran from the corner of his mouth. A knotted scar ran up the side of his throat, half-healed.

He says he's sorry for lying to you, came the text a moment later. *He promises not to do it again.*

Slate laughed despite himself.

At least someone was having a worse day than him.

Sighing, he dialed room service, ordering a bottle of something old and smooth. He considered having them send him someone to fuck.

He shouldn't have left Anthony with Cunningham. It was the bigger thing to do, but who knew what promises that little slut was whispering in his ea—

Slate froze, that hot, sharp little emotion twisting again.

He was getting an idea.

CHAPTER TWENTY

∞

August 2014

M icah's shoulders were killing him, and it was making it hard
to count.

It wasn't as bad as the solstice party; he *could* fail here, and failing
was sort of the point . . . but it wouldn't help him, and it would ruin
the show.

Reaching thirty, he rose up onto his toes, taking some of the
pressure off his arms.

It was difficult to breathe this way. With his arms tied behind
him, wrists tethered to the ceiling, he already had trouble inhaling
all the way. Well, that, and the toy he couldn't get out of his mouth.
The thick, veined dildo came straight down from above, and even
when he stood with his feet flat, he couldn't duck out from under it
without dislocating his shoulders. And when he stood on his toes, like
he was now—

Focus. Breathe. Count.

Micah closed his eyes behind his blindfold, willing his mind to
keep the metronome steady, even as his calves and throat begged him
to hurry up, to give them a break.

Whatever *wasn't* happening always seemed easier to bear. It was a
lie, an illusion, and Micah was above it.

Twenty-six. Twenty-seven. Twenty-eight.

Reaching thirty, Micah let himself drop. Immediately, the torsion
in his shoulders began to burn, the stinging matched by the *other*
toy—the one buried between his legs. It buzzed intermittently,
but weakly, the extra sensation easy to ignore in the cacophony of

everything else. The toy's taper, though, that was significant, even in the bare few inches that standing on his toes bought him.

Micah couldn't help the gasp of breath that escaped his mouth as he sank back down onto it, feeling it stretch him even after how many times—

No. He didn't count how long it had been.

He was here, focusing on inhaling with his arms torqued behind him like this. He was focusing on keeping his balance as he rose onto his toes, the spreader bar keeping his stance uncomfortably wide. He was focusing on staying relaxed around the toys from above and below, knowing that being tense would only make it worse. He did not count these transitions.

He did not need to know how many there had been.

He would be here until his owner grew tired of it, and there was no way to know how long that would be. Speculation could *only* let him down.

That was where Anthony failed. Anthony couldn't stop trying to make *plans*—

Micah felt a stab of worry for the other slave. He hadn't come home when Slate had returned from the inn, not for weeks now, and—

And Micah had lost count.

He immediately stifled the little voice begging him to just call it thirty, to sink down and take the weight off his burning calves—

But that was the weak way out. It was the same voice that told him he didn't *need* to work out today, he'd be fine if he skipped just *once*. It was a voice that lied. Accepting one excuse would open the door to accept more, and Micah couldn't afford to tolerate that behavior. God knew no one else was going to.

Micah started the count over from one.

The floorboards creaked behind him, a subtle brush of footfall on the bedroom's plush carpet. Micah tried not to flinch as his owner took his hand.

When Slate let go, there was a hard metallic ball left behind in Micah's palm. Micah moaned gently. The ball only weighed a pound or two—but he'd needed to grip the strappado rope to keep his balance when he went up on his toes. With his hands full, he had no choice but to stay down, his twisted shoulders screaming out a protest as the rope and the weight pulled them in different directions.

With the silicone toy in his mouth, he couldn't even grit his teeth. He settled for squeezing the ball as hard as he could. His finger slid into a divot, and he realized he recognized it. It screwed onto a hook.

So he likely had *that* to look forward to.

No, Micah thought, clenching his eyes behind his blindfold. Later was later's problem. He had to focus on getting through now.

Now was bad. He wasn't going to pretend it wasn't. But now *never* got any easier by trying to suffer later's problems, too.

There were hands on him now, stroking his chest, his shoulders, the sides of his throat. The touch took him by surprise, and his flinch nearly took him off-balance. He wished he could lean forward, even a little bit—but it wasn't going to happen with this thing in his mouth.

Slate laughed, low and easy.

"Don't worry. I'm just admiring."

His touch traced down the line of Micah's jaw, twisting lightly in a loose strand of hair. Micah let out a breathless moan. The touch *would* feel good, if it weren't for everything else.

The warmth vanished, reappearing at his hips.

"I've been thinking of having you tattooed," Slate mused. His thumb dug into Micah's hipbone, opposite Arabelle's signature. "I was thinking of my initials. Right here."

Micah let out another weak sound, this one not entirely faked.

Slate was going to put initials on him?

Why?

Micah had to be reaching the end of his time here. It had been more than two years. Surely Slate was getting bored with him by now. Micah's novelty had long since worn off... or was that why? Was Slate trying to do something different, to keep Micah interesting?

It's not your job to figure it out, stupid, Micah chided himself.

The hands slid lower now, and Micah's heart sank as a single fingertip slid down the shaft of his cock. He whimpered in what he *hoped* came out sounding like pleasure.

"Not too big a fan of this position?" Slate asked, fake concern dripping from his voice. He cupped Micah's soft junk in his hand, fingers moving like he was testing their weight.

Please don't squeeze, Micah thought wildly. His palms were sweating, and without his fingertip shoved into the divot, the metal ball would probably have fallen to the carpet. *Oh fuck, please, please don't squeeze.*

His body was doing everything in its power to try to jerk out of Slate's grip, and Micah felt like he was having to hold every muscle in check, one at a time. He tried to inhale, trying to find *any* sensation that felt good—or at least, not bad.

Right now, that was . . . Slate's hand on his hip, as the other idly played with his dick. Either of those.

Micah could do this, he *could*. It didn't matter how much it hurt; this was what he *did*.

He began to harden in Slate's hand, the fondling feeling marginally better as he flushed.

Good, he could work with that, he just needed to focus on that sensation, that *one* feeling, and he could—

Slate's hand vanished.

"I bet I know the problem," Slate said, from somewhere to Micah's left. "My mistake—this setup wasn't built for you, and I know you like things a particular way."

There was a mechanical clicking sound, and the toy in his ass got *bigger*. The stretch burned, and Micah had to fight to keep from tensing against it. It wouldn't help.

"It doesn't hurt enough, right?" Slate said, and Micah let out a low keen. He started trying to raise onto his toes, and almost immediately lost his balance, sinking back down onto the thick taper. He could feel tears soaking into the blindfold.

"If you wanted it to fuck you, you should have said," Slate said amiably, and then the clicking noise was back. It didn't get wider this time—but it did begin plunging slowly, inexorably upward. Micah was almost forced back onto his toes, but he managed to keep still, groaning as the widest part of the toy pushed deeper into him.

Just when he was sure he couldn't handle any more, it stopped and dragged back out of him with a warm burn. A moment later it was repeating. Where before, he'd had to choose which toy he wanted a break from, now each thrust pushed him up, making him struggle to cope with being impaled from both ends.

"That's better," Slate said, and the voice was in front of him now. "Isn't it?"

A new, sharp pain as one of Micah's nipples was pinched, then rolled between invisible fingertips.

This is a lot, Micah realized, in the quarter second he had to think before the toy in his ass began its upward journey.

Had he *actually* fucked up? Slate wasn't even bothering to disguise this as a "punishment," wasn't bothering with the game, the pretext he usually gave. Did that mean Micah had done very *well*, or very badly?

Micah didn't know, but there was nothing he could do now. He was inanimate, trapped in a cage of rope and silicone. All he could do now was hurt prettily.

But, to be fair, that was all he was being *asked* to do.

He could do that one thing.

With an exhale, he let himself feel it, the deep ache in his shoulders, his throat, his thighs, his ass, *everything* hurt, and with a sob, he let himself feel all of it. It blended together into a bright white noise that left him trembling and panting.

The metal ball thumped onto the floor. *Shit.* He'd forgotten he was supposed to be holding it.

He didn't try to apologize, just let his hands stay limp, focusing on breathing and not collapsing.

Inhale. Exhale. Inhale. Exhale.

A brief flicker of thought, wishing everything would just *stop*, and Micah shoved it down.

Everything seemed so much worse when it was happening.

Was this really, *really* worse than when he'd been in training, and they'd given him the lists of tasks to do each day? He'd spent months exhausted, sure he couldn't coax another twitch out of his protesting muscles—but he could always do *one* more sit up. Take *one* more hit. Deep throat a *little* further. And really, was he going to *die*?

He could bear this a *little* longer.

There was a crack, and fire raced across his palm. Micah couldn't help it; he screamed, his fist clenching.

"*Do not*," Slate hissed in his ear, and Micah forced himself to relax, his fingers peeling back one at a time. Immediately, the strap crossed his palm again.

Micah focused on not biting down on the toy in his mouth. That was an important skill; it wouldn't do to ruin the toy, and it wasn't always a toy. Biting down on his owner or their guest would be *unacceptable.*

He hadn't bitten when he was startled, and he wasn't, now, and he held on to that as his hands tried desperately to clench. He let himself scream, assuming that Slate was probably fine with that.

Three strikes in rapid succession, and then they stopped. Micah waited, trembling, for whatever would come next.

He flinched hard as the metal ball was pressed against his sore palm.

"You can have it in your ass later," Slate said graciously, and Micah saw a long day ahead of him tomorrow—kneeling in the corner of Slate's office for hours, the hook held in place with a lattice of ropes around his body.

That's what he needs from you, Micah reminded himself. *That's why he bought* you.

That helped him back into himself.

Any indent could suck a dick. Most of them could handle a couple of swats with a crop or a paddle.

This was something else, something that needed someone special. That was why Micah had proof of his training inked right into his body, why he sold for so much *more* than the others.

Because he could take what they couldn't.

"It hurts me that you don't appreciate this. I worked hard on it."

Something scratched him, right above the curve of his ass, circling around to the front of his belly. Slate had a weird fascination with the spot below Micah's belly button. It was toned and flat like the rest of his body, nothing particularly noteworthy about it . . . but Slate loved it, pressing his hands and mouth and cock against it every time he took Micah to bed.

He's going to have it tattooed, Micah thought, and it gave him a shiver even through the pain.

It wasn't *real* permanence—people like Micah didn't get *real* permanence, but even playing at it made the rest of it hurt a little less.

Micah focused on it, trying to angle his hips a little differently, and—there.

He could work with that.

Feverishly, Micah ordered his body to feel pleasure. Or at least, focus on something that didn't hurt.

His owner needed him to love this. So that was what Micah needed to do.

The new angle made it harder to keep his balance, forcing his thighs to pick up the difference, but it didn't matter. He could do it.

"There we are," Slate purred at him, the scratching edge of the paddle tracing a slow line up the side of Micah's hardening shaft. Micah's heart rate went through the roof as his mind was suddenly consumed with the image of his owner drawing back and landing the paddle across his cock. He'd done it before.

Micah flexed his belly, trying not to let his erection flag, trying not to brace against the inevitable blow. There was a click, and a moment later the dildo was being removed from his mouth. It was replaced with something hard—at first he thought it was an ice chip, but a moment later it warmed, and he realized that it was fingers, pressing into his tongue and pulling his jaw open.

"Ready for it?" Slate asked, withdrawing his fingers, fake sweetness in his voice. "I'll give you what you want. Bend over." Micah's blood went cold. There's no way Slate was going to try to—

The paddle landed on his ass twice as he tried to figure out how to do what Slate was ordering. Was Slate hoping to punish him for refusing? He could do that, but—

"*Now*," Slate said, his voice going suddenly hard, and his hand was fisted in Micah's hair, yanking him down and hitting him with the paddle again.

Several things happened at once, and Micah became aware of them in a particular order.

The first was that he was forced to bend at the waist. The toy inside of him was not prepared to handle that angle, and continued shoving its way upward, forcing him onto his toes. The position was unsustainable, and for a moment, he was only held balanced by the hand fisted in his hair.

And then he went down, shoving forward into his owner, and Micah screamed as searing pain ran across his shoulder and down his arm. This wasn't the paddle. Not at any strength. This pain was *deep*, accompanied by a sickening sort of pulling sensation. He'd felt this before, this was—

Oh, he thought, as Slate yanked him back upright with an angry shout.

He'd dislocated his shoulder.

CHAPTER TWENTY-ONE
∞

August 2014

The sound that Micah let out as he fell was *orgasmic*. Slate shuddered, doing everything he could not to come into his own hand.

It was only a moment later that he saw *why* Micah had screamed that way. It was obvious, in retrospect. He should have realized what would happen, but he'd gotten wrapped up in the way that Micah held every muscle in his beautiful body tight and trembling, waiting to take whatever it was that Slate would throw at him.

Even now, he was gorgeous, standing bent slightly forward to take the pressure off the strappado, his whole body tense as he tried not to let the fucking machine shift his balance.

Slate sat on the bed and reached for his phone to call the medic.

He paused with his hand in midair, looking at Micah. The way he stood there trembling, his breath coming in shuddery gasps as he tried to keep his shoulders still. The fucking machine was still buried inside him, his pink hole stretched so prettily around it . . .

Slate leaned forward, flipping the switch to retract the toy completely. Micah let out a little gasp as it slid wetly out of him, leaving him stretched and slick.

Micah needed a medic.

But . . . another ten minutes wouldn't *kill* him.

Slate unbuckled the spreader bar and then, holding Micah's wrist steady, the strappado cuffs.

The slave almost immediately stumbled, leaning into him as he cradled his limp arm. Mindful of the blindfold, Slate led him to the bed, pushing him back against the soft coverlet. Micah's whole body was tense and trembling. Slate picked up the paddle from the floor, tossing it carelessly onto the bed beside the slave. Micah winced at the sound, but otherwise didn't move.

Slowly, Slate unbuttoned his shirt, letting Micah hear as he stripped out of his suit. Then, naked, he climbed over the slave, bracketing Micah's body with his own. He leaned in, letting his lips brush Micah's ear as he spoke.

"Can you get it back up for me? Or should I call the medic."

Micah let out a wordless plea. He had to be in agony, but he refused to admit that he couldn't do what was being asked of him. Slate shifted, one knee sliding between Micah's thighs. Micah spread for him, moaning as the motion jostled his shoulder. Dark bruises were forming around his shoulder and collarbone, and Slate leaned down, pressing his lips to the marks. Micah let out a jittery breath, but whether in pain or something else, Slate wasn't sure.

Micah's good hand slid past Slate's thigh, coming to rest wrapped around his own shaft. Slate grinned, shifting a little to watch.

"You gonna touch yourself for me? Get ready so you can come on my cock?"

And fuck if that didn't *work*. Micah's dick hardened in his grip, even as he spread his legs wider in anticipation. His hole was still stretched open, puffy and sore from the fucking he'd taken earlier.

Slate reached between his own legs, gripping the base of his cock hard to keep himself from going off early.

He pushed Micah's knees further apart and then, slowly, slid himself inside.

Micah shuddered, stroking himself faster, his hole immediately going tight as he clamped down the way he'd been trained to do. Slate noticed a lot of little hallmarks of Micah's training now, mostly in things that Anthony had never done before he'd gotten his tattoo.

Slate groaned and stilled, thinking of Anthony. Anthony, who had mouthed off once too often and now never would again.

Slate couldn't hold still for long. He'd been sitting here hard for the last twenty minutes, idly stroking himself while watching as Micah endured the predicament of his bindings, and now, actually *inside* him . . .

Incredible.

Slate moved again, driving sharply into Micah's trembling, overworked body, his fingers running up Micah's side, toward his bad shoulder.

He imagined the noise Micah would make if he set his palm on that jutting collarbone and *pushed*.

His hand roved higher, covering those thunderhead bruises, and Micah went *so* tight and still beneath him. He whined out a wordless plea that he'd never dare to vocalize, and Slate went over the edge. He pumped furiously into Micah as he came, imagining how it would feel to press down just a *little* harder.

In the low light, Micah's bruises went blurry, seeping over Slate's hands until his fingers were a deep black.

The medic was giving him looks. Pointed, almost accusing looks, and Slate . . . well. Slate couldn't really blame him.

Slate was a man well familiar with the concept of post-nut clarity. When he'd been young, it had meant jerking off to pornography that was embarrassing and tacky when exposed to the light of day. Then it had become pornography of things that were likely illegal—things Slate told himself were scripted or faked.

The first slaves he'd owned . . . his dalliances with them had been few and far between, and he only continued after the first because he'd been sure he was going to jail. In for a penny, and all that.

Things had calmed down for a long time, after that. He'd gotten used to being serviced by indents and slaves, and his post-nut world had stopped taking him by surprise.

It was back now.

A bit.

Slate sat in a wingback chair angled toward the bed, a towel wrapped loosely around his hips, watching the medic tend to Micah. The medic had shown up six minutes after being summoned, taken one look at the restraints and toys still staged beside the bed, and understood exactly what had happened. He'd called a member of the security team to hold Micah steady, then slowly aligned the slave's arm back into the socket with a sound that had left Slate shifting uncomfortably in his seat.

Micah's whimpers were rough and hoarse as the medic laid poultices over the bruising on his shoulder.

"This is going to heal the strap marks on his back," the medic said. He wasn't asking for permission, and Slate considered taking issue with his tone—but then Micah shifted again, and one of those marks actually came into view and . . .

And he'd really done a number on him, Slate realized.

Micah trembled under the magic, twitching and wincing as the medic put a cloth over the poultice and taped it in place. The tape had ikons on it, but Slate didn't know what they did.

When the medic stood, he inclined his head toward the hallway. Slate raised an eyebrow but followed him out.

"How did you think that setup was going to end, exactly?" the man asked the moment they were out in the hallway.

Slate responded by shoving him into the wall and holding him there. "Watch your tone with me," Slate hissed, "or I'll have it watched for you."

"I just mean, you're lucky I was here," the medic amended. Apparently Slate was doing a good job of being imposing, at least for a guy wearing nothing but a towel. "His muscle tore straight across his shoulder. He was looking at the beginnings of nerve damage. That kind of injury can be very difficult to treat if it's not tended to immediately."

"And it was tended to immediately," Slate said, forgiving himself the white lie. He released the medic, and the man glanced back at the bedroom door.

"He's a slave," the medic said carefully. "But he's still human. He has innate biological *limits*."

Slate scowled. He was willing to admit he might have fucked up a bit with this one, for certain values of *admit*.

"Why do you think I keep *you* on staff?" he asked.

"I assumed it was to wipe your canvases clean from time to time," the medic snapped at him, and Slate almost laughed.

The medic wasn't a doctor. Not anymore. He had been, once, but then he'd gotten involved with drugs. Not the medical kind.

He'd traded jail time for a barcode, which was how he'd ended up with Slate. Slate liked the way his thickest connections were sharply truncated: people he'd betrayed or stolen from, and of course, the two daughters who hadn't spoken to him since the DUI that had killed their mother.

Slate wasn't taking advice on domestic relations from this man.

"When I break something you can't fix, then we'll talk," Slate said, then turned and stalked back into his room.

Micah was sitting up on the bed, slowly flexing and unflexing his hand.

The medic had given him something strong for the pain, without asking, of course . . . not that Slate was sure he would have denied it.

"You can go back downstairs," Slate said, going into his closet for a pair of pajamas. "Unless you'd rather sleep up here."

"Thank you," Micah said quietly. He was still watching his fingers move. Slate loved him when he was stripped down like this. Somewhere inside him, Slate knew, there was a man of indomitable will clawing like hell for control. But here on the outside, Micah was as docile and helpless as a kitten.

Slate lay beside him, not bothering with the blanket. Micah was sitting on it, anyway, and Slate didn't feel like making him move.

With one last look at the bruises crossing Micah's bare back, Slate shut off the light.

CHAPTER TWENTY-TWO

∞

October 2014

As blood dripped slowly onto the floor, disrupting his concentration, Slate was willing to concede that maybe things *had* gotten a little out of control.

Anthony was making a hoarse whispering sound that might have been *please.* It was hard to tell with him these days, of course.

"I can keep going," Slate said, cutting a glance at the Gestalt.

The angel stood with his arms half raised, the bands glowing softly as he fought one of the orders he'd been given. Probably *stay.* His face was pale, his eyes wide.

"He's . . . he's one of *yours,*" the Gestalt almost whispered. "Why . . .?"

"I'm not convinced that you can feel pain," Slate said, raising the whip again. The wire braided into the length caught the bright light with a feral gleam. "Not the way you pretend to, anyway. I wondered if you'd show a little less bravado when your disobedience comes out of someone *else's* skin."

Quite literally, Slate thought, looking at the sorry state of the man in front of him.

The whip had been specially made for the Gestalt—the angel's feathers were surprisingly protective. Regular leather did little more than impact damage, so he'd needed something special. The wired tail had served that purpose beautifully. The first stroke had cut cleanly through the vanes of his secondaries, the severed ends fluttering to the ground amidst the first drops of blood. Forty minutes later Slate had ruined his suit, rutting up against the angel's bloody back like a teenager on fucking prom night.

Coffey had been pissed. The cut feathers didn't heal—they'd needed to be plucked out one at a time before a new, unbroken replacement would grow. Slate had been there the whole time, fingers twisted in his bloody shirt, listening to the angel scream.

And *still*, the Gestalt wouldn't tell him what he needed to fucking know. Wouldn't stop his fucking sabotage.

A week later, Slate had had the idea about Anthony.

No, that wasn't accurate.

Slate had had the thought about Micah. He'd had the thought about Micah first, because Slate had been in his bedroom, looking through his toys, and his eyes had settled on a whip—a long, single-tail leather beauty he'd purchased but never quite dared to use.

He'd instantly known he could use it on Micah, could even turn it into a game—promising not to give him another one if he could keep from screaming for this one—but something in him went cold at the thought. He needed to keep Micah; the not-connection of his still needed an explanation.

So, not Micah.

But he could use the whip on the Gestalt, and he could use it on Anthony. Anthony, who had been to visit Godfrey and now managed not to complain or scream much anymore at all.

Anthony thought he was so *clever*. If he couldn't get Slate to sell him, then he'd talk his last owner into buying him back. Cunningham must have had a soft spot for him at *one* point, after all.

"Another five?" Slate asked, glancing in the Gestalt's direction. "Or are you ready to have a conversation yet?"

The angel only stared at him, an expression of disgust on his face.

"Another five, then," Slate confirmed, turning back to Anthony. The slave hung almost limp from the chains holding his arms wide. In the bright overhead lights, the blood streaming off him was so red it didn't look real.

Coffey had had this room built for Godfrey, so that the doctor could do his experiments on the angel and report back. Everything in it was pristine, from the white leather upholstery, to the shining stainless restraints, to the pebbled, spray-clean linoleum floor. Also white, of course.

All the better to see you with.

But Godfrey wasn't here now. He didn't much care about what the Gestalt *knew*. His interest began and ended with the creature's anatomy and physiology.

And of course, *no one* gave a fuck about Anthony.

Growing bored with his back, Slate circled around to the slave's front, which was still mostly clean. Anthony stirred just long enough to realize what was happening, then shook his head as hard as he could. His broken voice choked out unintelligible pleas for mercy. Slate shrugged.

"Ask the angel," he said, gesturing to the Gestalt. "He's the one who can make it stop."

"I can't," the Gestalt said weakly. His voice was desperate. "Can't you understand, I cannot trade my *world* to protect one person—"

"What I don't understand," Slate said, laying a deep stripe across Anthony's chest, "is why the new magic didn't form the torus. If it was just about the damage *you're* doing, then why couldn't it be contained?"

The Gestalt was silent.

"Tell me so I can understand," Slate said, and the bands encircling the Gestalt flashed.

"You don't have the power to fix the problem you have," Gestalt gritted out.

"My method was right, but there wasn't enough energy?"

"No."

"Then what?"

"You don't have the power to fix your problem."

Slate sighed. They'd been doing this for months—the Gestalt's answers were too simplistic to be applicable, too convoluted to be understandable, or comprised of nonsense words that the angel invented to describe concepts that humans weren't even aware of. The precious little freak had even invented a special word for his species: the *daiyura*.

"Have it your way," Slate said, and swung the whip again.

"This is what you do to your own," the Gestalt said, his nose wrinkled. "You display your savagery with every passing moment and you think it will convince me to open *my* doors to you?"

"I've offered to stop, if you do," Slate said simply, and the third swing crossed Anthony's lower belly, bisecting the thatch of hair above his cock. Blood ran down his thigh in a rivulet, and Slate wondered what it tasted like.

That was a new thought.

Slate was having a lot of those, these last couple of months. Last year, really, if he was being honest. He apparently wasn't immune to whatever motivator was making the parties progressively wilder.

It wasn't like it mattered.

He wanted to lick the inside of a man's thigh. That wasn't that extreme. There were people who would cook and eat someone, given half a chance.

It's fairly extreme . . . a voice inside said, but he ignored it.

Anthony's chest was starting to heave in a way that looked different from his silent screaming. Beneath the dripping blood, his legs were beginning to go limp.

"If he passes out, he'll die," Slate said conversationally. "He won't be able to keep breathing, hanging from his arms like that." He cut a look over at the Gestalt. "I only mention it because I know oxygen deprivation doesn't work on you, so, you might not know."

"There is no *reason* to do this to him," the Gestalt said. To Slate's surprise, he dropped to his knees. "Please. I can heal him for you. He can live."

"He has two more before we can negotiate again," Slate said, gesturing with the whip handle. "Those are the rules."

Slate had idly curled the whip around his hand and he realized that the leather polish had rubbed off on him. His hand was black, all the way to the wrist.

The Gestalt was silent, and Slate sighed, delivering the last two lashes in quick succession. Anthony's breath was coming in feverish gasps, his rib cage pulling the skin of his belly taut. The stripes across his front gaped open and closed, soft and wet and red.

Pressing uncomfortably against the inside of his slacks, Slate realized he wasn't bluffing.

If the Gestalt wouldn't give in, Slate . . . actually *could* let Anthony die.

It sent a little thrill through him, how sure he was. He could do it.

No, more than that, he realized, switching focus to look at Anthony again.

He was *going* to do it.

Slate didn't tolerate connections in his slaves, and this one had managed not one, but *two*. He'd talked his way back into that jackass Cunningham's heart, but beneath that, the slimmest beginnings of a gossamer thread traced out a path Slate knew well.

Micah.

Slate wasn't ready to get rid of Micah. He was *more* than ready to be done with Anthony.

A strange, reedy laugh escaped him as he thought about how *easy* this would be.

He could have Anthony's barcode removed, could have his body left out in the woods, and no one would ever find him. No one would go looking for him, not with the police tucked safely into the circle's various pockets. No one would miss him, no one would ever know what Slate had *destroyed*.

Well. No one but Cunningham, who apparently *had* developed some nostalgia for his errant fucktoy.

"*Please!*" the Gestalt shouted at him, and Slate was snapped out of his fantasy.

"Fine," he muttered. "Heal him."

The Gestalt was on his feet in a moment, crossing the room to cradle Anthony's face in his hands. Where they touched, Anthony's skin glowed. The power was the same inky blackness that Slate saw inside the portal, but while that was a darkness beyond the capacity of light, this blackness was . . . bright.

Slate stared at it, awed by its beauty even as it dimmed and went out. The Gestalt grunted in frustration, nearly *shoving* his hands against Anthony before the glow reemerged. It glittered purple along the tears of frustration in the angel's eyes.

Beneath the blood, Anthony's wounds began to zip closed, edges vanishing like a tight-lipped smile.

"Wake," the Gestalt commanded, and the light beneath his palms dimmed and stuttered again. "*Wake.*"

The purple-black light went out.

The room was silent, broken only by the slow drip of blood into the room's central drain.

"He's gone," the Gestalt said. His voice was quiet. Empty.

Something twisted through Slate's stomach, so violently that he looked down to make sure he hadn't been struck.

There was nothing there—just a tense excitement. The idea that something had *changed*. That things were *different* now. That a door had been opened—maybe not the *literal* door he was trying to fix, but certainly a *metaphorical* one, and—

And Anthony was *dead*.

Turned from a whining little prick into a dripping slab of torn meat.

Slate had done that.

He bolted for the counter, barely making it in time to be sick into the pristine sink.

Almost absently, he realized that the hand gripping the rim was clean.

CHAPTER TWENTY-THREE

∞

November 2014

The call was answered on the second ring, and Slate was so startled he didn't know what to say.

"Hello?" Christopher said again, a little louder.

"It's me," Slate said. With the hand not holding the phone, he toggled the lock/unlock button on the car door, watching the pin by the window go up and down.

Up and down.

Up and down.

"I know it's you," Christopher said shortly. "I have caller ID. What do you want?"

Slate cycled through the list of icebreaking comments he could make to try to smooth over the fact that they hadn't exchanged a single word in eighteen months.

"I need to talk to you," he said instead. "It's . . . it's about something important."

"What."

Slate rubbed a hand over his face, trying to figure out if he should summarize or just spill the whole fucking story. There had been a time, not that long ago, when that wouldn't have seemed so absurd. But now . . .

"I need to ask you a favor," he said instead.

"A favor," Christopher said, incredulity in his voice. "A favor. I had to *move*, Adam, because there was a bloodstain on my front path that *wouldn't come out*." His voice was high and close to breaking as he went on. "I will have nightmares about that creature for the rest of my life. What could you possibly want my help with?"

"It's not to help . . . *me*, exactly," Slate said, trying not to let the guilt into his voice. He thought of the look the medic had given him that morning, when Slate had finally opened the bedroom door. The medic and Carol had both been waiting in the hallway, their faces pale. They'd heard.

"I . . . I'm afraid if I don't ask, I'm going to lose my nerve."

"I think you could do with a little less nerve, in general," Christopher said. "I think we all could have."

There was silence on the line, silence in the car, broken only by the quiet *think-thunk* of the door locking and unlocking.

Locking and unlocking.

Locking and unlocking.

"Would it help if I said I might have been wrong?" Slate said, wincing, and while it wasn't the truth, it wasn't *completely* a lie.

The gateway wasn't closed. Or at least, not closed to everywhere. And by touching it, he'd . . .

His heart beat faster just considering, but he was fairly sure of it now. He'd let something through. Not something like the Gestalt, who spoke of colors and harmonies and walked in a stolen body as though it were his own.

No, Slate had brought something from another place. An empty, hungry thing that told him to clutch and squeeze and *pull*, even as Micah's skin bruised as black as the stain making its way past Slate's elbow.

Christopher sighed. "It wouldn't hurt."

Slate offered to host; Christopher didn't. Slate wasn't sure he blamed him. They agreed to meet somewhere neutral. Christopher picked the place, a tiny candle-lit restaurant with pastries and spoon steaks and salads made of colorful shredded unidentifiable plants, no lettuce to be seen.

There was no one else inside, because Slate had paid the manager to make sure they weren't disturbed. She wasn't used to that kind of request, but a couple members of Slate's security helped her do an admirable job of improvising. Even the waiter was nowhere to be seen—he'd left them their food and a pitcher of water and then vanished.

Christopher said nothing until he was gone, letting Slate fill the silence with trite observations. And then, suddenly, he spoke.

"Things have been bad, haven't they?"

"They aren't ideal," Slate allowed. "I'm having some . . . some trouble with certain aspects of . . . of the magic we did."

Christopher nodded slowly, his face pale. "I know it's hypocritical of me," he said quietly, "to pass judgment on you. You didn't even *do* the spell. I did. I did . . . *that*, and as much as I want to be angry at you, I know you didn't exactly have to *force*—"

"I want you to take Micah," Slate said, getting the words out before he could talk himself out of it. A part of him was hissing that he needed to take it back *now*, he could just get up and leave, he could—

"What?" Christopher said. "Micah? You mean, your, um . . ."

"The hospitality slave, yes," Slate said, trying not to be charmed by the way Christopher's cheeks were turning pink beneath his glasses. "I'm giving him to you."

"Oh, no." Christopher put up his hands. "No, you can't just fix all this with a *present*. I don't care how, uh—"

"It's not *for you*," Slate said, surprised at the anger in his voice when he said it. "I don't care if you never talk to me again after today. I'm doing it for him."

Christopher looked hurt, which was pathetic, considering he was the one who'd been on the offensive since he'd first picked up the phone.

He did pick up the phone, though, the little voice of reason chimed in. *And he agreed to meet.*

"Things have been . . . escalating," Slate said, his voice going back to normal. "Since we summoned the Gestalt—the angel. The creature." He'd forgotten he'd need to explain that. Gods, but it had been a long year. "The sense of decorum has slipped, to say the least, and I don't . . . I don't want to sell Micah on. I don't know who it's safe to sell him *to*."

There was more to it than that, *so* much more, but it was nothing he could explain to Christopher. How to explain the kernels of excitement and terror that had been burning in his belly since Anthony had died? The way the parties and exhibitions had been getting rowdier and more dangerous? How they'd used the silver cuffs and the spell Christopher had forged?

Or the way Micah had looked last night, drugged and bound and fully at Slate's mercy, and what Slate had *done* with that power—

How could he explain the fear he felt when he thought of what he might do next?

"I know," Christopher said quietly.

Slate frowned, switching focus. "How do you know? No one's talked to you, you've severed every contact three degrees deep—"

"I saw it," Christopher said dully. He picked at the napkin left crumpled on the table. "When I opened the gate, before we brought the creature through, I . . . I looked. And I saw."

Slate's eyes widened, and he leaned forward, suddenly eager. "What was it? What did you see? Was it the place we pulled the Gestalt from? What did it look like? He describes it as 'a place between colors' and won't tell me any more than—"

"I saw something horrible," Christopher deadpanned. "And if I hadn't, we would have died that night."

Slate frowned. "Why?"

Christopher pushed his napkin around the table, fabric soaking up the condensation left by his glass.

"Do you believe in souls?" Christopher asked the table.

"I've . . . never really seen anything that compels me to."

"That's what blood magic is," Christopher said confidently. "It's the power of a human soul. We pretend it's just science, but science can't tell us why blood magic can't be worked with animals, or with the blood of the unwilling."

"And . . . that's what you saw, through the gateway?"

For a moment, Slate worried that Christopher wasn't going to continue. He twisted the fabric anxiously around his fingers.

Slate reached out, laying his hand over Christopher's fidgeting one. It was a risky move—if it was too fast, Slate could have just ruined everything.

Christopher looked up sharply, his eyes wide behind his glasses. "Adam, I bound that creature with blood magic. *His own blood.*"

"It wasn't his, it was the slave's—"

Christopher brought his hands together, clasping Slate's between them. "*It was his*, Adam. But his soul didn't mesh correctly into his body, the way ours do, there was the tiniest little crack . . . and I was able to work my magic into that crack." His face was pale, and he shook his head. "I didn't even think about it until after it was done."

"You saved our lives," Slate said. "I don't understand the problem."

"Because in that crack was *darkness*," Christopher exclaimed, loud enough that Slate was grateful for the empty dining room. "*Evil.* Showing me how to turn a spell that *no one ever should.* The darkness inside that doorway is something *else*, something we should never know, let alone *use*, and I recognize it now, I hear it all around me, *in me*, whispering *possibilities* I never would have—"

"But you saved our *lives*," Slate repeated, louder.

Christopher looked back at him, face pained. "I shouldn't have," he whispered, and his voice cracked. "Everything you're afraid of now, I knew it was coming. I knew it the moment I saw."

"Is *that* what you saw?" Slate asked, breathless. "The future?"

Did the far side of the gateway contain a break in time somehow? Was that why he could see a connection to Micah that didn't exist yet?

"No," Christopher said, shaking his head as he stared down at the table. "No, not any more than you can see the future when a vase hurtles toward the floor. I don't know what's going to happen. What they'll do. But that gateway is woven from souls, and I know the darkness inside chafes at them, hour after hour, day after day . . . And I know no one can withstand that. Not forever."

Slate blinked, puzzle pieces slotting into place inside his head. The slow escalation he'd seen from others—and the faster one he'd seen in himself. And even those who hadn't given their blood—Locke, Coffey . . . they had been pulled along with the current.

"That's why you left," Slate said quietly, lacing his fingers through Christopher's. "Because you knew what we would become. But why didn't you say anything? We could have—"

"That's just it. I'm afraid of what *we* could do." Sighing, Christopher pulled his hand back. "I let you give me permission to do things I never would have done on my own. Things I *knew* were wrong. It started with what I did to Micah, but it wasn't until I bound that creature that I realized..." Christopher looked up, meeting Slate's eyes in a hard stare. "I realized how far gone I really was."

Slate opened his mouth to protest, but the words weren't there. Christopher was right—and it wasn't just him. The whole group *fed* off each other, like vampires, siphoning off every last shred of human decency.

"But you got away," Slate said instead. "So there has to be some hope."

"My blood isn't in the spell," Christopher said dully, scratching at his napkin. "I don't have that excuse. I made my own choices. And I don't like the reasons I made them."

There was a pause, long enough that Slate thought that maybe Christopher wasn't going to continue.

"I've been angry at you for a long time," Christopher said finally. "But all you ever did was ask. I could have said no. I could have walked away. So I think when I'm angry with you, I'm really angry with myself."

"You can be angry with me," Slate said. He considered reaching for Christopher's hand again, but decided against it. "Blame it all on me if you want. I'm not trying to trick you into coming back, I *know* this situation is fucked. The shit that's happened since you left, it's monstrous, it's—"

"I can't tell you what a relief it is to hear you say that," Christopher said, a tired smile in his voice. The seam of his napkin was beginning to come loose. "I knew it was going to come apart, but I couldn't bring myself to do anything about it if it wasn't . . . if that wasn't what *you* wanted." He let out a cynical laugh. "I see the dark everywhere, I feel it creeping into my mind in a way I know I'll never be able to escape, and even with all that, every choice I make is still for you. It's *always been* for *you*."

Slate blinked, leaning back in his chair.

He'd known they were friends. He hadn't been surprised when Christopher had kissed him the night of the summoning. And if he was being honest with himself, he'd known that Christopher would answer the phone, would agree to meet him if he asked. So maybe this confession shouldn't come as such a surprise.

"So . . . you'll help me?" Slate asked cautiously. Christopher might be haunted by what he'd seen, but it was clear the empty darkness wasn't *inside* him, not the way it was inside the others. Certainly not the way it was inside Slate.

"I've been waiting for you to ask," Christopher said, looking up at him with a smile. "I thought, of all of them, if anyone was going to put a stop to it, it would be you."

"I don't think I can *stop* it," Slate said, frowning. He puzzled over the magic he'd come to know well, even with its inconsistencies and unknowns. If Christopher was right about the doorway chafing at the souls it was made of, then there was nothing to be done. Anything strong enough to form a protective barrier would *also* need to be made of blood magic; it was the only thing strong enough to work on forces this grand.

"That's where you're wrong," Christopher said, reaching down for the leather messenger bag at his feet. He laid out a thick binder, paying no attention to the crumbs and condensation on the table. Unlike the ancient leather tomes Slate was used to working with, this looked like it had come from Office Mart. Rather than thread and glue, the college-ruled pages of this book were held in place by snap-shut metal rings.

"There's no way to stop the decline," Christopher said, standing and flipping through page after page of handwritten notes and complex illustrations. "But we can still save everyone another way."

He reached the center of the notes and triumphantly jabbed his finger right in the middle of the diagram.

Diagram was a generous word. It was a manic drawing of the doorway in ballpoint pen and black permanent marker, ink lines so thick and overlapping that they broke through the paper in some places.

"I haven't been able to do much on my own, not against that many souls," Christopher was saying, "but with your help, I'm certain we can figure it out."

"What are you talking about?" Slate said, flipping the book around so he could see. "I don't need your help with the gateway, I'm not *asking* you to come back, I just want you to take a slave off my hands, someone . . ." He trailed off, flipping backward through the pages. "Someone who . . ." He skipped slower, reading the words on the page. He looked up, to where Christopher was watching him with a wide smile. "What the fuck have you been *doing*?"

"I think of it as stapling," Christopher said, turning a half-dozen pages and pointing to a series of equations. "I can't *close* the gate on my own, but by drawing it crosswise along itself, I can prevent the passage of—"

"It's you." Slate's blood drained out of his face as he studied the papers. "None of my spells worked the way they should . . . because of *you*?"

Slate had blamed it on the angel, and that stupid fucking monster had taken the blame, refusing to give them solutions because he didn't *have them*—

Christopher was looking at him curiously now. "Of course it was me. You didn't recognize my work? I used the circle pattern, each interlocking spell reinforcing the one before and after—"

"And that's why the damage couldn't be contained in the torus," Slate finished. He slumped back into his chair, rubbing his face. Everything he'd worked on, all his experiments, would have to be redone. He knew even less than he'd thought.

"But I know how it works now," Christopher said proudly, flipping through to the back of the book. "Lilin and I figured it out. Look, there's a linchpin at the base of the magic; you break this one point and the gateway will collapse."

Slate didn't need the diagram. He knew the pin in question.

"You can't pull that," he explained patiently, "because everyone will die. If the gate collapses, everyone who put their blood into it *dies*."

Christopher looked pained. He circled the table, settling down into the seat closest to Slate.

"Adam, I *know* that," he said softly. "But you've seen what I saw. What's happening now is only going to get worse. We have to stop it while we can."

So it gets worse, so what? Slate thought, trying not to think of Anthony's naked body, the way it had sagged in the restraints. "We knew we would have to break some eggs to make this omelet. We *knew* that."

Christopher reached out, taking his hand again. "You called me because you know that's not true. You know that the cost is getting too high, and Adam, it will only get higher. What I saw through there was Hell. We summoned a demon, from *Hell*."

Unbidden, Slate recalled the Gestalt's face, tears on his cheeks as he tried to shove his failing magic into Anthony's battered body.

There were demons to contend with, sure, Slate thought. But they hadn't come through the gateway.

"I know you're afraid of the path you're on," Christopher said earnestly, looking at their entwined hands. "But none of you can die so long as the gateway is open. Imagine the depths you'll have sunk to in a hundred years. Two hundred." His eyes were wide and earnest behind his glasses. "You know I'm right. This is how we save everyone, Adam."

Slate stared at his friend in disbelief. He'd thought *he* was slipping, that Christopher would be a safe haven . . . but Christopher was worse off than any of them. He was delusional. The doorway was incredible, but it wasn't the fountain of fucking youth.

"You need to stop the magic you've been doing," Slate said bluntly. "I *need* to see what's on the far side. I don't care what it takes."

Christopher shook his head vehemently, clutching Slate's hand harder.

"No, I'm telling you, you don't want to see. You don't want to know. It's *Hell*, Adam, it's horrible and insane and—"

"*I don't care*," Slate hissed, leaning in. "I *have* to see it."

It couldn't be that bad. It couldn't. The Gestalt had come from there and he was fine—intelligent, well mannered, and saner than he honestly had any right to be. He knew things he'd never reveal if Slate tortured him for a millennium—and Slate didn't have that kind of time.

He *had* to get that gate back open.

Christopher tried to withdraw his hand, and Slate realized he'd been holding on too tight. His nails had left crescent indents in Christopher's skin. Still, he didn't let go.

"Stop. The magic," Slate repeated.

A pained look crossed Christopher's face, and he yanked his hand back, rubbing at the divots Slate had left. "No." His voice was harder than Slate had ever heard it. "I'm not going to let you do this to yourselves."

Slate was almost impressed. He wouldn't have thought Christopher had it in him.

"I'm not asking permission," Slate said, standing to look down on his friend. "I'm telling you: it stops now, or you won't like what happens next."

Christopher rose as well, leaning in, and for a moment Slate thought the man meant to fight him. His eyes searched Slate's from inches away, and Slate prepared to dodge a punch.

Instead, Christopher's hands came up to cup Slate's cheeks. He closed his eyes and pressed his forehead to Slate's.

"I'd go with you," he said quietly. "I'd be there with you, when— when the door closed. I wouldn't make you do it alone. It sounds horrible, but . . . I'd go with you, into the dark. If you wanted."

"Your blood wasn't in the spell," Slate said dully.

"But I'm in Hell nonetheless," Christopher said, and Slate could feel wetness on his cheeks. It wasn't from him. "I lost something that night I can't live without. And I know I'll never get it back."

Slate took Christopher by the shoulders, pushing him back to stare at him from arm's length.

"I'm telling you to walk away. Now. From all of this. Whatever you lost, *live without it*."

"I don't *want to*!" Christopher shouted, and the air reverberated in a way that had little to do with sound. Slate drew back, switching focus as he did.

At first he thought there was something wrong with his eyes, something that left shifting starbursts twisting across his blurred vision—but no, Christopher was still there, in the center, clear as day.

He was connected to *everything*.

Slate wasn't sure what this meant. He'd never seen this before. He wasn't even sure that Christopher knew what he was doing. The man stood beside the table, his face a mask of sadness and anger, breathing deeply. Even the *air* was connected to him.

Slate's hand inched toward his knife, forgotten on the table beside his half-eaten steak. He switched focus and the restaurant came back into view, ambient lighting on the empty tables and chairs.

"What are you doing, Christopher?" Slate said, keeping his voice level as his fingers curled silently around the handle.

"I'm trying to talk some sense into you!" Christopher shouted, and his words echoed in a way they shouldn't, as if the air were reluctant to let them go. "You know there's something wrong, you admit you're even scared of *yourself*—and your solution is to save Micah? *Micah*? One hospitality slave, and everything else can burn?"

Slate did have to admit that his priorities on that one might be a little skewed.

It probably wouldn't help his case if he argued that he didn't even really care about Micah, per se, it was just that the medic kept giving him these *looks*, after, and he didn't have any excuse, really, for the things he did. If it were any slave but Micah, he could just kill them and not have to summon the medic at all . . . it had worked with Anthony, it could work again . . .

Okay, yes.

There might be something *very* off about his priorities.

"I don't have to explain myself to you," Slate said in a low voice. "You're the one who left. You're the one who's been undermining me from the shadows this whole time—"

"To save you from the demons you'd pull through!" Christopher protested, and Slate laughed. It was dark, and low, and it sounded very small in Christopher's atmosphere.

"I've been blaming *the demon* for the gate failures," Slate said, his grin flavoring the words. "And *Hell* is what I've put him through, trying to force him to fix it."

Don't antagonize him, said a small, scared little voice in Slate's head, but it was drowned out by a larger one, an angry one that said *he had no right.*

"I killed someone," Slate hissed, and it was so easy to say it now. "I told the *demon* that I'd stop if he fixed the gateway, and would you know it? He refused. He refused through the beatings, the amputations, the *rapes*, Christopher. Oh, I'm sure you can imagine those."

Christopher's face was turning white, and he'd taken a step back. Good. Be afraid. *Be* disgusted.

"You're lying," Christopher said, and Slate shook his head, grinning. He could feel that little tendril of excitement curling in his belly, the one that purred when he had someone dead to rights.

"Swear on the gods. How does it feel, knowing that you let a *demon* suffer all that, just to protect *you*?"

"You're *lying*!" Christopher shouted, pushing him backward, and Slate almost dropped the knife as he stumbled back. He caught himself on a chair before he could go down, and he sat there, laughing.

"I don't need to lie, Christopher. Whatever lie I could spin to hurt you, the truth is worse." Slate looked up at him, a grin playing at his lips. "Now the question on my mind is, what do I need to do to *him* to make *you* stop?"

"You wouldn't," Christopher said, his voice as thick as the air, tight and oppressive around Slate's chest. "You're not that kind of man. I *know* you, Adam—"

"Do you hear yourself?" Slate asked, almost laughing. "We *killed* someone together, Plant. Or, wait . . ." He paused, tapping a finger on his chin. "Do you mean I'd never do something like that *to you*? Because you're *different*?"

The expression on Christopher's face let Slate know he'd struck truth. He stood, laughing, and set the knife back on the table. He gestured for his jacket, before remembering that he'd told the staff to leave.

Annoying.

He settled for buttoning his suit coat, not looking at Christopher as he did so.

"He heals very quickly, so bear that in mind when I tell you this. I'm going to go home, and I'm going to cut his tongue out for lying to me. Then I'm going to start repairing the gate. And every time I get the *suspicion* that it's not working the way I *hope* it will, I'm going to take one of his fingers off with a bolt cutter."

Christopher was shaking his head, the air reverberating with the frantic motion. "I can't, Adam, I can't let all of this go just for him—"

Déjà vu, Slate mused, settling his hands into his pockets with a nonchalance he didn't completely feel.

"—but I'm not giving up on you. You do . . ." Christopher swallowed hard. "I can't stop you from doing what you feel you have to. I'll just have to trust in the good I *know* is in you."

The air shifted, telegraphing Christopher's intent far ahead of his motion. It parted for him with ease, candles flickering and almost going out.

Slate didn't resist as Christopher pressed their mouths together, magic swirling around them like a cool breeze. The air rushed back into the room, pressure relenting until Slate became aware of Christopher's hands on his hips.

One, two, three gentle pecks as the air-starved candles rose again to their full height, chasing away the oppressive darkness. It was like a physical weight had been lifted off his shoulders. Christopher stared up at him, hope written plainly over his features. Slate gave him a small smile, then leaned in, pressing a soft kiss against Christopher's temple.

"When he runs out of fingers," Slate whispered, his lips brushing the shell of Christopher's ear, "I'll cut off his cock."

His business thus finished, Slate didn't wait to revel in Christopher's wide-eyed stare. He simply turned and walked away.

Or at least, he tried to.

Two steps away from Christopher, the air turned to stone. Slate froze, midstep, the space beneath his foot becoming stone.

"I tried, Adam," Christopher said, his voice choked. "I want you to remember that. I want you to remember that I *tried*."

"With what?" Slate snapped. At least he could still talk, even if he couldn't move. "Your stupid fairy tale kiss? You thought I was going to give up everything I worked for because I'm in *love*?"

"*Shut up!*" Christopher screamed. Tears spilled from his eyes, making him look younger than he was. He dropped to his knees, rummaging through his bag. "I didn't want to have to do this! You *made* me!"

Slate had no idea what "this" was, but considering the current circumstance, he couldn't imagine it was anything good. The smug tendril of warmth in his belly twisted into something not unlike fear.

But, no, Christopher wouldn't hurt him. Christopher was in *love* with him. Or at least, he thought he was.

Then again, Christopher was also a couple piñatas short of a party and had started the meeting under the impression that Slate wanted his help committing mass murder and suicide, so, it was hard to predict *what* Christopher would do, really.

From his bag, Christopher withdrew an intricate wooden box, no bigger than a deck of cards, and set it on the ground. He didn't open it. Instead, he retrieved a grease pencil and began drawing on the floor: square, geometric characters that Slate didn't recognize.

Slate took the opportunity to shift his weight, testing his reach for the table and the knife resting on it. It might have been his imagination, but he thought he moved a few centimeters.

"It's not forever," Christopher said, to himself or to Slate, it wasn't immediately clear. "It's just until I find a better plan. A way to close the gate on my own, or someone to help me. Someone who isn't afraid of you."

Slate wished him luck with that. Magic tended to make money, and people with money tended to like each other. The circles Slate ran in tended to keep an eye on their enemies—while they lasted.

Christopher had only escaped their notice because the Gestalt had been taking credit for the shit he pulled.

Slate's fingertip brushed the knife just as Christopher finished drawing and looked up.

"What are you doing?" he asked, his eyebrows furrowing. The air around Slate's hand turned solid, just as his fingers closed around the handle. He had it—uselessly.

"You were going to—to stab me?" Christopher asked, his voice layered with hurt, and Slate actually had to think about it. Before *this* unfortunate meeting, Christopher had been the one person whose company Slate really enjoyed. He'd been the person Slate trusted to keep Micah safe. And mass murder aside, his misguided heart really did seem to be in the right place with this "gateway to Hell" thing.

Could *he kill Christopher, if he needed to?*

Slate looked down to the engraved wooden box and the containment spell it sat in the center of.

Yeah. Yeah, he could.

Christopher must have seen it in his eyes, because he sighed and picked up the box, setting it on the table. Slate tried to pull away, but he was frozen in place so tightly he didn't even twitch.

"I've done this before, don't worry," Christopher said. "On an incubus I tried to summon as a familiar. You'll meet him when we get home."

"I'm not going home with you," Slate said, too loud, but the bravado fell flat when they both knew he wouldn't have a choice.

"This might hurt," Christopher said apologetically, and Slate got out a single shout before the air cracked. The solid restraints around him turned intangible, leaving him stumbling. His ears rang, and he checked the box, expecting to see that it had exploded or something.

It sat silently on the table, innocent and unopened.

"What . . .?" he started, and then Christopher collapsed forward against him, almost taking them both to the ground. Fortunately, Slate's chair was still behind him, and he dropped into it, Christopher's limp bulk on top of him.

"Sir?" someone asked, and Slate looked up, confused.

Justin stood in the doorway. The guard's gun was drawn.

Of course.

Slate's brain worked backward through a chain of realizations as the bloodstain bloomed across the back of Christopher's shirt.

The security team had been here, waiting outside to make sure he and Christopher remained undisturbed. He'd brought them to keep away intruders, but they would have heard the commotion. They would have recognized the danger.

And Justin . . .

Slate watched the indent re-holster his gun, his scarred hands strong and sure.

Justin could do what needed doing. He'd killed men for less than this; that was why Slate had bought his contract.

"He'll live, if we get a medic in here fast enough," Justin told him. It wasn't an order, or even a suggestion. Just information for Slate to use as he pleased.

Christopher's head lolled against Slate's chest. Hot blood was seeping into the space between them, ruining Slate's jacket.

Christopher's eyes twitched, and he let out a pained whimper. His breath rattled wetly; there was blood in his lungs.

Could his magic heal him? Was that a power he had?

Slate didn't know.

He kept his eyes on the wooden box as his hand found the knife, slipping it into the space between two of Christopher's ribs. He could *feel* the resistance on the blade as Christopher's heart tried to continue beating, autonomous flesh unable to recognize the harm it did itself as it spasmed and flailed against the sharp edge. But what could it have done if it had known? The heart cannot choose contrary to its purpose.

Blood poured over his hands, and Slate waited for that twist of feeling, the joy in his belly that told him he'd done something real. That there was no turning back now.

It didn't come.

He waited as the motion of the blade slowed and stilled, as the blood between them cooled, as the candles burned to their prickets.

When he withdrew the blade, the hand that held it was black. Whether it came from blood or a deeper stain, he didn't know.

CHAPTER
TWENTY-FOUR
∞

November 2014

S late lay on the table, letting Micah's hands wander over him. He'd had a masseuse for this once—a woman whose hands hinted at a Gift, though she swore she didn't have one. She was a person, not an indent, though, and that had rankled at him. He'd asked her if she would consider a contract, a permanent placement, and she'd laughed.

Slate didn't permit many people to laugh at him.

She had a husband and hopes for a baby, and the money she made was too good to need a contract. So he'd gone the other route and paid off her mortgage in exchange for lessons. She'd given those lessons to three rounds of hospitality slaves now. She thought they were Slate's lovers; no one corrected her.

Micah wasn't *as* good as she was, but he was certainly better than nothing.

Part of it—and Slate realized he was partially to blame for this—was the hesitancy in Micah's hands, a softness where there should be force.

It frustrated him. When he'd first bought Micah, he'd expected that hesitancy—the meek, cowering submission that was the hallmark of most slaves. Most owners considered it a *feature*, and did everything they could to bring it about deliberately. Not Slate. Slate played games; he had no interest in a partner too timid to make a move.

Maybe that was why he'd waited a year and a half to reach out to Christopher. Christopher, who had retreated until it was his turn and then far overplayed his hand.

Maybe that was why he was still taunting Cunningham, pretending to wrack his brain for clues about where he'd sent that pretty little slave that Cunningham wanted back so badly.

And maybe that was why he'd killed Anthony, that whining little bitch who refused to play, insisting to the last that he could quit, take his ball and go home.

Micah had been fun while he'd lasted, but it seemed that Slate was destined to break even his favorite toys.

"Christopher's dead," Slate murmured. He wasn't sure why he felt the need to say anything; at the same time, he thought Micah should know.

"I'm sorry to hear that," Micah answered. His sadness sounded genuine, but then, sounding genuine was what he did best.

"Do you remember who I'm talking about?"

Micah hummed, his fingers playing over the muscles of Slate's lower back. "Yes. He borrowed me when he came to visit. He was . . . easily pleased."

Slate snorted. That had been one way to describe him, yes.

"He liked you," Slate said, crossing his arms under his chin. "I offered to gift you to him, but I guess he wasn't interested in actual ownership."

"We are a big responsibility," Micah agreed tactfully.

"Did you like him?" Slate asked, before he knew he was going to. Immediately he felt tired, because that was the start of a game he didn't have the energy to finish. Micah's ten moves of plausible denial, the inevitable punishment for lying—

"Yes," Micah said simply, and Slate turned to look at him. Micah had his eyes down, but his face wasn't set in the expressionless mask he usually maintained.

Micah actually sounded . . . unhappy.

Slate considered arguing, boxing Micah into a corner and forcing him to make a comparison that would form the cornerstone of his next punishment, but he didn't. He could still feel the rush of hot blood over his hands, the twisting little tendril in his belly satiated at last.

Micah waited, silent, until Slate lay back down, then resumed his silken presses.

"I'm not sure what to do with you, since he didn't want you," Slate said, once again resting his head on his arms. There was a minute break in Micah's rhythm. Someone who didn't know him as well might have missed it.

"I'm sure you'll find an advantageous placement," Micah said, diplomatic as always. Then, "May I ask who'll be taking on my duties?"

"I've told you not to question me," Slate warned.

"Of course," Micah said, but while his voice was deferential, the pressure from his hands increased. "I just wondered whether you'd want them trained before placing me elsewhere."

Slate closed his eyes, picturing the way he'd left Micah, the night before meeting Christopher. The drugged confusion on his tear-streaked face, the way bruises had blossomed over his hips—

"No one's taking on your duties," Slate said, and at the moment, he could almost tell himself it was true. He told himself that he could *stop*, could throw himself into his work and a future divorced from everything happening here, now.

"But someone *needs* to," Micah said, the words accentuated by a hard roll of his knuckles, so perfect that Slate groaned.

"Give yourself the out, Micah," Slate said. He was past games now. "Don't pretend to enjoy it, it's not believable. Not at this scale."

"Love it or hate it, you need to do it to *someone*," Micah said, moving his way back up to Slate's shoulders. "If you can't get what you need, then what's the point of having us?"

Slate rolled to his side on the table, and Micah took a few steps back, his hands crossing behind him, his eyes on the ground.

"Are you fucking with me right now?" Slate asked. Phrasing aside, the question was sincere. "No bullshit, I'm telling you you're getting out of here and you're *arguing* with me?"

"No bullshit?" Micah asked, still looking at the floor. "You need things you can't get from other people. I don't *like* it, but it's my job. I like to think I bear it well. And if I don't do it, someone else will have to." Micah raised his eyes, and for a moment, Slate saw the gladiator Micah easily could have been. "So, no bullshit? I'll do what needs to be done. Sir."

One thing, Slate thought, as the moment passed and Micah lowered his eyes again. *If I was going to have one thing in my fucking life go right, of course it was going to be him.*

Slate lay back down, his mind idling in the warm den that Micah's loyalty had provided.

A moment later, he felt hands return to his back.

The touch was no longer hesitant.

CHAPTER
TWENTY-FIVE

∞

April 2015

"This is going to hurt," Tyler said apologetically, and Micah nodded rather than ask his sore throat for favors. If it had been Slate, he would have given a verbal confirmation, but it wasn't. Tyler was just an indent, albeit a lifer.

Tyler took Micah's biceps in one hand and his wrist in the other and tugged them apart, slow but sure, until the broken ends of the bone settled back into place. Micah almost screamed as the bones grated against each other. He managed to keep the sound in, panting hard as he tried to keep the bubbles of color from overwhelming his vision. He couldn't pass out. He hadn't passed out when it broke, he wasn't going to pass out now.

Tyler retrieved a splint and an ace bandage with sigils pre-printed along its length. Once they were activated, they'd begin knitting the bones back together, and he'd be healed by morning. Micah knew this from experience.

"Don't move," Tyler instructed him, and Micah nodded again. His head ached. There was a ring of bruises around his throat. He was bleeding from at least three places, one of which was between his legs.

He'd noticed, anecdotally, that the job was always harder in the winter. People were more difficult to please when they were cold and miserable. The sky got gray when it wasn't black, and the owners sat inside with nothing to do but demand amusement.

Privately, Micah celebrated the winter solstice for his own reasons. It was a hopeful reminder that easier days were on the way.

Or at least they should *be*, Micah thought, as he watched Tyler wrap his arm.

They were well into spring now, and things weren't getting better. At least not consistently.

Slate had started to have . . . Micah hesitated to call them *good days* and *bad days*. Slate had days during which he was easier to please, days when he wanted a quick fuck and for Micah to fall asleep in bed beside him. And he had days when Micah's duties were . . . more difficult. Days like today.

Tyler secured the bandage and moved to Micah's back. Micah hissed in pain as Tyler probed the welts with gentle fingers.

"Two of them are bleeding?" Micah asked.

"Five." Tyler's voice was flat. Micah let his eyes drop, even though the medic couldn't see. Tyler had a low opinion of Micah's job.

"It's been a while since that's happened, though," he said, trying for reassuring.

"This tends to spread," Tyler said, dabbing some kind of salve across the torn skin. It tingled as the magic set in. Micah could have sighed with relief as the throbbing, stinging feel of the welts began to dissipate. "I wouldn't be surprised if it covers your whole back, and probably your neck besides."

He punctuated the statement by reaching around, dragging one slick finger down the column of Micah's throat.

Micah froze. "I'm supposed to wear them," he said, trying to keep his voice level. Already, his voice was smoother, and it hurt less to breathe. The bruises above his collarbone would already be fading. Slate wouldn't be happy with that.

"I told you, *that's how the salve works*," Tyler said firmly. Now that the area wasn't one throbbing blanket of pain, Micah could feel him dabbing the salve onto the smaller welts as well, not only the ones that needed help not to scar.

Micah turned, catching Tyler's hand in a grip strong enough to discourage resistance. "They're just bruises," he said, meeting Tyler's eyes. "And I'm supposed to wear them."

"Let me help you." Tyler's voice dropped as he leaned in. "There's people I can get you in contact with."

It took a moment for Micah's aching head to connect the dots. His eyes widened. "Is that what happened to Anthony?" he blurted.

Slaves generally didn't enquire after another. After a lifetime in the system, Micah was used to people disappearing from his life without explanation. Frankly, it was a miracle *he* hadn't been traded in after this long.

But before he'd left, Anthony had talked about his old owner, had gone on at *length* about how Walter was just *playing*, Walter was going to buy him *back*—

Slate had certainly developed some sentimental affects since Christopher's death last fall, but Micah couldn't see him making that sale. He couldn't see Slate allowing the possibility that anyone *else* would make that sale. It left Micah with an uneasiness he hadn't quite been able to shake.

Tyler was frowning at him, confused. "Anthony? Isn't he at the inn still?"

"I don't know," Micah admitted. He released Tyler's wrist. "Never mind."

"When was the last time you saw him?" Tyler pressed.

"I don't remember," Micah said firmly.

Tyler waited a long moment. "He'll kill you too, you know."

"Don't be stupid," Micah snapped. His voice was too loud, and it was all he could do not to wince at the sound. Micah's owners were often violent. He wasn't going to defend them on that front. But that was why they kept medics like Tyler on duty. It wasn't just to take care of their slaves' scrapes and boo-boos. They were there for when things went *really* wrong. "It's just a broken arm."

"That you got while he was strangling you."

"It's my job," Micah said. He already knew it was useless. Tyler was a lifer, but he was still an indent. He wouldn't understand the value of having a use. "Just like the bruises are my job. I don't need help trying to get out of it."

"Even if it kills you."

Micah set his shoulders. "It won't."

CHAPTER TWENTY-SIX

∞

June 2015

On the eve of his success, Slate had Micah pierced.

He still liked the idea of having Arabelle's signature mirrored by his own, a small *AS* in the hollow of Micah's hip, but he never quite settled on how to do it. No design felt right. In the meantime, gold rings and studs accented the slave's body nicely.

Slate sat in his own dining room, surrounded by people for whom *friends* was the wrong word. He nursed a drink and watched Locke silently gesture to Godfrey. The silence was critical—Micah was blindfolded, and verbal suggestions might have given him a hint as to where Godfrey's hollow needle might strike him next.

Micah bore it beautifully, even under the influence of the drugs that Slate now used more and more.

Slate liked games, but Micah played them *too* well. At least, he did when he had his wits about him.

Slate watched Godfrey put a neat ladder of gold barbells up the underside of Micah's cock. He'd have to find someone for Micah to fuck later. Maybe not today. Next week, though. Slate shivered at the thought of Micah trying to stay stoic through that. He could pull it off if he was sober. Or if a little blue pill made its way into his food, rather than a white one.

The possibilities were endless, really.

Slate didn't realize he was hard until he felt a hand in his lap.

He turned to see its owner—not a slave, no slave would be so presumptuous. No, this was a friend of Arabelle's—her protégé, if rumors were to be believed. A pretty, young brunette named Heather, or Sage, or something. She was new to the circle, punch drunk on the freedom of it all. She didn't always use the freedom responsibly, as evidenced by her decision to try to draw Slate into a sexual interlude without so much as a *hello*.

He decided to let her.

Why not? Things were going well.

He'd had low points this year, but they'd stopped right around the time he'd followed through on the threat to cut the Gestalt's tongue out. It had grown back, obviously, but the angel was a lot less sarcastic afterward. It had done something to him, learning that the *real* saboteur had been discovered and summarily killed. It was only a matter of time now, and the creature knew it.

Or maybe it was just that he was still starving. Godfrey continued to report slowing healing times, but that wasn't a problem.

This time tomorrow, the gateway would be open, and the angel could be easily replaced.

Slate pictured it, the thought of tomorrow's work exciting him as much as the woman in his lap or the glinting jewelry on Micah's naked, writhing body.

Two years. It had taken him two years, but he knew what was wrong with the gate now. He had Christopher's notes, basically an instruction manual for fixing the problem Slate hadn't known he had. He'd been going over the binder for half a year, waiting for the stars to align back into a position he could use.

Lavender was blocking his view, and he shifted her to the side as Locke pried Micah's jaw open. The slave would have opened without protest, if asked, but Locke *liked* the protest, and so Micah protested. He whimpered in genuine fear as Godfrey closed forceps over his tongue, drawing it out until the needle could reach.

When Locke released him, Micah held his mouth open, the gem on his tongue glinting in the darkness.

Twenty-four hours later, the gateway was open.
Really open.

Slate didn't know how he could have been confused earlier. The kaleidoscope of emptiness inside now was *nothing* like the blank, hungry nothingness he'd been seeing the past two years.

Looking through the stone gateway now, Slate saw what Christopher must have seen.

He supposed it could be Hell, if you were small-minded enough. It was like the Gestalt had said—what existed beyond that doorway couldn't be experienced with anything so paltry as *flesh*. If one were particularly *attached* to their flesh, the concept of what it would take to pass fully through that doorway was . . . well it was maddening, in the original sense of the word.

Staring through the sparkling black, Slate saw how Christopher had become what he had.

For a moment, he felt something akin to pity.

Reaching out, his hand passed effortlessly into the boundary. It wasn't a full crossing—just a harmless taste. The eddies of the universe rippled harmlessly through his fingers. Smiling, he pulled his hand back, holding it out to Coffey.

Coffey, who didn't believe, and who wouldn't try summoning another angel until Slate could prove he could get results.

"Satisfied?" Slate asked, wiggling the fingers on his unharmed hand.

Coffey looked suspicious.

Shrugging, Slate went back to his books. Coffey's misgivings about liquidating his slaves were his own problem.

The universe beckoned, and Slate had a course to chart.

CHAPTER TWENTY-SEVEN

∞

December 2015

Micah waited to see if the other shoe would drop.

He lay on his back in Slate's bed, the slab of foam beneath him creating the illusion of weightlessness. The sheets held bunched in his fists were buttery smooth, the color of a warm summer sky.

Slate's cheek was pressed to his, breath hot in the hollow of Micah's throat. He wasn't far from his climax—Micah could tell by now, he'd brought this man to orgasm literally hundreds of times—and despite that, Micah was . . . unbroken.

His throat was a little sore, sure, and given a choice he'd have used a *little* more lube . . . but overall it looked like this was going to be one of the good days. Slate hadn't even given him a perfunctory *spanking*, just gone for a cocksucking and now this. Micah was surprised to learn that Slate could even *get* hard doing something so . . . vanilla.

It wasn't disappointing, exactly. It wasn't like Micah *enjoyed* stress positions or the drugs or the wire-knotted flogger; he'd just come to expect them. Their absence made him uneasy.

Micah counted off the movements of his hips, ferrying his owner along the current, keeping him on the edge. If it weren't for the familiar surroundings, he'd almost think he was confused—that this wasn't Slate, but a guest, or even an indent.

Eventually they reached their destination, and Slate rolled off, lying panting on the bed beside him. If Micah ignored the sound, he would never know the other man was there. The mattress truly was a wonder.

They had memory foam down below, waterproof slabs that made the bunks tolerable, but there was foam and then there was *foam*.

Micah let himself enjoy it, his bare skin languishing over the sheets as he stretched. He didn't *need* to stretch, it was aesthetic, but it still felt good. His cock had hardened at some point and still stood erect, putting on a good show. If he were feeling bratty, he could roll onto his stomach, rub the pierced length into the satin coverings—but that would do nothing but leave a wet spot, and Micah didn't think Slate was really in the mood to punish him.

Micah cast a glance at his owner. Slate was lying back, arms crossed behind his head, looking up at the ceiling with a satisfied grin. It was vaguely unnerving.

Slate liked to multitask. His idea of foreplay was to introduce some impossible contrivance and then ignore his hapless slave while they struggled. It aroused him to ignore them. That was all fine. Predictable.

Micah had a tidy little roadmap of variables he kept in his head to help him prepare for a given scenario. Bedroom scenes were less frequent, but generally worse. Sober scenes were usually, but not always, less intense. If Slate's suit coat was on, Micah was probably just in for a couple hours of cockwarming. Coat off, there were going to be restraints. Shirt sleeves rolled up, Micah was going to have a long night.

It did not help him to predict these things—but he couldn't stop himself from marking the patterns anyway. It was something to work on.

Ignorance would prevent the unease he was feeling *now*, as he counted on one metaphorical hand the number of times he'd seen his owner *naked*.

"I'm going on a trip soon," Slate told him conversationally. Micah took the cue to roll onto his side, his head resting on one hand, giving every appearance of listening attentively. Slate didn't look over at him, just stared at the ceiling. "I think I'll be gone quite a while."

"Should I pack for warm or cold?" Micah asked, and Slate laughed.

"No, I'm not taking anyone with me on this one. This is something I have to do alone. Though . . ."

Slate reached out, fingertips trailing lightly over the curve of Micah's shoulder. Micah's hair stood on end at the touch. He looked toward Slate's hand to avoid meeting his eyes.

"I've very much enjoyed you," Slate said, thumb stroking light circles over Micah's skin. "I think maybe if things had been different, you might've . . ."

Micah's heart beat faster. He didn't have a map for this. This was a *new* variable, and he didn't know what it meant. His usual strategy with Slate would be to fuck up a little, get the scene moving along—but he wasn't sure how to manage this interaction with someone who'd already fucked him.

But then Slate dropped his hand, rolling back to look at the ceiling.

"If you were more than a toy, maybe," Slate said, and the soft note was gone from his voice. Micah relaxed. Back on stable ground. He waited, patiently, to see if Slate would say more.

"I'm having a party tomorrow," Slate said, after a while. Micah hummed. "For the new year. I think you'll find it interesting."

He cut a glance over to Micah, who met his eyes for just a moment. He had an expression that Micah didn't know how to parse. It wasn't a threat or a warning. He seemed almost . . . hopeful?

Micah didn't dare to guess why Slate would be *hopeful* about taking him to a party.

When Micah didn't respond, Slate turned away from him, rising off the bed and fetching pajamas from the bureau.

"You can stay if you like," he said, not looking back at Micah. "Just don't make any noise."

Micah smiled at that, remembering not to thank him verbally, in case it counted as noise. He burrowed under the blanket, soft sheets against his skin.

Slate had been letting him stay more often, but only when he'd done a particularly good job. He wasn't sure what he'd done to earn it today, but the praise still left him feeling warm and happy as he pulled the comforter over his shoulders.

CHAPTER TWENTY-EIGHT
∞

January 2016

S late was so sure of himself, he let Mercia handle the actual summoning.

Coffey had become a *coward*, putting him off with one excuse after another until finally, at the solstice, he got drunk enough to admit that he wasn't sure anymore. He didn't think Slate could do it again. He didn't want to see another doorway start to bleed.

Slate told him to go fuck himself and bought a pair of slaves at the next auction. A man and a woman. He did everything he could not to think of one of them as a spare. Just in case.

No. It would work. He was sure of it now. Christopher's notes explained everything, every inconsistency he'd been unable to account for in his experimentation.

The gateway was open, and they could summon the angels now.

Slate gave Mercia the spell, and Mercia, predictably, went completely over the top with it. A massive gathering, black robes for everyone, matching costumes for the staff in attendance—everything.

It didn't annoy Slate nearly as much as it normally would. Maybe it was because, after today's proof of concept, he'd know for certain the gate was safe to travel through. The culmination of years of work, crystallized in two silver-feathered pairs of wings. Or maybe it was just a pleasant buzz and the fact that Micah looked good in nothing but a collar and an ivy skirt. It didn't leave much to the imagination—Slate could see the slave's jewelry glinting between the leaves.

Arabelle was around here somewhere. Her protégé had brought an interesting group of friends, one of whom was just thrilled with Micah.

It occurred to him once again that maybe, *maybe*, he *could* take someone with him—he still hadn't figured out Micah's connection to the gateway—but he shook it off.

Micah was an exemplary fucktoy, but, as he continually reminded himself, still just a fucktoy.

Slate smiled graciously as the woman straddled Micah, watched Micah flirt, falling perfectly into the role. A new master, a new mask. There was nothing *to* Micah—he was just a hole to be filled, in every sense of the word.

Slate told himself this as Mercia made his way slowly through the summoning, adding unnecessary flair and drama to every step. It wasn't how Slate would have done it, but then again, Mercia's audience was packed, while Slate's last attempt had been for an audience of, what, twelve?

As the painted slave was shackled to the dais, Slate couldn't help looking over at Micah.

He couldn't help it. He wanted to see the slave's reaction.

Fucking hell.

Slate forced his attention back to the dais for the spoken lines of the ceremony, waiting to see what form the possession would take. This magic wasn't opening the gate, so there would be no reason for the gore that had marked—

The skin beneath the painted wings bulged, then ripped. The man let out a throat tearing scream. Slate leaned forward, waiting for the silver blade that had signaled the genesis of the Gestalt's wings. The glint of metal didn't come. Instead, what burst forth was heavy and misshapen flesh, sodden with blood as it flopped to the ground and went still.

Slate's stomach dropped. A murmur went through the crowd.

Mercia was on top of the situation immediately, drawing everyone's attention to the second slave as the first was quickly bundled into a blanket and vanished off the dais. Arabelle's friends were looking questioningly at Slate.

"That's why we prepared a spare," he said, feigning a nonchalance that covered his growing panic. What had just happened? Had Mercia fucked something up? This wasn't half as difficult as opening the gate, and the gate was *open*. All Mercia had to do was reach through and pluck an angel out. Easy as a cookie from a cookie jar.

No, his pronunciation had been perfect. Slate knew it backward and forward. Was there something in the sigils on the floor? Slate had done those *himself*—

The second slave was howling like a banshee as she was shackled into the place the other one had vacated. Slate signaled a passing waiter, trying to ignore the murmurs of the crowd. Then, just to his left, there was an indignant yelp too loud to be ignored.

Micah had shoved Arabelle's friend to the ground. He was looking desperately back and forth between the dais and Slate. He started to say something, but didn't get it out before Slate grabbed him by the collar and yanked him down.

"The *fuck* do you think you're doing?"

Micah's eyes were wide, and fuck if he didn't look *hurt*. "What are *you* doing?" he hissed back.

People were staring, and that bitch on the dais seemed to be getting louder by the moment.

Micah tried to pull away, but Slate didn't let him. He forced Micah onto the couch beside him, twisting the collar around his fist until the leather bit into Micah's throat, cutting off his air. The slave stilled immediately, and Slate relaxed. At least *something* was acting predictably tonight. Micah had just forgotten himself for a moment.

Slate turned to the others, beginning his apology, when the wind was suddenly driven from his body.

It took him a moment to realize what had happened.

Micah had *hit* him.

Him.

His body remembered how to breathe and he dragged in a ragged breath. Micah stood, taking barely a step before stumbling. In Slate's peripherals he could see security converging, a combination of his men and Mercia's, but he wasn't going to wait for them. In his breast pocket was the tiny syringe he'd been carrying ever since his last meeting with

Christopher. Instant and nonlethal, it began working barely three seconds after the hypodermic punctured Micah's thigh. Slate watched the slave hit the ground, then gestured for Mercia to continue.

The entire ballroom was staring at him. Micah's outburst had drawn their attention even away from the woman on the dais, who should *also* have been drugged and for *fuck's* sake, Slate was never leaving anything to Mercia again.

And this was the last time he'd try to impress *Micah*. That was for fucking sure. Slate had thought the slave might have an appreciation for the incredible. If there was anyone in Slate's life he thought he could count on not to get *squeamish*, it was Micah. But no, apparently that, too, had only been one of Micah's illusions.

Slate muttered his apologies to Lavender, helping her back into her seat as security dragged the insensate slave away. She and Arabelle's other sycophants quickly engaged themselves in a twittering discussion of suitable punishments, leaving Slate to watch the second summoning.

It didn't go any better.

CHAPTER TWENTY-NINE

∞

Fucking *fuck*.

The Gestalt grinned up at him with bloody teeth.

"I told you that you didn't understand," he sneered, and Slate gave him another kick. Coffey protested, and Slate rounded on him with fire in his eyes.

"I don't give a *fuck* that he's dying; he's brought this on *himself*."

Like Coffey had any right to complain about the dying angel's dwindling energy; he'd certainly burned through enough of it himself.

"What did I miss?" Slate demanded, staring down at the huddled creature. "*What did I miss*?"

Christopher's notes had described his sabotage in detail. It had explained *everything*: why the torus didn't work, what damage the Gestalt had done coming through, *everything*.

So *why* were those slaves dead?

"The summoning was misshapen," the Gestalt said. "Because your magic is misshapen. *You* are mis—"

Slate hit him again, trying not to remember the disgust in Micah's eyes as he'd stared at the dais. The way he'd stared at the syringe in his thigh and had the audacity to look *betrayed*.

Him.

Slate scowled, resisting the urge to rub the spot under his arm where Micah had struck him. It'd been healed of course, only a few minutes after it was inflicted, but still. *Still.*

Anger washed over Slate's body like a boiling rain, and it must have shown on his face, because the Gestalt paled, flinching. Fuck him. Slate had known he was unreliable.

Everyone was unreliable, as it turned out. He'd had two people he'd thought he could lean on, and both of them had turned on him with the same wide eyes and *left*.

Well. Tried to leave, anyway.

He still *had* both of them.

Christopher languishing in the ground, six feet under a headstone with a name he would have found funny, if he could have read it.

And Micah, well.

Micah thinking about what he'd done, in a tiny cell so dark and cold he wasn't much better off than Christopher.

Cold, real cold, the unrelenting cold of stone within the earth, not the vague *absence* Slate now felt in his empty bed.

Slate turned and stalked out of the Gestalt's room, disgusted with the angel and disgusted with himself.

CHAPTER THIRTY

∞

February 2016

Slate reached through the doorway, his hand vanishing at the wrist as if severed.

He couldn't reach further than that.

There was nothing preventing it. No physical barrier, no unendurable pain. There was nothing, *nothing*, between him and what he'd always searched for.

Nothing except uncertainty. The nagging fear that the Gestalt was right, that his sneering condemnations were celestial truth rather than speculative cruelty.

Slate couldn't imagine what it would be like to exist *beyond* what he knew now—what mechanisms would comprehend the experience when his eyes and ears and synapses had vanished into the void. He wanted to know. Wanted it more than *anything*.

Almost anything.

Strands of the unknown slithered through his fingers, gossamer and silk, and what they funneled back through skin and nerves and neurons, carried through atoms of potassium and sodium to a computer of flesh and blood, was the sensation of *cold*.

And Slate couldn't shake the fear that, beyond the doorway, cold was all that awaited him.

What if a life of touch and taste and warmth and satiation had left him unable to appreciate, unable to *comprehend* the wonders of what waited for him within?

What if he was unable to return? Or worse.

What if he missed what he'd had?

He withdrew his hand, watching it emerge healthy and whole, none the worse for its jaunt through eternity.

He steeled his shoulders, staring through the careening darkness to the other side.

Just because he couldn't pull anything else here, didn't mean he couldn't go *there*.

He'd go. He'd see for himself. He *would*.

But not today.

Something dark roiled in him as he turned away.

CHAPTER THIRTY-ONE

∞

March 2016

Three months.

Slate managed to punish Micah for three months.

And it *was* a punishment for Micah, Slate knew that. That was the worst part, for Micah. Even worse than the beatings and fuckings Slate had the security team deal out, worse than the cold, the isolation, the darkness, worse than any of those things, Micah hated that he *needed to be punished.*

And after three months, Slate decided he had learned his lesson. Probably. Only one way to be sure, of course.

Micah was up the moment the door opened, on the floor in a supplicant's pose that showed off the scarring on his back. He did that on purpose, trying to remind Slate that he'd suffered for his transgressions. It worked—partly because of the clean, even lines, and partly because it was all Micah could do.

"Are you ready to return upstairs?" Slate asked, and Micah nodded vigorously, his hair brushing the concrete floor. "Learned your lesson?"

Micah's arms trembled, his fingers twitching against the cold floor.

"I can't hear you," Slate said, a smile in his voice. "I need you to promise that you're going to be obedient if I let you return to your duties."

Micah said nothing, though his shoulders hitched in what might have been a sob. It was impossible to tell, with what Godfrey had done to him.

Slate had wanted his tongue taken out. Micah's behavior had *humiliated* him, almost worse than the absolute fucking shit show of Mercia's summoning. Slate had had to use an emergency sedative, for fuck's sake. Taking Micah's tongue would have been something he could point to, a nice visual for what happened when people let him down.

Godfrey had been hesitant, which was a little shocking; Slate hadn't thought the man was capable of *comprehending* restraint, *and yet*. The doctor had pointed out that while medical technology could do wonders with superficial scars, they weren't quite at the point of regrowing body parts that had been fully amputated. He'd do the surgery, of course—at the end of the day, Godfrey did what he was paid to do—but once done, it might be difficult to undo.

Slate had struggled with that idea. More than he'd liked to admit.

It was in the middle of that internal struggle that Godfrey had mentioned another factor: without a tongue, Micah would be a significantly worse cocksucker. Slate had immediately conceded the point. That was what Micah was really for, after all. His banter was a perk, but if he couldn't take a dick, might as well take him out to pasture and shoot him.

So Godfrey got his way, and Micah lost his voice.

"If you can't bring yourself to tell me," Slate chastised, turning to the door, "I'll give you the chance to show me. Come on."

He didn't look at Micah as he walked away.

The test was simple, for all the time it had taken Slate to come up with it.

A mere two steps: Slate borrowed a slave off Coffey and told Micah to flog them. It was easy enough, not much different from what he'd had Micah do to Anthony.

Well. It was a little different. *This* flogger would do far more damage. But then, it wouldn't be a punishment, or much of a test, if it was easy, now would it?

Slate handed Micah the flogger, then stood back and waited. Waited for his will to fill the empty space within Micah, molding him into exactly what Slate wanted.

The braided tails slipped between Micah's fingers as he stood, motionless, staring at it, and a slug of ice began forming in Slate's stomach. Micah, whose sole identity trait was his eagerness to obey, *Micah* was going to hesitate now?

He snatched the flogger from Micah's hand before the man could do something irreversible like *refuse*. Micah flinched, waiting to take the blow, but Slate wasn't that stupid. Micah would always rather take a punishment than dole it out, and Slate didn't miss the way he cringed as the tails laid stripes across the other slave's skin.

He *did* miss the lightning-fast movement of Micah's hand, snatching the flogger and tossing it to the side before Slate could even begin to react. Their eyes met, and Micah looked almost surprised with himself.

Slate opened his mouth to give an order, but before he could, Micah struck him on the temple and ran.

Slate's ears rang. All he could see was white, and it took him a moment to realize that was because he was staring at the floor. He'd fallen to his knees. A bright red orb appeared, then another, then two more as blood dripped from his nose onto the tile. Far away, past the ringing, Slate heard a muffled shout as Micah met the security team *again*. Two more drops of blood before the sound of Micah's body hitting the floor. Slate couldn't even bring himself to be smug about the clicking rattle of the taser they'd used.

For a moment he was on a different floor, blood on his hands, gasping for air and watching a piece of his heart walk away from him.

Another drop of blood, this one black as coal, and Slate grit his teeth.

He didn't have time for this. He had *work* to do.

CHAPTER THIRTY-TWO

∞

April 2016

In the end, Slate told Megan to get rid of him.
He'd thought of doing it himself.

Hell, he'd thought of doing it himself a number of *ways*.

Drowning was the one that kept coming back to him. Holding Micah under the water, watching the panic overtake his features, feeling his body writhe as he finally lost his composure and began to *fight*.

Since banishing Micah back to his cell, Slate had resolved to kill him on four different occasions, and on four different occasions, Slate had changed his mind. He told himself it was because Micah still might be useful. The mark on his body might still be a clue in all of this. *That* was why Slate was hesitant to kill him, not because of any attachment he'd formed over their time together.

Slate sighed, leaning forward to run his fingers through the gate again. The ether was cold and soothing and indifferent to the lies he told himself.

He couldn't keep Micah.

He told himself it was because Micah had disobeyed, because Micah was dangerous to keep, and that might even have been the truth. Another truth was, if he kept Micah, sooner or later, he'd kill him. He wanted to. He looked *forward* to it, sometimes.

Another truth was, Slate didn't think he'd get over that.

And so he'd sent Micah away. He'd signed the paperwork to transfer Micah to a work site, the sort of place that chewed through indents and slaves alike, leaving nothing but neat, bureaucratically accurate death certificates.

In six months, maybe a year, Micah would be dead. He would be dead because he had tried to leave, and as much as Slate couldn't keep him, he couldn't let him walk away, either.

Not him.

Slate knew that, just as he knew he couldn't kill Micah himself.

It was another door he couldn't bring himself to step through.

And then word came back that Micah had never made it to his destination, that he and Megan had simply vanished into the ether, and Slate realized his fate wasn't that easy to avoid.

CHAPTER THIRTY-THREE

∞

May 2016

Slate kept his composure long enough to make it back to the car. It was parked on the broken blacktop of the Selina police department, where he'd come to collect the errant little *slut* who'd thought he could walk away.

It answered one question. Slate had never seen a connection between the two runaways because there had never been one. They hadn't run away together at all. Megan had seen an opportunity and taken it.

Megan was still nowhere to be found, but Micah.

Micah.

Micah had been unrecognizable.

His face had been the same—hair curling over his collarbones, hazel eyes bright, and wide full lips that begged to be parted—but the man behind them was different.

The driver got the door, and Slate slid casually into the back seat before pounding his fists into the upholstery, over and over until blood rushed in his ears and he saw red at the corners of his vision.

Micah had been ruined. That was all there was to it. Micah, the perfect reflection of his owner's needs, had found someone *rotten*. Someone who told him to stand proud and stare his betters in the eyes. That beautiful empty connection was obscured by a new one, turgid and thick, drawing poison like an umbilical.

"*Ohhh*," Slate growled, diving for his computer.

He couldn't remember who he owned at this department—he'd mistakenly thought the answer was *everyone*, but he hadn't managed this situation personally in *years*—but whoever it was, they were about to get a fucking earful.

He found the officer's name five seconds before the phone rang. Caller ID showed the house number.

Slate stared at it in horror, large and dangerous puzzle pieces sliding into place. That son-of-a-bitch detective had called him all the way down here knowing *full fucking well* he wasn't going to release Micah.

Why?

To get him out of the house, of course. So it could be searched without his interference.

Slate didn't answer, just chose a different number. A burner whose ring would set off alarm bells in estates and businesses all over the world.

When those alarms began to ring, the *hiding* would begin. People would vanish. People who had already been vanished would die. Favors would be called in, bribes paid. Influences shifted.

Taking a deep breath, Slate pressed Call.

It didn't save them.

The party at the inn was over. People no longer wanted to be where People were—not when the backstabbing began. And it began fast.

Godfrey's aliases weren't as bulletproof as he thought. He rolled instantly to save his own skin. Arabelle's phone numbers began deactivating.

Coffey liquidated his collections. The Gestalt slipped through Slate's fingers twice, first when Coffey killed him and again when his surprisingly animate corpse was taken into the custody of—of all the fucking people—the *Selina police department*.

Slate was only slightly surprised when Coffey's attempt to retrieve the angel was, in a word, *unsuccessful*.

When Locke and his lover were found dead in their bedroom, Slate began making plans.

Slate sat in the ballroom of the inn, cross-legged as he stared into the gateway. The shadows within twisted enticingly, beckoning like cheap whores.

He could see the cracks now, the ones Christopher had spoken of. The ones that existed in the middle grounds of reality, glimpses around the proscenium to where the props and rigging waited to be used.

Upstairs, Micah was creeping down the hallway, looking for the way into the basement. He was using some kind of talisman to evade the visible light spectrum, but the thermal cameras showed his progress as clear as day.

Slate sat patiently, listening to the shadows, until the security team reported they'd caught him. He'd come right down the stairwell on his own, just as Slate had predicted. He knew what Micah was here for. The Gestalt wouldn't be far away, back again to wreak the havoc that had been his purpose all along.

Slate rose slowly, slapping life back into his tingling limbs. He'd been here longer than he'd thought. Justin waited, watching from his post near the door, paying no attention to the muffled sounds of pain coming down the hallway.

"You want me to go get Jasmine?" Justin asked, and Slate nodded, waving him off before following him down the hall.

Micah lay on the floor, barely five steps from the stairs, twitching under the ministrations of a stun gun jammed into his side. A small crowd had already formed, watching hungrily.

The clicking stopped and Micah collapsed, meeting Slate's eyes as he tried to catch his breath. Slate could see the fear there, and he gave Micah a little smile.

"Here to do the angel's dirty work, hmm? We thought he might show up himself."

"Just me, you son of a bitch," Micah lied. There was defiance in his eyes, and Slate's heart broke a little. Micah had been *so* promising, rising so perfectly to the occasion when utilized by those who knew how to use him properly. He was wasted on this.

Slate gestured for the guards to search him, watching as they retrieved and discarded various weapons and tools. Micah kept up the bratty glare the whole time. When they hauled him to his feet, Slate noticed, maybe for the first time, that Micah was *taller* than him.

"I'm free. You can't hold me and you know it," he snapped, vitriol on his tongue like acid.

"Someone gave you your voice back," Slate said, frowning. He lifted Micah's hand, pushing his sleeve down, and Micah at least knew better than to resist. His barcode was gone, tattooed over with the image of a forest. "I'll have to have that fixed."

He took hold of Micah's shirt and yanked, tearing it down the front. He kept his focus on the real world, not wanting to see that grotesque new connection that Micah had formed. Instead, he let his fingers play over the unbroken skin of Micah's chest. Before Megan had taken him away, Slate had scrawled a message there—*damaged goods*. He hadn't realized how far Micah could fall. It gave him an idea of where to start.

"I remember putting my mark here, last time I saw you. Apparently I should've used something more permanent."

The gathering crowd shifted, trying to get a good look as Micah's hands were shackled together and he was bustled over to a restraint post. Slate didn't know when it had been installed. He'd lost track of the crowds that milled through here. This wasn't the first time the space had been used for a show like this. Around here, this was just another weeknight.

Looking around, Slate counted a couple of dozen people, mostly dregs, hangers-on who had been left behind when those they'd hung on to had gone into hiding. He didn't recognize most of them, and didn't particularly care. They weren't important.

Micah's bound hands were hauled above his head, immobilizing him on his toes. A little further, and he'd quickly lose the ability to breathe—but it wasn't time for that yet. Slate let him bear his weight on his feet, for now.

He searched the crowd, trying to find Jasmine—that was her name, not Lavender, *Jasmine*—and beckoned her forward. She had the kit from Godfrey's makeshift office, and looked eager to use it. Slate held out his hand, not bothering to verbalize, and she reluctantly handed it over. She'd get her chance.

Slate sterilized one of Godfrey's scalpels, enjoying the way Micah's eyes widened when he saw it.

"Normally I'd get a doctor to do this," Slate said, "but we seem to have a shortage of those lately. As I'm sure you know."

Micah remembered his training, keeping his jaw clenched as the scalpel bit into his skin. Only the quietest whimpers escaped his lips as Slate worked. No one else could see the rot that had filled this lovely vessel to its brim, so Slate made sure it was obvious.

DAMAGED GOODS. The block letters dripped blood down the planes of Micah's belly, mixing with the perspiration beading there.

If he were still Slate's, it wouldn't be so bad. They'd ache for a few days and then Slate would pay to have the scars removed. Worst-case scenario, he'd carry them until his next sale.

Slate was absolutely certain that Micah's new friend, the controller who lived in a tarpaper shack, didn't have the kind of money it would take to treat these. If Slate let him live—and that was a big *if*—he'd carry these scars the rest of his life. And he *knew* it.

Someone picked up the bottle of alcohol Slate had used to sterilize the knife, and doused Micah's chest in the clear liquid. Slate almost winced in sympathy as the slave screamed. He'd been silent through worse.

"Shouldn't have let Godfrey talk me out of taking his tongue."

Jasmine stepped forward, tired of waiting for her turn. She unzipped the case, lifting it so Micah could see the shining needles within. Slate had had the jewelry made special for this.

"A free man, hmm?" she said, tilting her head at him. "I think you just need a bit more training."

Slate watched, relishing the tiny motions of Micah's body as Jasmine pierced him. He thought of the last time he'd had this done to Micah, all those months ago, when he'd been sure that everything he wanted was in his grasp. It was all falling down around them now— but to be sure, it was falling down around Micah *faster*.

She did his septum and his nipples, his hands balling into fists and his jaw clenching, but not much more than that. There was a purpling bruise forming over his ribs, courtesy of the security team no doubt. Compared to their tender ministrations, a needle through a nipple was nothing.

But Jasmine wasn't to be denied her due. She clipped a gold chain to the nipple rings, grinning into Micah's face as she tugged it ever so gently forward. Micah struggled to rise higher, but the manacles already left him with little slack. He hissed as the chain went tight, pulling against the tender wounds.

She laughed and leaned into him, her tongue slipping past his lips in a deep kiss he couldn't pull away from. The crowd jeered and she turned toward them, grinning. "Ready for the fun part?"

Slate crossed his arms, watching as volunteers stepped forward to strip Micah out of his jeans. The material was ruined with blood and isopropyl, and Slate felt a petty sort of satisfaction knowing that he'd cost Micah that.

Jasmine crouched down, then looked up at Slate, frowning. She'd been prepared to pierce the head of his cock, replacing the barbell that any free man would *surely* have removed by now.

"The other one's still here. What do you want me to do?"

The satisfaction vanished as Micah smirked, his eyes meeting Slate's like a dare. He quickly wiped the expression away, his face regaining that same blankness that Slate knew so well.

Had that smirk been there all along?

Slate strode forward, one hand fisting in Micah's hair, the other yanking at the gold chain. He forced Micah to look at him.

Those hazel eyes stared up, blank as glass.

"You think that's *funny*," Slate realized. "You think this is your choice."

How long had *that* been there, beneath the surface, hidden behind the masks that Micah wore so well? Months? Years?

Micah's empty eyes gave him no answers.

"You still want to tell me I *can't*?" Slate snapped, giving the chain another tug. Micah shook his head once, and Slate released him. He leaned in.

"You're the same as you've ever been." His voice was too low for the rest of the crowd to hear. This was just for Micah. They wouldn't understand. "You say you're free and strong because those are the desires of the man who *fucked you last*." Micah stiffened beneath him, and Slate knew he'd struck pay dirt. "He takes you to bed and you pretend to love it. Maybe even pretend to love *him*, because that's what he needs from you. I bet sometimes you even believe it. *That's how good you are.*" Micah tried to shake his head, but Slate tightened his grip. "How convenient for him, to fall in love with exactly the man who could do this job for him?" He dropped his voice one more time, letting the words carry on his breath. "I bet coming here was your idea, and everything. No. You're not free. And you never will be. You don't know *how.*"

Slate released the chain, backing up and raising his voice so the crowd could hear. "I'm gonna pass you around like a fucking party favor." He looked to Micah. "By the time I kill you, you'll forget you were *ever* free."

The laughter of the crowd buried Micah's groan as Jasmine buried one of her needles in his cock. Someone produced a blindfold, dropping it over Micah's eyes as the rope holding his wrists was released. Slate stepped back, letting the crowd have their fun.

He'd let other people fuck Micah before, obviously, but never so many at once. They descended over him like locusts, spreading and pulling and shoving as Micah did his best to remain pliant beneath them. The bruising was spreading, and Slate suspected Micah had at least one cracked rib. He couldn't help but dwell on that, how much it would be hurting the slave to draw in those deep gasps on the occasion that someone took their dick out of his mouth. They'd put a ring gag on him, leaving him helpless as they took him deep and hard.

The sight didn't arouse him the way it once might have.

He had something more interesting planned for this evening. Something he'd bought the day Godfrey was arrested.

Leaving the party behind him, Slate returned to Godfrey's office, retrieving the two electric brands. They were custom orders, the *A* and *S* stylized just so. They made a lovely pair.

By the time he returned, Micah was unconscious. It seemed like a waste to Slate.

He plugged the irons in, setting them on a low table so he could watch them heat.

By the time his guests bored of their new fuckdoll, the irons were hot and Micah was conscious again. He was laid out on a table, his arms and legs held down by various people. Slate gestured for them to turn him onto his stomach. Micah tried to do it gingerly, but no one here was taking it easy on him. Slate didn't envy him the feeling of his full weight on those new piercings.

Someone produced a length of rope, using it to tightly bind Micah's leg to the leg of the table. It wouldn't do to have him moving *at all* during this process. Micah could hold still if ordered to do so—usually. This, though . . . this was something else.

Slate turned the brand slowly in his hands, knowing that Micah could see it. He remembered a time when he'd planned a different way to put his initials on Micah. He suspected Micah remembered too.

"I got it for the angel, of course," Slate lied, looking up at Micah. "Figured if I was going to have to mark him up again, might as well do it in style." He twisted the brand around in his fingers, watching it turn. He cut his eyes back to Micah. "There's an *S* too."

Micah tried to vanish, tried to turn on that blankness, but there was too much fear now.

"Two strikes," Slate instructed, handing the brand over to Justin. He sauntered slowly out of Micah's field of vision, taking in the sight of his trembling body. It reminded him of the good old days. Considering a moment, Slate slapped him hard just above the line where his ass met his thigh, the handprint instantly turning red.

"Right there," he directed Justin. "Right on that red mark."

Justin complied, pressing the burning metal against Micah's flesh in a single, sure stroke. His face didn't change as Micah screamed.

The crowd moved in, hands holding Micah still as he thrashed despite himself. Slate regretfully admitted it was the right move. Usually he loved this part, the moment where Micah's training failed, where his body struggled and fought without his permission—but the brand would have smeared, and Slate really wanted the mark to be legible.

If Micah lived, everyone he ever fucked would know Slate's name.

Micah let out a low keen as the first brand was removed, and Justin lined up the second. His eyes were shut tight, his breath coming ragged through his clenched teeth. His hair fell across his face, damp with sweat, and Slate resolved to fuck him at least once more before he died. Not here, but later, somewhere where it was just the two of them and Micah could focus a little better.

The second brand made contact with a hiss, and Micah keened, high and desperate. His body arched, the audience laughing as they almost, but not quite, lost the struggle to hold him down.

"So you can remember," Slate said, leaning in close, listening to Micah's ragged panting. "Exactly where your freedom will *get* you."

Micah didn't respond, and Slate realized he was unconscious. The security team had given him a hell of a beating, and they'd probably need a medic to rouse him again. Slate almost called for one, then closed his jaw so fast he nearly bit his tongue.

No. No. This motherless bastard had spent the last year tearing Slate's empire apart brick by brick, and if Slate couldn't bring himself to kill him outright, he could at least *let* him die.

"Party's over," Slate announced. "Throw him in a cell. He can go another round if he wakes up."

There were some halfhearted protestations from the gathered crowd, but Slate ignored it. They had their own slaves, or the creatures Coffey had stashed here—hell, they could take their boredom out on each other, for all he cared.

Two of the staff dragged Micah off toward the barracks, and Slate turned back toward the security team.

"Anything on him that could be tracked?"

Justin shook his head. "Even if there was, it wouldn't work within the perimeter of the warding. This building's a black box." He gestured to the phone they'd taken off Micah. The battery had been removed, the phone itself snapped in half. It lay, screen cracked and dark, alongside the collection of items they'd found in the various pockets of Micah's tactical jacket. Nothing looked particularly dangerous, though Slate was amused to see that his errant whore had apparently learned to pick locks.

Something blue caught his eye. "He had this?"

Justin shrugged helplessly. "In his pocket, yeah."

Confused, Slate switched focus.

CHAPTER
THIRTY-FOUR
∞

The world wasn't that complicated, once you had a handle on it. Even the unsolvable mysteries weren't that mysterious once you had the courage to pull back the curtain.

Slate sat on the floor in front of the gateway, leaning against the black stone frame, one leg hanging over the edge, into the abyss. The winds beyond ruffled his pant leg. Gazing out across the infinities, Slate saw answers and answers and answers, but never to the question he'd asked.

He'd made this, torn this hole in the universe, to solve the mystery of Micah's missing connection. Something that could not be and yet was.

The answer wasn't in there. It was here, in his hands, in the blue plastic cap of a milk bottle.

To anyone else, it would be an unsolvable mystery all on its own. Why would a man on a suicide mission bring a piece of cheap garbage? Why *this* piece of cheap garbage? But Slate knew, and only Slate *could* know.

He switched focus, a smile playing at his lips as the tendrils spread like calligraphy, into the portal and out of it. The whole story, playing out at last.

Slate had been wrong about Micah's new owner. Wrong, and wrong, and wrong again.

Micah's mysterious connection hadn't been obscured, it had simply been incomplete, waiting for everything to fall into place. Waiting for Slate to pluck a piece of darkness into the world. It wasn't Micah's bottle cap at all. It belonged to the Gestalt, who had saved it for the nostalgia of its *color*. He'd given it to Micah this morning. A good luck charm. A joke between the two of them.

Slate could see it all as he turned the bottle cap over in his hands, the connection between Micah's lovers forming a starburst all of its own. A connection strong enough to appear before they'd even met.

It had nothing to do with Slate after all. And it never had.

Sighing, Slate cast the cap into the darkness, watching it vanish from view. Micah's new friends were nearby, waiting for the signal to make their next move. They were with the detective, that motherfucker that Slate should've had shot after the incident in Selina. Another mistake to add to the tally.

The cap reappeared, and Slate caught it easily, the cold stinging his fingers. He could see what had thrown it, as easily as if the creature still gripped it between its myriad talons.

The wind whispered to him, and Slate reached out, taking hold of a breeze. It flowed over his fingers like gossamer, showing him where it had come from and where it wanted to go.

Slate couldn't see the future, but the writing on the wall wasn't blurry. He didn't have time for more testing. His cowardice was about to make the decision for him.

By morning, this place would be overrun with police, and Slate would lose his chance. The gateway would become police property, if the Gestalt didn't manage to close it first. That wouldn't do. That wouldn't do at all. Something would need to be done about that.

The wind twisted between his fingers, and Slate's fist tightened.

The power went out, and as the generator brought the red emergency lights to life, Slate closed his eyes and slipped into the darkness.

Explore more of *The Powers That Be* series at:
riptidepublishing.com/collections/series-the-powers-that-be

Dear Reader,

Thank you for reading Hazel Domain's *Broken Contracts*!

We know your time is precious and you have many, many entertainment options, so it means a lot that you've chosen to spend your time reading. We really hope you enjoyed it.

We'd be honored if you'd consider posting a review—good or bad—on sites like **Amazon, Barnes & Noble, Kobo, Goodreads, Twitter, Facebook, Tumblr,** and your blog or website. We'd also be honored if you told your friends and family about this book. Word of mouth is a book's lifeblood!

For more information on upcoming releases, author interviews, blog tours, contests, giveaways, and more, please sign up for our weekly, spam-free newsletter and visit us around the web:

Newsletter: riptidepublishing.com/newsletter
Twitter: twitter.com/RiptideBooks
Facebook: facebook.com/RiptidePublishing
Goodreads: tinyurl.com/RiptideOnGoodreads
Tumblr: riptidepublishing.tumblr.com

Thank you so much for Reading the Rainbow!

RiptidePublishing.com

ALSO BY HAZEL DOMAIN

∞

The Powers That Be
Any Price
Any Cost

ABOUT
THE AUTHOR
∞

Hazel Domain is a cryptid who escaped Ohio and can now be found roaming the woods of eastern Maine. Hazel spends their time fixing computers, fiddling with databases, making renaissance faire costumes and, when all alternatives have been exhausted, writing.

Hazel has five Nanowrimo certificates, a doctorate in parapsychology, and a cat.

Tumblr: tumblr.com/hazeldomain
Twitter: twitter.com/HazelDomain
TikTok: tiktok.com/@theehazeldomain

Enjoy more stories like
Broken Contracts
at RiptidePublishing.com!

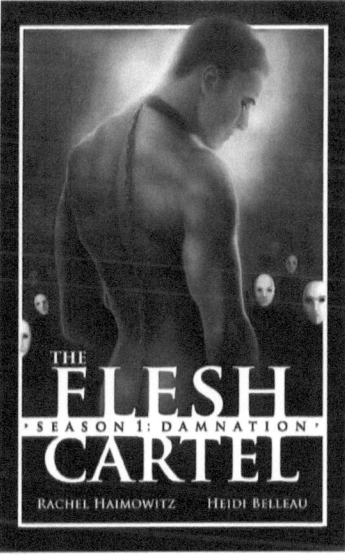

Anchored

ISBN: 978-1-62649-236-3

Flesh Cartel, Vol 1

Sublime service, made to order.

ISBN: 978-1-62649-064-2